Praise for Stephanie Lehmann's novels

You Could Do Better

"Perfect pitch and a wicked sense of humor . . . more addictive than any prime-time soap."
—Johanna Edwards, national bestselling author of *The Next Big Thing* and *Your Big Break*

"Turn off that TV and pick up this book—*You Could Do Better* is witty, warm, and irresistible."
—Sarah Mlynowski

The Art of Undressing

"In this spicy drama of cooking, stripping, and family values, Lehmann shows that love conquers all—even awkwardness between a mother and daughter."
—*Houston Chronicle*

"Witty."
—*The Orlando Sentinel*

"Worth buying just for the shopping scene alone."
—*The Seattle Times*

"hmann dresses her writing with humor, wit and insight."
—*Summit Daily News*

"his is a wonderful book."
—Eyecandyzine.com

"Near the very top of my list of favorite writers . . . another delightful and touching tale."
—Rian Montgomery, Chicklitbooks.com

continued . . .

Thoughts While Having Sex

"A poignant look at the troubled relationship of two sisters and the surviving sister's guilt. Stephanie Lehmann does a tremendous job developing Jennifer's inner turmoil. Readers will also find themselves immersed in a behind the scenes look at how a play is produced from start to curtain call."

—The Romance Reader's Connection

"You'll be scouring the bookshelves in the hopes of finding that Lehmann has published another novel to follow this debut."

—womenwriters.net

Are You in the Mood?

"A darkly compelling portrayal of what happens when two roads diverge in the wood, and you try to take both of them. Stephanie Lehmann is brilliant."   —Cathy Yardley, author of *Surf Girl School*

"Are you in the mood for fun? Then Stephanie Lehmann's got just what you're looking for."

—Jennifer O'Connell, author of *Off the Record*

"An exhilarating, emotional rollercoaster ride—I simultaneo laughed and cried as I read this new page turner."

Michelle Cunnah, author of *Confessions of a Serial Da*

"Take this book to bed to find yourself in the mood . . . for laugh ter, love, and sex! A delightful, revealing portrait of women edging toward marriage and motherhood. I couldn't stop reading!"

—Josephine Carr, author of *My Very Own Murder*

You Could Do Better

STEPHANIE LEHMANN

 NEW AMERICAN LIBRARY

MAIN

NEW AMERICAN LIBRARY
Published by New American Library, a division of
Penguin Group (USA) Inc., 375 Hudson Street,
New York, New York 10014, USA
Penguin Group (Canada), 90 Eglinton Avenue East, Suite 700, Toronto,
Ontario, M4P 2Y3, Canada (a division of Pearson Penguin Canada Inc.)
Penguin Books Ltd., 80 Strand, London WC2R 0RL, England
Penguin Ireland, 25 St. Stephen's Green, Dublin 2,
Ireland (a division of Penguin Books Ltd.)
Penguin Group (Australia), 250 Camberwell Road, Camberwell, Victoria 3124,
Australia (a division of Pearson Australia Group Pty. Ltd.)
Penguin Books India Pvt. Ltd., 11 Community Centre, Panchsheel Park,
New Delhi—110 017, India
Penguin Group (NZ), cnr Airborne and Rosedale Roads, Albany,
Auckland 1310, New Zealand (a division of Pearson New Zealand Ltd.)
Penguin Books (South Africa) (Pty.) Ltd., 24 Sturdee Avenue,
Rosebank, Johannesburg 2196, South Africa

Penguin Books Ltd., Registered Offices:
80 Strand, London WC2R 0RL, England

First published by New American Library,
a division of Penguin Group (USA) Inc.

First Printing, August 2006
10 9 8 7 6 5 4 3 2 1

REGISTERED TRADEMARK—MARCA REGISTRADA

LIBRARY OF CONGRESS CATALOGING-IN-PUBLICATION DATA:

Lehmann, Stephanie.
   You could do better / Stephanie Lehmann.
      p. cm.
   ISBN 0-451-21854-X (trade pbk.)
   1. Man-woman relationships—Fiction. 2. Mate selection—Fiction. I. Title.
   PS3612.E355Y68 2006
   813'.6—dc22   2005035666

Set in Didot LH
Designed by Elke Sigal

Printed in the United States of America

PUBLISHER'S NOTE
This is a work of fiction. Names, characters, places, and incidents either are the product
of the author's imagination or are used fictitiously, and any resemblance to actual per-
sons, living or dead, business establishments, events, or locales is entirely coincidental.
   The publisher does not have any control over and does not assume any responsibility
for author or third-party Web sites or their content.

You Could Do Better

One

I was in bed watching *Supermodels* on TV. Niles and Ashley were in a horse-drawn carriage in Central Park. They gazed at each other with rapture.

"Evidently," my boyfriend, Charlie, said, "she's selling her house."

"What?"

He was on the bed next to me. "Have you heard anything I've been saying? My grandmother decided to move to Florida."

"Good for her." My eyes were still on the screen. Ashley had her hair up and was actually wearing a tiara. Niles looked suave in a black tuxedo. "I hear there's a great dating scene down there."

His grandmother's house was in New Rochelle. The only intriguing thing about New Rochelle was that Dick Van Dyke used to live there. Or should I say Rob Petrie.

Interesting trivia: Carl Reiner, who wrote and created and produced the *Dick Van Dyke* show, actually lived in New Rochelle with his wife and son. Carl Reiner is said to be the first writer who deliberately based a sitcom on his own life, going so far as using the same street address that he actually lived on, changing one number so people wouldn't drive by his house to ask for autographs.

"Um. Daphne, would you turn that off?"

"Now?"

I looked at Charlie. He was so cute, in an Adrian Grenier from *Entourage* sort of way.

"There's something I want to talk about."

"But I've been looking forward to this all week." My eyes were drawn back to the screen. *Supermodels* was a guilty pleasure in the tradition of some of my past favorite trashy nighttime soap dramas like *Beverly Hills, 90210* and *Melrose Place*. But, like *Desperate Housewives*, it did not take itself completely seriously. Niles was now telling Ashley how gorgeous she was, especially since she got her cheek implants, chin augmentation, crowns, and veneers.

"I hate that show," Charlie said.

"You aren't exactly its demographic."

"That would be high-school girls, prison inmates, and you."

"Just because it's idiotic doesn't mean I can't enjoy it. Can you hand me the peanuts, please?"

He handed me the jar on his nightstand. "You're a mental case."

"Then you must be one too, seeing as you choose to live with me."

I had him there.

I poured a small handful of peanuts into my palm and gave him back the jar. He took some too. "You care more about your shows than real life."

"Niles is finally going to propose to Ashley."

"Really?" He actually turned his attention to the screen. "Right now?"

"Uh-huh." I was surprised at his interest. Maybe we could cuddle up and watch together. We both munched on our peanuts and I filled him in. "She's going to quit modeling and have his baby."

"Really. Maybe you can tape it. There's something I want to talk about."

So much for my cuddling fantasy. "Can't it wait for a commercial?"

"I've been thinking. I could talk to her about selling it to me."

"Selling what? Who?" Niles was telling Ashley how he fell in love the first time he ever laid eyes on her at a photo shoot in Nova Scotia when it was five degrees out and she had to wear a bathing suit.

"My grandmother. The house."

What was he saying? Charlie, not Niles. I pressed the mute

button and forced myself to focus. "Could you go back a little? I think I missed something."

"I bet she would finance it. And give me a good deal."

We'd been to his grandma's house a couple times for Thanksgiving Dinner. My main associations were dry turkey, a gold brocade sofa, figurines of people from the eighteenth century waltzing, and aqua wall-to-wall carpeting. "You're thinking of buying her house?"

"It would make a lot of sense."

My god. Was this going where it seemed to be going?

This was Charlie's first year of teaching high school after finishing all his requirements to get certified—a humbling and utterly practical move he made after all but giving up on his dream of writing for television and his reality of bartending at the Gotham Comedy Club. Now Charlie hated everything that was on. Of course, none of it was his.

"We'd get more space," he said. "Lots of it."

"That's true." Our one-bedroom apartment was on the Upper West Side in an old building on Broadway and One Hundred and Twelfth. I'd lived there since graduating from The New School, where I got my MA in Media Studies. The thing that really made this apartment so special was because it was in the same building as Tom's Restaurant. From *Seinfeld*. Not that they ever actually went there, seeing as the show was shot in L.A., but the exterior shot was of this very building. Which gave it a certain cachet, at least in my TV-addled brain. And I liked imagining them downstairs sitting over coffee talking about "nothing." (The food was so greasy and the coffee so bad, I never actually went there myself either.) Another plus: The apartment was a quick subway ride to my job at the Museum of Television & Radio on Fifty-Second Street.

"So . . ." Charlie took my hand. I looked into his eyes where the green flecks blended into brown. His expression was serious. Totally. "We could buy the house."

My stomach fluttered.

"And get married," he said.

My stomach went from fluttering to all out losing its horizontal hold. "Is this a marriage proposal?"

He cleared his throat. "I do finally have my certification. And teaching may not be the most glamorous profession in the world, but it is somewhat secure . . ." He was straining to make his voice sound casual, which made it anything but. "And . . . well . . . I love you. And I love the idea of living the rest of my life with you. And having a family together . . ."

"Really?"

"Yes."

I blushed. My palms were perspiring. "I love you too."

"So . . . will you marry me?"

I was aware by my peripheral vision that Niles was most likely proposing to Ashley at that very moment. It took a heroic amount of concentration not to undo the mute and turn my head toward the screen. I also made the judgment call that Charlie would not be amused to know he was proposing at the same moment as Niles.

"Yes," I said. "Yes. I do. I mean, I want to. Let's get married. Yes!"

"Are you sure?"

I smiled. "Of course I'm sure." We'd been together for four years, lived together for three. I couldn't imagine my life without him. "But do we have to live in New Rochelle?"

"It's just an idea. We can think about it."

I nodded quickly. "We'll think about it."

"It's impossible to imagine raising a child here," he said, his eyes sweeping the bedroom walls as if they might actually prevent his sperm from reaching my egg.

"But you know how much I love it here." Not that the apartment was more important to me than having a child.

Eventually.

I did want to have a child.

Eventually.

As a matter of fact, that would've been a good name for my child, since I'd been thinking of it that way for so long.

Eventually, go clean up your room right now!
I will clean it, Mom. When I actually have a room.

"We'll figure it out," he said.

"Yeah, we'll figure it out."

I wasn't sure if we were done talking. I glanced at the screen. They'd cut to Mirage, the ultradiva model on the show. She was in love with Nigel, but he'd already told her (in last week's episode) he was going to propose to Ashley. She knew he was doing it right this second, and it was tearing her apart. But she was a professional—determined to get through this shoot without letting it show. I didn't need the sound on to know she was struggling to smile into the camera when all she really wanted to do was cry.

"My mom will be happy," Charlie said.

I turned back to him. "Yep." Charlie was an only child, and his mother was worried that he'd stay shacked up with me forever without making it legal. I wondered if he'd talked about all this with his parents already. Seemed that way. His parents lived in Rye, a few stops up from New Rochelle on the Metro-North railway. They would love having their son nearby—that was for sure.

"Mom might want to help you with planning the wedding and everything. So be prepared for the onslaught."

I nodded quickly. "That's fine with me." No need to actually say out loud that it was painful for me that I had no parents to get involved. There'd be enough chances to wallow in morose thoughts later. "It'll be nice to have her help." And it would be. I liked Charlie's mom. She was really smart and kind—had worked as an emergency room nurse for many years until the stress got to her. Now she let Charlie's dad support her (he was an executive at IBM) and did a lot of volunteer work for local charities. She'd always made me feel welcome. She reminded me of Ruth on *All My Children*. "I probably won't want anything too big and elaborate, though."

"That's fine. It's up to you. Whatever you want."

"Wow." I snuggled up to him. "This is so exciting!"

"Of course, I'm sure your sister will have her own ideas."

"Mmmm."

My sister. Billie. I *really* didn't want to think about her. The two of them did not get along. As a matter of fact, they actively disliked each other. And she would most certainly look down her nose at New Rochelle. "I can't believe this is happening." I stole a look at the screen. They'd cut back to the carriage ride. Nigel was now presenting Ashley with a huge rock.

"I was going to surprise you with a ring," Charlie said, his eye on the screen too. "But since you're going to be the one wearing it . . . I thought we could go to Forty-Seventh Street and look around so you could pick out your own."

"That sounds like fun." God. We were actually going to do this! "I love you." I leaned over and gave him a tender little kiss on the lips.

"I love you too." He gave me a tender little kiss and then put his arms around me. And we hugged. And I looked over his shoulder and checked the clock on his nightstand. There were still twenty minutes of the show left. Would Charlie want to make love now to celebrate our engagement? Was it wrong that I preferred to watch the end of *Supermodels* than have sex with my husband-to-be? Well, if he wanted to, I'd go with it. At least I could check later on televisionwithoutpity.com and read about what I missed.

Oh. And—ahem—at least I'd gotten my own proposal.

He went to the bathroom to brush his teeth. They cut back to Mirage, who was now in the photographer's bathroom snorting cocaine. Mirage was played by Jessica Cox, and everyone knew she'd left the show to pursue a movie career. The only question was if they were going to kill her off at the end of the season or just get rid of her temporarily. I hoped they'd put her in rehab so she could come back if her movie career flopped. Mirage was my favorite character on the show. I loved getting sucked into the drama between the wild, promiscuous *Vogue*-chic bad girl (Mirage) and the good, steady, J. Crew sweater girl (Ashley).

Charlie came out just as the commercials came on. He undressed down to his boxers and got in bed and leaned over to kiss me. "I love you."

"I love you."

We kissed again, a little longer. And then once more. Uh-oh. Could I stall him till the end of the show?

"Well," he said, "I should get to sleep. I have to get up early tomorrow for a conference with some parents."

"Poor thing. They work you too hard."

I felt relief. What was wrong with me? I should've been hot to make love after being proposed to. But, truth be told, our sex life was on the mediocre side. We weren't married yet, but we were already past the honeymoon stage, and our honeymoon stage had never been all that hot. Charlie was a good guy. Sweet, cute, and smart. But not the best lover I'd ever had. Did that mean we shouldn't get married? The thought made me nervous. But there was time enough to work on all that. The important thing was that we loved each other.

"Good night, Sweetie Pie."

"Good night, Pumpkin."

I undid the mute. Charlie closed his eyes. Ashley and Niles were still in the carriage.

"I want a big wedding," she was saying. "At the estate. With a full orchestra dressed in white tuxedoes, white rose candelabra centerpieces, and a six-tiered cake decorated with white sugar roses . . ."

"Could you turn that down a little?" Charlie asked.

"Sure."

"Whatever you want, Darling!" Niles said. "Whatever your heart desires."

I lowered the sound. Niles put his arm around Ashley's shoulder. They merged into a passionate kiss. A hemorrhoid ad came on. I couldn't quite believe it. I, Daphne Wells, was engaged to be married.

Two

*B*y the time I dragged myself out of bed and hit the shower, Charlie was gone. He had to leave at some ungodly time like six in the morning to take the subway down to Grand Central, where he took a train to Pelham High School in time for the morning bell. The only good thing about his commute was that he could walk to the school from the station.

Why teach in the burbs? They paid $20,000 a year more than city schools, and he could correct papers on the train. Still, I really did not know how the guy did it. Having to face all those hormonal kidiots so early in the morning, every day, five times a week. But he was sick of bartending, and there weren't too many options for an English major who'd spent his twenties out in L.A. unable to get an agent or sell a script.

So, yeah. New Rochelle made a lot of sense. Plus, on some level, the whole "house with a lawn, kids, and family" thing appealed to him. He'd grown up that way and had a pretty happy childhood. But I didn't want him to give up on his dream of writing for television. He certainly was good enough. If anything, he was too good. Charlie loved shows like *The Sopranos* and *NYPD Blue* and *Curb Your Enthusiasm*. He'd never been able to bring himself to write the crappy schlock that might've helped him break in. As a matter of fact, Charlie and I met at JFK standing in the taxi line when he was on a trip home to stay with his parents. He was taking a break from L.A. and reassessing his situation. I was returning from visiting my sister at a photo shoot in Bermuda. We shared a cab into Manhattan, discovered our mutual interest in television, and exchanged phone numbers. He ended up moving in with me . . . and never returned to L.A. We'd talked a few times about moving out there together for the sake of his writing career. But I hated the idea of L.A. In any case, I couldn't imagine leaving Billie. And he seemed to be adjusting to the idea of being a teacher. At least it did make him feel good inside—when he didn't want to murder his students.

My own job as a curator at the museum was great. It gave me the perfect excuse to obsess about my favorite pastime. And who wouldn't love working in a place that promoted television as an important cultural phenomenon to be analyzed and studied and preserved? True, my $40,000 a year pay was a joke for Manhattan. Yes, I lived there, but could I afford to take advantage of the fact? And sometimes it could get boring—especially if I was working on a project that didn't really interest me. But there are worse things than having to watch ten seasons of *Happy Days* in the name of research.

I moved the showerhead so the water wouldn't spray all over the floor. Our bathroom wasn't much larger than a closet, and the tile floor was cracked with age. I loved the charm of our ancient fixtures, but no matter how clean we kept it, this could never compete with the appeal of a gleaming, modern, spacious bathroom. Yes, New Rochelle probably was the intelligent and sensible thing to do.

Taking the still-damp towel Charlie had used, I dried myself off. One of us had to buy some new ones. Was it my job because I was the woman? If we moved to New Rochelle, would I be in charge of keeping it clean? Did he have some fantasy of turning me into a 1950s housewife? I'd grown up on the Upper East Side, and the city was all I knew. I couldn't even drive, and with my terrible sense of direction, I'd probably vacuum in circles around the wall-to-wall carpeting.

I opened my tightly packed bureau drawer and pulled out a royal-blue V-neck top and my current favorite pair of black pants I'd recently bought at Urban. They had a not-too-high, not-too-low waist, slim leg, and a slight flare that hung perfectly over my black leather wedge-heeled shoes. I ran a comb through my hair, fluffed out my bangs, and glossed my lips. Billie had picked this shade for me at Sephora after I'd tried on almost every brand, and I was sure I'd get some kind of virus from all the testers I sampled. Miraculously, I survived without side effects. Even though this was the most expensive one, it really did look the best with my coloring, plus it had a nice scent that always gave me a moment of pleasure when I brought it to my lips.

It was late spring, and the heat I craved all year had not yet arrived, so I grabbed my black wool blazer and was almost out the door when my stomach growled. I made myself go to the refrigerator. One of my big ambitions was to stop buying a five-hundred-calorie muffin on the way to work and have something healthy at home. But toast sounded so boring. I stared at a carton of milk as if it were a crystal ball telling my future.

If only I could tell my mother the news.

So Charlie and I are going to get married.

I moved the milk aside. Maybe I'd have orange juice.

No, Mom, I haven't told Billie yet. There's time enough for that.

Forget the juice. Too acidic. I picked up the bread, but we were down to the heel.

You do like Charlie, Mom, don't you?

I could scramble some eggs. But was it worth cleaning the pan?

I know he's not like dad. He isn't ambitious—at least not anymore—but there's nothing wrong with that. Where does ambition get you? The higher you go, the farther you fall. Right?

No offense, Dad.

I closed the refrigerator door. Who was I fooling? It would be a muffin as usual.

I walked down Broadway toward the One Hundred and Tenth Street station. As I passed the flower shop, it really hit me all over again. Charlie and I were engaged! This was really happening! Maybe I'd been telling myself I was in no hurry, that marriage was just a piece of paper, that there really wasn't any difference between living together and holy matrimony. But now that we'd decided to actually do it . . . I had to admit to myself . . . I was glad to make it official.

The headline of a *Post* caught my eye. Tyra Banks was being sued by an ex "top model" from her reality show. Now that was gratitude.

Rumblings from underground signaled the pending arrival of a train. Years of subway riding had sharpened my senses. From up on the sidewalk, I could tell if they were coming from uptown or downtown. Express or local. This one was mine.

I skipped down the stairs, swiped my MetroCard, sailed through the turnstile, and slipped through the closing doors of the train. Just as it pulled out, I nabbed an orange seat in the corner and settled in for my short ride. A middle-aged woman in a tailored plaid jacket sat across from me. She was reading a *Post*. Tyra Banks smiled back at me again. The gentle swaying of the train lulled me into a half-awake trance, and I imagined breaking the news to my sister. *Guess what? I have some good news. Well, you may not think so, but . . .*

Billie was thirty-six, seven years older than me, and single as the day she was born. My nuptials would make her feel even more single. I'd have to find some way to make it more agreeable. Comfort her with the idea that it would be a small wedding. A subdued wedding. A subtle wedding that no one would take special notice of.

I gazed at a tired-looking mom with a little girl leaning against her, sucking her thumb. The mom held the handle of a stroller with a toddler—a girl, judging by the pink barrette—who was sitting very erect, giving me this big toothless grin. I smiled back.

The train lurched to a stop. The woman across from me turned the page of her paper. We all sat still, doing our best to be in denial about the fact that we were sitting underground in a dark tunnel. The brightly lit car with its ads for Calvin jeans and Gucci sunglasses gave the illusion of security. The toddler smiled at me again. I smiled back. Yes, we're sitting in a tunnel . . . isn't this fun?

The train finally inched forward, then gradually picked up

speed. When we reached the Seventy-Second Street station, the driver had to slam on the brakes. People poured in, and the quiet, almost intimate atmosphere was transformed into cattle-car claustrophobia. I could no longer see the kid in the stroller. I was now sandwiched between two people who didn't seem to have any problem taking up as much room as they could, even if that meant their butts were jammed against mine. I inched forward in my seat to give the wide part of my hips more room.

Lots of the train emptied out on Fifty-Ninth Street. At least you could breathe again. The kid in the stroller was still there, and gave me another big smile. I stood, smiled back, and then said "bye-bye" as the train pulled into my stop on Fiftieth Street. She was still smiling as I got off the train.

The exit was clogged, so I waited in line to get through the turnstile, then filed up the stairs behind a line of people. There was no choice but to stare straight into the butt of the woman in front of me. Emerging onto Sixth Avenue, I took a deep breath of fresh air, then swerved through the thick crowds on the sidewalk. It was a six-block walk to the museum past skyscrapers with corporate names like Paine Webber, Time Magazine, and Simon & Schuster. So many people—but I loved it. Why? I wasn't sure. Other than my small circle of friends, I didn't do anything about meeting any of these vast numbers of people who lived in my city that I didn't want to leave because I was afraid of being isolated.

I veered to my left to avoid colliding with a businessman yacking on his cell phone, then turned right to head down Fifty-Second Street.

I was probably clinging to habit. To the place I knew. It's not like Westchester was the other side of the world. It was just one easy train ride from Grand Central. And in some sense, city . . . suburbs . . . people were all the same, weren't they? Really, when you got down to it, weren't we all somewhat interchangeable? If you moved to a new place, you'd find new people. Let's face it: Half my social life was with my TV, and New Rochelle got the same channels as New York City.

Plus, I wouldn't have to cut myself off from my present life. It's just that *I'd* be the one who would commute. And the museum was walking distance from Grand Central. And his grandmother's house was walking distance to the train. So that wouldn't be so bad. So there really was no rational reason to have such mixed feelings about getting married.

So be happy, I told myself, as I stopped at a red light.

Be happy.

The light changed.

Be happy.

I crossed the street.

I *would* be happy . . . once I told Billie. That was the problem. I had to get that over with. She would be annoyed at first, but then she'd get used to the idea, and then she'd be happy for me. She'd probably get into the idea of planning the wedding, even if it was mine. Or maybe she wouldn't. In any case, she would be gracious, and congratulate me, and I'd see that it didn't have to be such a big deal.

I stopped into the Cafe Metro to get my coffee and muffin. I'd been going to this place for years. What was that *Cheers* theme music? Where everyone knows your name? The guy behind the counter barked out, "Whadaya want?"

I certainly recognized him — saw him almost every morning for the past couple years — but he didn't know my name or anything about me, and certainly never remembered my coffee order, even though it was the exact same thing every day. Another reason I loved the city. Anonymity.

"Large coffee with half and half . . ."

"Sugar?"

"No thanks."

Sad comment on sitcoms: Hardly any of them had theme music anymore. *Friends* was one of the last. Now they usually put the credits on during the last scenes of the show, on the side, in letters so small you couldn't read them. No time to acknowledge the creators of the show. No time for a cute, catchy tune. Too expensive.

"Anything else?" he asked, popping the cap on my paper cup.

"A muffin . . ." I eyed them. Blueberry, cranberry, banana nut, bran . . . Did I want tart or sweet? Whole-grain? Low-fat? There was a line behind me. The pressure was on. "Blueberry." As he put it in the bag, my gaze lingered on the banana nut.

The museum was in a beautiful sixteen-floor stark, modern, gleaming white building designed by Philip Johnson and commissioned by William Paley, who ran CBS for many years. He built it for the sole purpose of housing the Museum of Television & Radio. Other museums had Van Goghs and Picassos; we had Gleason and Ball. If Paley hadn't imagined the museum, it wouldn't exist, and there'd be no place dedicated to making sure the history of television was preserved. Maybe some people thought that would be fine, but to me, that would've been as heartbreaking as losing my own childhood home movies, and I had few enough of those.

I pushed through the revolving door into the spacious, high-ceilinged lobby. It was pandemonium out on the streets, but in here it was a retreat. Despite its location in one of the densest business centers in the world, the museum was sparsely attended and tranquil. My good friend Taffy was behind the admissions counter. Her red corkscrew hair framed a heart-shaped adorable face. My age and still living with her parents, she was a huge *Supermodels* fan.

"Did you not love the carriage ride through Central Park?" she asked.

"Very romantic."

Taffy was on the VS staff: viewer services. The VS staff rotates between selling tickets in the lobby, working up in the library, where people choose their shows, and helping in the console room, where they viewed them. I used to be on the VS staff when I first started working at the museum six years ago.

There were still ten minutes before the public was allowed in, so I took my coffee and muffin out of the bag. "Guess what happened while Nigel was proposing to Ashley."

"You finished off a tube of Pringles like I did?"

"Charlie proposed."

"You're kidding! Oh, my god! What did you say?"

What did she think I would say? "I said yes!"

"Well, congratulations."

"Thanks." Did she seem tentative, or was I imagining that? Taffy had only met Charlie a couple of times. She didn't really know him. Still, I did want her approval. "Charlie has this idea that we should buy his grandmother's house in New Rochelle. Can you imagine me living in the suburbs?"

"You'd get to be Laura Petrie."

"Maybe he'll trip over an ottoman when he comes home from work every day."

"From his job writing television!"

Oh, my god. I hadn't even thought of that. Rob Petrie did for a living what Charlie wanted to do. That qualified as slightly ironic.

"Have you set a date?"

"Not yet. I have no idea where I'd want it or anything."

"Whatever you plan, I'm sure it'll be wonderful." She was glossing over the fact that I did not have a mother to plan the wedding with. A father to give me away. I was about to say something to her about how scary it was to make such a big decision when Simon walked in. "Morning, ladies."

Simon was in charge of the VS staff and used to be my boss. He was wearing his usual dark suit and bow tie that went with his tiny round wire-rim spectacles. His shy and soft-spoken manner, combined with the fringe of short brown bangs that ran along the top of his forehead, was monklike. He was in his thirties, single, and Taffy had a big crush on him.

"Guess what," Taffy said.

I wasn't sure I wanted my news available for public consumption. It felt too fresh to be spreading it around. But she wasn't looking at me.

He opened the flap on his coffee and took a sip. "They're bringing back *The Bachelorette*?"

"God forbid." It was common knowledge that Taffy hated reality shows even more than she hated reality. "But you're on the right track, sort of. Daphne is engaged."

"Hey!" He looked at me and got this big smile on his face. "Congratulations!"

"Thanks."

"That's great." He pushed his spectacles up his nose even though they weren't falling down. "I really liked your Lucy tribute."

"Oh, thanks." I wasn't surprised he changed the subject so quickly. Simon was not good at "interpersonal." Rumor had it his wife left him for another woman about a decade ago, and he'd never been in a serious relationship since. His big passion was the museum. He was a lifer.

"I haven't watched it yet," Taffy said, "but I will today."

The tribute to *I Love Lucy* would be featured in the screening room every day for the next month. I'd put together the clips and written the narration spoken by her daughter, Lucie Arnaz. I'd tried to get across the incredible popularity of the show, and how it was the first time in the history of television that people connected emotionally with this electronic picture flickering in their living room. Old episodes of *Lucy* were still *the* most requested shows in the museum library.

"To tell you the truth," Taffy said, "I can't stand Lucy."

"But she's incredibly important." I snuck a piece of muffin out of my bag. "Do you realize she insisted on casting Desi and having the show shot in L.A.? So she could keep him home, so she could keep an eye on him, so he'd stop cheating on her with other women. Think about it: The show about a loving but quarreling couple was created in order to keep a loving but quarreling couple together."

"But she gets on my nerves. I hate how she's always breaking down into tears."

"Yeah," Simon said, "but women totally related to her. Stuck at home, constantly rebelling against Desi, dying to break into show business. If that doesn't speak to what's going on right now, nothing does."

"I suppose," Taffy said, leaning across the desk toward Simon. "But I feel bad for Vivian Vance. I read somewhere they made her gain twenty pounds to look frumpier than Lucy. Plus she was stuck with Fred."

Simon took a sip of coffee. "The real question is: Who loved Lucy more? Ricky or Ethel?"

"Ethel," I said. "Definitely." Was Taffy my Ethel? Was I hers? Every woman needs an Ethel.

"In a way," Simon said, "we have Lucy to blame for the end of live television. If she hadn't insisted on doing the show in L.A. and *filming* it, they would've gone on doing shows *live* here in New York. No one thought anyone would ever want to see a show twice. The rerun never would've been born."

"Isn't it amazing?" Taffy gazed at him like he'd come up with an incredibly profound comment, but then she didn't know that had all been covered in my tribute.

"Anyway," Simon said, nodding to me, "congratulations again." He headed to the elevator.

Taffy waited until he was out of earshot. "He must be picking up on my signals, don't you think?"

"If not, someone needs to adjust his antenna."

"Or maybe he's tuning me out. So did you tell Billie yet?"

Taffy was well aware of my sister problems. "Nope."

"She'll be happy for you."

"Ecstatic."

"She will! She wants you to be happy, silly."

"Theoretically." I opened my bag and tore off another piece of muffin. There weren't many berries in this one. I should've gotten the banana nut.

Three

I rang the bell to my sister's apartment to warn her I'd arrived, then let myself in with my key. The door rammed into a cardboard box full of dusty old *Seventeens*. The top one had Twiggy on the cover. I shoved it aside with my foot and passed through the parquet-floor entranceway. Her apartment was a luxurious two-bedroom in a postwar, white-brick doorman building on the Upper East Side. "Billie?"

"In here!"

I followed her voice to the second bedroom, or "study," as she called it, as if she ever studied anything other than her own appearance. Okay, I love my sister, we're very close—really—and maybe that sounded harsh, but I swear, that's pretty much her overriding concern in life. Oh, and she also put quite a lot of research into the accessories that enhanced her appearance, but there's no real reason to distinguish, is there? I found her staring into the computer screen, carousing with her virtual lovers—the eBay community. Oh, well. It was better than her past addictions. Alcohol, cocaine, bingeing, purging, laxatives . . . Now she compulsively bought used designer clothing and dusty old fashion magazines—particularly ones from the early nineties that had glossy pictures of her.

"Look at this," she said. "A Gucci handbag for twenty-five bucks. Think I should bid?"

She was in lilac silk running shorts and a white short-sleeve top. Her long, tan eye-magnet legs, bony arms, and lanky body (with boy hips that I coveted) barely fit into the space under the desk. I was a perfectly respectable five-seven and hovered between a size six and eight, but next to my five-foot-eleven, size four sister,

I felt squat. Ridiculous, I know, but I guess it's all relative when it comes to relatives. We both had our mom's small straight nose and almond brown eyes. But Billie also had mom's full pouty lips and mahogany brown hair. She liked to keep it long and cascading and parted in the middle. I got Dad's more delicate lips and his thin black straight hair. Billie was always trying to get me to grow it out—especially my bangs, which she hated, but I liked them.

"Sounds like a good deal." I moved a pile off a chair of unopened parcels she'd ordered online or "won" in eBay auctions and never bothered to unpack, pulled up next to her, and took a look. "It's nice," I said, trying to sound positive because I knew, soon enough, I'd be sounding negative.

When I went to my sister's place, I usually had the same progression of feelings. First came jealousy for all the space she had. Then relief that she at least had the space. And then anxiety that she would lose the space.

Charlie and I could've existed quite happily here. There was a fantastic thirty-second floor southern city view that included the Chrysler building, the Empire State Building, and the Fifty-Ninth Street Bridge. At night, with everything all lit up, it was downright, if deceptively, glamorous. But perhaps most exciting were her huge double-door closets (crammed with clothing) and two, count 'em, two bathrooms! And we could've put a crib right in the corner of this study, right where she had her ironing board set up.

But (to follow my progression) *thank god* Billie had a place to live. My worst fear—and it was not completely unrealistic, despite appearances—was that she would end up homeless and begging for change on the streets.

"I love the purple trim. Isn't it gorgeous?" She stared into the screen. "On the other hand," she scrolled down, "there's a really nice Fendi bag, but it's already bid up to a hundred. Look! Gold silk lining."

At least she was in one of her good moods. In a bad mood, I would've found her in bed having an existential crisis because she couldn't find anything to buy and was losing her looks. She was till quite gorgeous, of course, despite the ever darkening circles under her eyes and newly etched crow's-feet when she smiled. "Laugh lines," she liked to quote from that play *The Women,* "tragic."

"Very nice. But . . ." I hated being a killjoy, yet felt compelled to kill her joy when it came to the three c's: clothing, cosmetics, and consumeritis. "Do you really need another bag?"

"You can never have enough handbags, Darling. And it makes me feel so good to open the door and see a package waiting for me. It's like giving yourself a present. Every girl should buy herself a present at least once a week—don't you think? Especially if *he* doesn't."

He being Max.

"But look at all these boxes you haven't opened."

"I know what's inside, and just thinking about it makes me happy. Stop being such a grouch."

Ever since our parents died, it seemed that I had to be the grouch. My translation? The sensible one. After getting the call from some official at the airport on Martha's Vineyard, we were both wrecks. Our parents had been flying up there to look at a summerhouse they wanted to buy.

My father loved his little Cessna. I'd only flown with him a few times, but my last excursion qualified as the most horrifying half hour of my life. I'll never forget sitting in the passenger seat while he frantically looked back and forth at his maps and the ground because he couldn't find the runway. Talk about sweaty palms. Parts of my body I didn't even *know* could perspire sweat moisture. He did eventually locate the thing, and oh my god, was I glad to have the privilege of walking on the earth again.

That fateful day we got the call, a gust of wind had flipped the plane when he was approaching the runway. Just like that, our parents were gone. Gone with the wind. Ha-ha.

I dealt with it by showing everyone I could be incredibly mature about the whole thing. I was sixteen and Billie was twenty-three, but I was the one who called the funeral home to make arrangements. I discussed the plans for transporting their badly bruised bodies to the cemetery in Westchester. I decided on the $4,000 caskets because the $3,000 ones were unfinished pine and looked like crap and the more expensive ones seemed to exist only to gouge guilt-stricken mourners. I went down the list of friends and family, made the calls, talked to the lawyers. Billie could barely stop crying long enough to listen to the rabbi who didn't really know my parents say words that didn't really help. But I was not going to crack, even when I realized that my comfortable Upper East Side childhood was behind me. Billie was already supporting herself as a model-actress-whatever, and a fairly successful one at that, at least as far as the modeling was concerned. I was suddenly dependent on her. And it was just the two of us.

Now she was more dependent on me, though, at least in an emotional sense. At least, that's how I saw it. And it was no longer just the two of us. I had to tell her about Charlie. And deal with her disapproval. And this was the moment to tell her. And I was about to, really, as soon as we were done admiring the Fendi bag. But she jumped up from her computer and gave me a hug. "So guess what. I have the most glorious news. Max asked me to go to Monte Carlo with him."

"Cool!"

"I haven't been there since I did a shoot for French *Vogue*."

There weren't many places she hadn't been. Her work had taken her all over the world when she was in demand, which had been a lucky thing after our parents were gone, because our finances changed so drastically. My father, a tax shelter lawyer, had died with all sorts of leveraged business deals that left his investments a tangled mess. What had seemed to be major assets boiled down to almost nothing after all the lawsuits were settled. Our mother left us with a lot of jewelry, perfume, makeup, and clothes that didn't fit. A Second Chance—the Salvation Army for the Upper East Side set—had a field day with her closets. She definitely had a flair for the glitz. My mom had given up on a singing career to have kids and ended up with two tone-deaf daughters.

"I brought some strudel from Balducci's," I said, holding out the bag, aware that she would not totally welcome this. "Apricot."

She ignored my offering and got back in front of the computer. "You're evil."

I was. "You can have a little. It won't kill you."

"I need to lose two pounds."

"You always need to lose two pounds."

I couldn't remember a time when Billie was not dieting. When our parents' brownstone had to be sold off, I moved into her place, and there was never anything in the refrigerator. That's when I took to ordering in. The diner down the street was on speed dial, and the guy who answered the phones knew my voice just from "I'd like an order delivered." Billie was away so much on jobs, it was practically like I was living on my own. Not that I didn't appreciate the fact that she was successful at what she did. Billie paid my tuition at private school so I wouldn't have to switch. And she was totally generous with cash. She gave me clothes all the time. Still, I finished out my last few years of high school in a haze.

And watched a lot of TV.

The dependability of the prime-time schedule anchored me. The wryness of Letterman was my lullaby. I often slept through the night with laugh tracks scoring my dreams. In the morning, I'd get dressed to the morning shows. Who needed parents? I had Charlie Gibson and Joan Lunden.

"Good news about the trip," I said. "Has Max ever vacationed with you before?"

"Only if you count the week we spent in the Plaza Hotel when his wife was out of town."

"Maybe he's getting more serious about you," I said, more to humor her than anything else.

"He's always been serious about me. He's *crazy* about me! It's just been hard because of his kids. But he's definitely beginning to realize he can't put off his own happiness forever."

"Uh-huh."

"He's had enough of living this double life."

Yep. Billie was in one of her up moods. In her bad moods, she would go on and on about how he didn't care about her and was just using her until she got too old, and then he'd find a replacement.

There'd been a time when she was almost always in an up mood. When I was in high school, she seemed to be living a stunning, magical existence. Flying off to St. Thomas to do a swimsuit shoot. Off to Milan to do a runway show. Paris for a ten-page layout in *Vogue*. I was unaware of all the drinking and drugs. Okay, maybe not completely unaware, but none of it kept her from functioning, and I had enough to worry about what with Murphy Brown getting pregnant and Sam Malone losing his bar.

Those years were crazy. But sometimes I longed for the glamour she'd radiated. Now the jobs were petering out, and she didn't bring in nearly enough to support herself in the style she still aspired to. The bulk of her current work was body-parts modeling. Hands, mostly. She still had beautiful, long, tapered fingers and was an expert at manicuring her own nails.

"Been doing any work recently?" I asked, as she checked the feedback on someone selling a Coach leather tote.

"I did that job last week."

"The hand job?"

"Yep."

"Did it go well?"

"Darling, you know I give the best hand jobs in the industry."

Old running joke.

"Oh, and I had that audition. For the casting agent at ABC, remember?"

"How did it go?"

"Don't ask."

Billie had always fantasized about being an actress, but she'd never been practical about it. Her biggest paid acting job was a voice-over for a limo commercial that she'd done ten years ago. It was sort of funny, because it still perpetually ran on TV. *"For quick service to the airport, dial 777-7777."* She'd gotten a flat fee for doing it. Something like $77. On any given day it seemed to be on about 777 times. Too bad she didn't get a residual every time it aired. She'd be about $7,777,777 richer.

So how, one may wonder, did Billie manage to live in this fabulous two-bedroom apartment with very little discernable income? It's not like she'd saved a penny from her heyday years. No. The truth was . . . she kept up appearances courtesy of Max. In other words, she was a "kept woman." And Max was her "sugar daddy." Not that she referred to him that way. She clung to the concept that they were "having an affair." But the guy hardly ever spent time with her other than coming by for sex. He owned the apartment. Paid the maintenance. Gave her a credit card. Was always slipping her cash. I'd never met him, not once, and I didn't want to. If Max got sick of Billie and cut her off, I had no idea what she would do.

"So now," she said, "I'm in a major panic. We're going next week, and I have to put together an entire new wardrobe."

"You have tons of clothes."

"It's all old and ugly. Don't worry, Max gave me a thousand dollars to rectify the situation. Not nearly enough, of course—he has no idea. You want to come shopping with me tomorrow?"

"Um . . . some of us work for a living?" But that reminded me. At some point, I was going to have to think about a wedding dress. And Billie was going to want major input into picking it out. Was this a good moment to tell her my news?

"Oh, yes, your job. How is that going?"

"Fine. I just need a brilliant idea for a seminar or a special event."

"I'm sure you'll think of one." Billie scrolled back to the Fendi bag. "Max has no idea what things cost. This bag retails for $4,000. It's bound to get bid up. Maybe I should 'Buy it now.' "

"I don't know . . ." They wanted $299 if she bought it immediately.

"Let me just put a watch on it." After a few more clicks, she got up from the computer. "Shall we have your sinful strudel, you evil witch? I'll put on some tea."

I followed her to the kitchen. It had oak-wood cabinets and was equipped with a mini-size washer–dryer (luxury in the city), a stainless steel refrigerator with a water spigot in the door (I always wanted one of those), and a spiffy dishwasher (forget the spigot— I *really* wanted one of those). Purple tulips drooped in a green teardrop-shaped vase on the granite countertop. She put a kettle on the Wolf stove. "So how are you?"

It was my moment to tell her. "Pretty good . . ."

"What would you like?" She'd opened her cupboard. There were stacks of almost every flavor of tea you could think of: Orange Spice, Apple Cinnamon, Almond Vanilla, Green, Decaffeinated Green, Red Zinger . . .

"Lipton is fine."

"You're so easy to please."

The way she said it, I wasn't sure if it was a compliment or criticism.

"So what's new?" she asked.

Tell her, a voice inside my head said. "Not much." *I'm getting married.* "So things are going well with Max?"

"He was just here last night. Speaking of hand jobs. He does like my hands . . . do you like my new shade?" She showed me her nails.

"I love that pink."

"Bergdorf's. Yves Saint Laurent. $19.99."

I showed her my hand. "Duane Reade. Wet 'n' Wild. $1.99."

"Groovy."

We took our snack to the table in the small living room and cut pieces off the long stick of strudel. Billie's piece was about the size of a quarter.

"What happens," I asked, "if you don't feel like servicing Max?"

She laughed. "I'd recommend the gas station near the Lincoln Tunnel."

"No, really, what would happen?"

"It's not a matter of feeling like it. If I won't do it, he'll go to someone else, so I make sure I feel like it. It's really not a big deal.

As a matter of fact, Max was supposed to come over tonight, but he canceled. Used to be, he needed a good blow job every few days to keep him going. Now he can go a whole week."

"Huh." Charlie certainly liked his blow job now and then, but we basically relied on missionary sex, which made us total geek-nerds, I know, but there you have it. Plus, I might mention (in our defense—am I getting defensive?) it wasn't bad missionary sex. He knew how to bring me to orgasm, and I knew how to bring him. But still. We seemed to need to stay pretty much within a well-defined script for our lovemaking, and he was so not into going down on me. I was tempted to ask Billie if she thought it was a problem. But I didn't. Because I knew she'd say it was a big problem, and it would become one more reason for her to disapprove of Charlie.

"It's fine. Really," she said. "I'm glad he didn't come. I'd rather be with my little sister eating strudel."

"Aw, shucks. But . . . so . . . do you really think he's getting more serious about you?"

"Definitely. It's becoming less of a sex thing. We're starting to get really close. The fact that he's taking me on this trip is major. So romantic. We're going to stay at a hotel right on the Riviera."

"Wow."

"And you thought he was losing interest in me."

"It is a good sign that he's willing to wake up next to you."

"No need to get catty."

"And you can actually go out in public." I cut another slice of strudel. "Without worrying about his wife."

"Fuck you—you're jealous."

"I *am* jealous." I wasn't, but it was better to let her think I was. "I can't remember the last time I got out of the city, much less the country. Except for going to Rye to visit Charlie's parents, and that doesn't count."

Maybe I was actually a little jealous.

I took another slice of strudel. *Tell her*, that voice insisted. But now it seemed odd to bring it up. After all, a marriage proposal was something you blurted out at the beginning of a conversation. It's really not a "by the way" kind of thing. No, we'd let this visit focus on Max. I'd bring up Charlie next time. "Monte Carlo really sounds like fun."

"At the risk of jinxing it . . ." She flattened a piece of the cheese filling with her fork. "I think, when we're there, he's going to ask me to marry him."

"Really?" Could it be true? Oh, god. If only Max would leave his wife and marry her. I wouldn't have to worry anymore. . . . "Did he say something to make you think that?" I wanted a fact. Something specific. Billie could manufacture hope out of almost nothing.

"He keeps saying how important commitment is. His oldest daughter is going off to college, you know. I can't wait to walk down the beach in the glorious sun as naked as possible. And then we'll spend the evenings at the casinos playing blackjack and screw all night. . . ."

"Maybe you *should* go for that Fendi bag." I swallowed some cream-cheesy apricot filling and washed it down with some tea.

"You think I should?" She looked at me in a panic, and then, as if drawn by a powerful force field, got up and ran back to the computer. "What the hell. I can always sell it on eBay after I get back."

"Now you're thinking." I moved to the couch and flicked on her TV. What would we do without our screens?

Four

"It's so beautiful back here," I said, sipping white wine from my plastic cup. Charlie and I were sitting on folding chairs in the back garden of Taffy's brownstone enjoying the sunshine and the shrubbery. It was actually Taffy's parents' brownstone. She lived on the top floor. Her parents lived on the bottom three floors, and they were throwing themselves an anniversary party.

"Yeah," Charlie said, taking a sip of his wine, "it's really nice."

Taffy's mother taught Women's Studies at Columbia. Her father was a stockbroker, but the nice kind you would trust your life savings with and not worry that he'd churn your account and then take your money to Reno to gamble away at the craps table. (This happened to my parents once.) They basically left Taffy alone and let her stay rent-free.

This setup was admittedly virtually the same as still living with your parents, and she was mortified that she still did at twenty-nine, but I totally understood why. It was a beautiful home on West Eighty-Eighth Street near Central Park West. A quiet and residential street lined with gorgeous tall trees. The park was right at the end of the block. You could often hear birds tweeting. Not that I cared that much about nature, but it was nice to have it around now and then.

"If we moved to New Rochelle," Charlie said, "you could have a garden five times this size."

"And you could spend all your spare time maintaining it."

"I'd like that."

"No you wouldn't." This conversation was annoying me. I wished it wasn't. Lots of couples moved out of the city to start a family; it was almost impossible not to these days if you weren't rolling in money. Charlie was being practical. I was being unreasonable. Except . . . "What about my job?"

"You can commute in."

"I think the train fare would eat up about a quarter of my salary."

"You can quit," he said. "We could start on babies right away."

Right away? Was *eventually* coming so soon? "But if we move out there, I'll need my job more than ever. I don't know anyone in the suburbs." I gazed at the happy partygoers standing near us, chattering away happily. Why were we talking about this now, at a party, when we were supposed to be enjoying ourselves?

"You'll meet other moms at those baby classes," he said. "I mean, face it: Add up the train fare and the babysitter, you'll barely be breaking even."

"Maybe we should deduct the babysitter from *your* salary."

"That doesn't make any sense."

"It makes as much sense as what you said."

Neither of us spoke. I took a sip of wine. So did he. We had arrived at a proverbial cul de sac.

Taffy emerged through the sliding glass door of the kitchen and pulled up a chair. She looked great in a fuzzy lime-green sweater that set off her red curls. "Isn't it lovely? I never come out here except when there's a party or some sort of function. Isn't that ridiculous?"

"It is lovely," I said, trying to wipe the sour look off my face. The brownstone dated from 1890, and her parents had lovingly restored it. I'd grown up in a very similar house, but on the East Side, where it was, in general, even more wealthy and more uptight. I never understood why my parents wanted to live in that neighborhood. Seemed like no matter how much money people had, they were desperate to have more, desperate to look good compared to everyone else. Why bother to impress when all anyone else cared about was how impressive *they* were? But my father had grown up poor, managed to get into Yale, made a lot of money, and wanted the world to know it. I certainly didn't remember him as a happy man. Always working, always worried about something, always trying to lose twenty pounds but unable to stop eating fattening meals in fancy restaurants. "It's so amazing," I said, "to think your parents have been married for thirty years."

"I know. Charlie, yours have been together a long time too, right?"

"Thirty-five years."

"Wow." Now Taffy looked around the garden as if it was a prison courtyard. "Sometimes I wonder if I'll ever leave."

"It would certainly be understandable. Great space. Nice neighborhood. Pleasant parents." I shot her a teasing look of pity. "You're trapped."

"I'm going to end up an old maid with ten cats."

"You don't have to get the cats," Charlie said.

"But I will. Because that's what happens to people like me."

It's true that her love life had been static for years. There'd been one heated love affair a couple of years back with a guy named George. She'd thought he was going to be the one. But George ended up moving to California for a job and didn't ask her to go with him. Now she rarely dated. Or met anyone new. She'd invited Simon to this party, but so far he was a no-show.

"There's a prospect for you." Charlie nodded toward a very tall, slim man with a huge forehead and almost no hair. He'd just stepped outside and was admiring the garden.

"Him?" Taffy sighed. "An old friend of my mother's who happens to be gay. But you should talk to him, Charlie. He's an agent at William Morris."

"That's okay."

"He's very nice."

"He'll think I want him to read my scripts."

"Yes," Taffy urged. "You should ask him."

"So I can experience more rejection?" Charlie scowled. "No thanks."

He was so negative. I wished he wouldn't be, but I understood where it was coming from, so I kept quiet.

"I'm sure it happens to him all the time," Taffy said. "Don't be shy."

Charlie shook his head. It wasn't shyness holding him back. More like bitterness, disgust, resentment, and rage.

"Come on," she said. "Go for it."

"Thanks for trying," I said, "but Charlie's pretty much not into it anymore."

"You mean you've given up?" Taffy looked at him with astonishment. "How can you do that? You can't do that."

"Can't give up on failure?" His whole face tensed up.

"You aren't a failure," Taffy said, "unless you give up."

He sneered and said nothing.

Piano playing drifted from an open window. "Oh, good." Taffy got up. "My dad. I love it when he plays. It's so hard to get him to do it in front of guests."

"He plays so beautifully," I said, fighting off an attack of sentiment. My mother loved anything by Gershwin. Hearing the music made me pine to hear her sing. She'd always planned on getting back to it professionally, but that never had a chance to happen.

Taffy looked at Charlie and nodded toward the agent. "In case you change your mind, his name is Gordon Fineberg."

As soon as she was inside, I switched from defense to offense. The truth was I didn't want him to give up. His television writing was a big part of what had attracted me to him in the first place. When we'd first started dating, I'd gotten a vicarious thrill out of reading his scripts and giving him feedback. It was exciting to be part of the creation process for a change. And I was impressed that he could see himself succeeding in that world.

Now he was so bitter. And supercritical of everything that was on. When he first moved in, we always used to watch TV together. It was fun and cozy. *Seinfeld* reruns. *Law and Order. Saturday Night Live.* These shows had been a vital part of our courtship. Now he scorned everything, and practically the only thing he watched was the Yankees.

"She's right, you know. You deserve to get your work out there."

"I'm not going up to a stranger to sell him on how 'wonderful' I am just so he can avoid me the rest of the party."

I looked at the agent. His expensive leather jacket, air of confidence, gloss of authority—it was intimidating. But Charlie needed him. "One minute of groveling," I said. "That's all it takes. Then it'll be over with."

"If you're gonna keep this up, let's just leave."

I exhaled a stream of air out my nostrils that could've snuffed a candle. Honestly. Charlie needed an agent to get him an agent. Well, maybe that had to be me. I would have to step in. Truth was, I had the most pressing motive. New Rochelle. Wall-to-wall carpeting. Lawn mulch.

I downed my wine and psyched myself up. Our prey was now smiling and nodding to an attractive but tiny, slim woman with a bleached-white pixie cut, a white T-shirt, and white jeans that showed a hint of butt crack. I waited until she walked away, and he went to peruse the cheese tray. Then I descended on him just as he was putting a cracker with Brie into his mouth.

"Hi."

"Hello." Bits of cracker crumbled out of the side of his mouth. "Excuse me."

"No, excuse me, I didn't mean to—"

"Not at all. My name is Gordon Fineberg." He held out his hand without the cracker. A firm grip.

I made small talk, mentioning how I was at the party because I worked with Taffy at the Museum of Television. I figured that would break the ice.

"I've heard of that place."

"Ever been there?"

"No, but I do always plan to get there. . . ."

That's what everyone says. "You should come. We have more than 120,000 shows. Lots of rare copies of kinescopes from 1948 and on, like *Your Show of Shows*, *Texaco Star Theater*, *This is your Life. . . .*"

"Really. I definitely will."

"So, what do you do?" I asked, as if I didn't know.

"I'm an agent."

"Real estate?"

He laughed. "William Morris."

"Oh." I pretended not to be impressed. And noticed Charlie walking past us, heading inside. "How fascinating. What kind of things do you represent?"

Mr. Fineberg spoke as if he was telling me his PIN number in front of an ex-con. "Mostly television writers."

"You know, my boyfriend—he's written a number of wonderful scripts."

"Really." His eyeballs instantly darted past me as if looking away would transport him to another party in another garden in another town. The sounds of Gershwin tinkled out the second-floor window. I proceeded to list some of the more recent existing shows Charlie had written spec scripts for, peppering my delivery with exclamations on how talented he was. Then I added, since he was barely listening, how I was sorry he couldn't meet him because he happened to be at the running of the bulls in Pamplona.

"Wow, great! Congratulations!" he said smiling but clearly not intending to ask if said boyfriend was represented, had sold any of these scripts, or was at all anxious about getting trampled or gored.

"He's actually looking for an agent," I said. "He has a pilot for a new sit-com."

The smile that had been on Mr. Fineberg's face became strained, but he had the grace to keep it pasted. "That's great!"

"It's called *Sitting Comics*. It's a cross between *Seinfeld* and *Cheers*, and it focuses on a bar at a comedy club and the depressed comics who hang out there."

He'd used his experiences from working at the club, and it was his best piece of work, in my opinion. Or, at least, his most low brow and accessible. I liked to take some credit for it (at least in my own mind) because I'd come up with the idea and helped him work out the story. "He's sent it to some agents in L.A., a few production companies, but hasn't had any luck yet. As you well know, it's hard to break in, but it's just so good. . . ."

"You should tell him to send it to me. I'd love to take a look."

"Really?" Phew. He'd actually made the offer. Spared me the final humiliation. "That would be great. I'll tell him."

"Let me give you my card."

His card. I knew he was probably just trying to get rid of me, but I couldn't help but feel a thrill. Oh, yeah. This was why we lived in New York! This was the way things happened!

As he removed it from his wallet, I thanked him as graciously as I could. "I know how busy you must be."

"No problem."

"And I'm sorry to foist this on you at a party. It was really nice talking with you."

Grovel, grovel, grovel.

"You too."

"Thank you so much . . ." The sound of my own sickeningly sweet syrupy voice emanating as much goodwill as possible, as if I was the nicest person in the world, and my niceness was soft, warm butter oiling up his entire body . . . it made me cringe.

He excused himself and went back to the cheese tray.

I followed the sound of the piano upstairs. People were gathered around, listening to Taffy's dad play "Summertime." I felt a moment of jealousy at how wonderful it must be to have a father who could play such beautiful music. But I knew she was sad that Simon hadn't shown up. I at least had Charlie. I stood next to him and whispered into his ear. "I spoke with the agent."

He looked sideways at me and kept his face dour.

"I have his card," I whispered. "He wants you to send him something."

Charlie whispered. "He was just being polite."

I frowned and rolled my eyes and shook my head.

"But thanks," he said quietly. "That was nice of you." He gave me a kiss on the cheek. I felt good inside.

We stood there and listened to the sad, sweet song. It probably was true. Mr. Fineberg probably was just being polite. But I fingered the piece of card stock in my pocket. . . . You never knew.

Five

I was sitting at my desk, trying to come up with an idea for a really good special event. My office, like all the private offices, was small and in the shadow of the high-rise next door. But I'd made it as cozy as I could, with posters of Luke Perry, Daria, Marlo Thomas as *That Girl*, a rare subway poster of *Dharma and Greg*, and a cardboard stand-up of Spike from *Buffy the Vampire Slayer* (a gift from Taffy) that I really had to get rid of because he took up too much room.

Ben Kaplan, the other curator, appeared in my doorway with coffee cup in hand. "So have you decided what you're working on?" He was in his early fifties, had graying hair and blue eyes, and wore a light gray suit. We had completely different tastes — which was part of the reason we worked well together.

"Still bouncing some ideas around in my head."

"My seminar on *Meet the Press* is ready to go."

"Great."

What could be more boring? Okay. Granted. *Meet the Press* was *the* longest running show ever, period. It premiered in 1947, was still on, was still a public affairs "radio show" with talking heads, still serious, and *still seriously dull.* There's a reason why it's relegated to Sunday mornings: That's the only time of the week when people voluntarily don't want to watch television.

"And the Bochco project is falling into place," he said. "Just working on getting the actors to show up."

"Good luck." That was always a major scheduling nightmare. "So what are you working on next?"

"I'm thinking about Westerns. Why they're dead and how police dramas took their place. From *The Gene Autry Show* to *Gun-*

smoke. I'm delving into them now. They're great fun. You know what they say: They paid the horses more than the actors."

"The only horse I ever got into was Mr. Ed on Nick at Nite reruns."

"In the late fifties there were something like thirty westerns on the air."

"Wow."

"And now? None."

"Sounds like a good topic."

"Thanks. If you want to bounce some ideas off me . . ."

"Thanks."

He headed to his office.

Pretty much all I knew about Ben Kaplan was that the daughter in the picture on his desk liked soccer, the son in the picture on his desk liked baseball, and the wife, who did not rate a picture, liked spending too much money on remodeling their West Village brownstone.

I arranged what was left of my muffin and coffee on my desk and eyed my huge pile of unread books. Maybe I'd look through and see if something sparked my interest. *Media Moguls, Four Arguments for the Elimination of Television, Late Night Talk Show Wars.* Nothing was calling out to me. When the phone rang, I was glad for the distraction.

"I need you!"

It was Taffy. "What is it?"

"Jonathan Hill."

"What about him?"

"He's here."

Jonathan Hill was an incredibly successful television producer. As a matter of fact, he was the writer, creator, and producer of *Supermodels*. His first show, *Boomers*, made him a darling of the critics, and his next three series were all characterized by a quirky intelligence and a New York sensibility. Admittedly, *Supermodels* was more quirky than intelligent. But the guy was so talented— even when he was making trash. "Are you sure?"

"Yes! He gave me his name. He's looking for episodes of *Models, Inc.*, and we don't seem to have any."

Models, Inc. was a spin-off from *Melrose Place*, which was a spin-off of *Beverly Hills, 90210*. I'd watched a few episodes back when it was on. Linda Gray of *Dallas* fame ran a modeling agency, and there was the usual backstabbing, murder, stalking, and decadence, not unlike what you'd find in *Supermodels*. But that show was canceled after one season. It just didn't have the magic combination of casting and writing that made a show fly. *Beverly Hills, 90210*, on the other hand, used to be one of my very favorite shows in the universe. I'd followed it religiously as the gang went from high school to college at pretty much the same time I did. "So tell him to watch some *Top Models*."

"He doesn't want that. And he insists there's another show about models. Something from the eighties. I've never heard of one, have you?"

"The eighties . . . ?" Hmmm . . .

"Would you just come down? Please?"

"Fine." I took the elevator down. Noticed I was trembling slightly. Felt relieved I looked good that day. I happened to be wearing my favorite outfit—a white lace camisole under a lilac sweater, short green corduroy skirt, and my black cowboy boots. There *was* a show in the eighties about models. But what was it? It would be so annoying if my brain failed me now. We rarely had industry people coming in to the library. Jerry Seinfeld came once to watch some Jack Benny, who was supposed to be one of his idols. One of the original writers on *Our Miss Brooks* came to see shows he wrote. He was, like, in his nineties. That was so cute.

I got off on the 4th floor and pushed open the glass door to the library. It was a pleasant space, with wood paneling, windows on both ends, and ten large, glossy wood tables where people could sit at computers and search for shows. Taffy was behind the desk. She nodded toward the wall, where there was a series of those cartoonlike prints by Al Hirschfeld—caricatures of personalities like George Burns and Gracie Allen, Sid Caesar and Imogene Coca, Rowan and Martin. . . .

There he was. Somewhere in his forties, quite tall, wearing a powder-blue short-sleeve linen shirt and white chinos. He was walking slowly past each print, clasping his hands behind his back, peering into each one.

Taffy mouthed something—I couldn't tell what, she seemed to be having some sort of panic attack—so I went over to him, stood behind him as he examined a grinning Phyllis Diller, cleared my throat, and said, "Excuse me?"

Jonathan Hill turned around and—I could've sworn—he noticed me. I mean, like, really took me in. Found me attractive? Dream on. This guy could have anyone he wanted. God, what would it be like to be that successful? To have this effect on people that he was having on me now just by being in a room. All that power. Did anyone treat him normally?

"Hi," he said.

My heart was pounding.

As if this meant anything in the scheme of my life.

As if I wasn't just doing my job.

"Can I help you?" I didn't tell him my name. You'd think I was scared I'd get it wrong. The thing was . . . he was so good-looking. Dark brown hair, dark brown eyes, healthy tan. He looked like he hadn't shaved in days. Considering the expensive clothes and healthy glow, it was obvious the stubble was fashion statement not lack of grooming.

"Maybe. Yes. I'm looking for episodes of *Models, Inc.*"

"We don't have any of those."

He made this disapproving "hmmmm" sound. Sometimes people assume we have copies of, like, every single show ever made. But just like any museum, we are dependent on donations. Sometimes they come from the networks (ABC was particularly generous), sometimes producers, sometimes people who just happened to find an old kinescope on the top shelf of their closet.

"Any suggestions how I could find it?"

Did he want to steal plotlines? Was he worried Aaron Spelling would think he was trying to rip off his idea? It was totally typical for story lines from old shows to be rehashed.

"You could try to contact Aaron Spelling." I smiled to let him know I was teasing.

He chuckled. "I don't think so. Do you know of any other series about models?" he asked. "I'm positive there was a show in the eighties . . ."

"Did you try a search?" I asked, going to one of the computers.

"Nothing came up."

Just in case, I did my own search for "model" and then "fashion," but there was nothing. What was that show? Think. Think. "Do you know who was in it?"

"Heather Locklear keeps coming to mind."

"No, she was Amanda on *Melrose Place*, and it was her mother who owned the modeling agency on *Models, Inc.*, but it was *someone* like that. . . ." And then, bing, it clicked in. "Morgan Fairchild!"

"Yes," he said, "I think that's right!"

"Now what was the name of that show . . ."

We were both silent for a moment as we racked our brains. He kept looking straight at me, and I had to look away because it was just too exciting to make eye contact. Morgan Fairchild. Morgan Fairchild. Morgan Fairchild. It was killing me. It was right on the edge of my mind. I was about to go ask Taffy to look her up on IMDB.com, a Web site with all the info on every movie and show—great resource—and then I looked at him, our eyes locked, and the planets aligned. We said it together at the exact same time.

"*Paper Dolls!*"

Then we grinned at each other like we'd just won the final question on *Jeopardy*.

"What a relief!" he said.

"I *knew* I knew it. . . ."

I quickly typed in *Paper Dolls*, doing my best not to make typos. "I think we have a few of those. But they're in the archive, not the collection, so they haven't been cataloged or cross-referenced yet.

That's why it didn't come up in the search. Here we go. There are twelve of them."

"Hey, thanks. This is great."

"You can select four to view right now. The limit is four a day. . . ."

"Would it be possible to check them out?"

"You mean like take them out of the building? We don't do that. Everything stays here."

He frowned. "I'll be happy to put down a deposit, whatever you need. I don't really have time in the middle of the day to come here, and I'm sure there isn't exactly a horde of people wanting to watch that show. . . ."

Here was a man used to getting his way. "This is a museum. You wouldn't go to the Whitney and take home a Warhol."

I'd meant to say it pleasantly with a smile, but it came out sounding snotty with attitude. And then I was too nervous to soften it with a smile because, once again, I really sensed he was *looking* at me, and it made me so self-conscious I felt like if I moved my lips they would explode into spasms of tics.

His expression changed to skepticism. "You would compare old *Paper Dolls* to a Warhol?"

"Warhol would've appreciated the camp, kitschy nature of the show, don't you think?" His eyes swept down my body. God. Did he like what he saw? Not that it mattered. I was an engaged woman, after all. With a boyfriend who had piles of scripts this man could produce . . . "I mean, television is a vital part of pop culture, and Warhol was all about pop art. Anyway, that's the policy." I hated sounding like a hard-ass, but, well, that was the policy.

"If that's the *policy*," he said, "I guess I'm stuck."

Was he mocking me? "Is there anything else I can help you with?"

"Don't think so. Thanks."

I got up from the computer and he sat down to pick out his four. Oh, yeah. I'd really charmed him.

Not that there was any reason to charm him.

But did I need to come off like such a prig?

I joined Taffy at the desk. She was practically panting. "Did you think of the show?"

"*Paper Dolls.*"

"Oh! Right! Never heard of it. You think he's stealing plot-lines?"

"He wanted to know if he could check them out. If only I could tell him about Charlie's pilot."

But it was hopeless. Producers didn't want pilots from unproven writers. Jonathan Hill came up with his own ideas and wrote them himself. And he didn't do sitcoms anyway. Not that there was any reason why he couldn't.

Taffy looked down at her screen. He'd entered his four requests into the queue. I braced myself as he came up to the desk. Taffy managed to do her part. "It'll just be a few minutes. You can wait on the bench, if you'd like."

We always tried to get people to wait on the bench by the window so they wouldn't be hovering over us while they waited. In his case, I wouldn't have minded if he hovered, though he probably didn't want to mingle with us "commoners."

But then, to my surprise, he did hover. And again, I felt him looking at me, and his gaze made my whole body go warm. "So what are the most popular shows people watch here?"

"Oh, you know . . ." He waited for my answer. I resisted the urge to ask him if that was a fake tan, and wondered what it would be like to feel those nubby whiskers against my cheek. "*The Simpsons?*" I looked toward Taffy, but her face was frozen in terror. "*Seinfeld,*" I added. "*Sex and the City. Friends. I Love Lucy.*" Now I couldn't shut up. "*The Sopranos, The Honeymooners.*" And then, I added, just to make him feel good, "*Boomers.*"

Taffy raised her eyebrows. *Boomers* was the show that had established his career, but hardly anyone ever asked to see it. Indeed, Jonathan Hill looked surprised. "Here at the museum, we're all very impressed by your work, Mr. Hill."

"Please," he said—I could've sworn he blushed ever so slightly—"call me Jonathan. And you are?"

"Daphne Wells."

He gave me a humble little Japanese nod. "Thank you, Daphne Wells."

"You're welcome," I said, and quickly added, because I was freaked out that he'd called me by my name, "and this is Taffy."

He nodded at Taffy. "I like that name. Taffy. Can I use it sometime?"

"Sure." She blushed. He'd just made her century.

"I'm always looking for good model names," he said.

Taffy seemed unable to form any words, so I said, "By the way, we'd love to add the first season of *Supermodels* to the collection—if you'd like to donate it."

"I'd be happy to. Though maybe I don't want people to remember me that way."

"Are you kidding? We love that show."

"You do?"

"I try to keep up with the story line." No way was I letting him know I never missed it.

"So people ask to see *Boomers*?"

"The pilot is very popular. And the episode where Lisa thought Dennis was cheating, but he was actually learning Hebrew to connect with his roots . . . a classic."

No one ever asked for those shows, actually. Okay, maybe occasionally. Rarely. But there went my heart again, pounding away. Thank god there's no volume control on body parts. "We at the museum consider *Boomers* to be a quality evening drama like *Hill Street Blues*, *St. Elsewhere*, *Moonlighting*, *Twin Peaks* . . . Real rule-breakers."

"Good company," he said.

"But of course none of them explored the dilemmas of that generation like *Boomers*. The way it challenged the ideals of the suburban home, the impossibility of balancing career and family, the need for men and women to step out of their traditional sex roles to find fulfillment . . ." Out of the corner of my eye I could see Taffy screwing up her face at me, and indeed, where was I coming up with all this? I'd hardly watched the show when it aired in the nineties. It was too much about marriage to interest me then. "And it had such great characters."

"Some called them whiney and complaining and self-centered."

"They were just jealous of the fantastic ratings."

He smiled. I'd just made a friend.

"So," he asked, looking around the room, "what exactly is it that you do here?"

"I'm a curator. I organize screenings, events, seminars. . . ."

"So you know everything there is to know about the history of television."

"Maybe not everything, but a ridiculous amount. That's one of the hazards of loving your job."

"Now that's unusual," he said. "Someone who loves her job."

"I guess I'm pretty lucky."

It seemed odd to be telling a successful man like him that I was lucky. He was the lucky one, right? But, well, it was true. I did love my job. At least, most of the time. And that did make me lucky. Most of the time.

"So this place," he said, "isn't full of frustrated television writers?"

"Not really." I decided this was not the moment to mention I was engaged to a frustrated television writer. "We all just happen to love TV."

Taffy handed his request slip to him, but was so nervous, she looked at me while she told him, "Your selections are ready. Take this and go down those stairs to the console room. They'll set you up."

It was frustrating to know he'd be sitting at a television console one floor below us for the next couple hours and then be out of our lives forever.

Except . . . he did want to see the other *Paper Dolls*. So he would be back. "If you need anything else, please let me know."

"I may take you up on that."

He reached out to shake my hand. I paused before taking it, as if he was holding out a live wire. When I put my hand in his and our skin made contact, my entire body warmed up. "Enjoy your shows."

"I'll try. Thanks for your help."

He nodded at me one more time before disappearing down the stairs. I kept a stupid grin on my face until he was gone.

"*You wouldn't believe how often people request it?*" Taffy aped me. "*Boomers?* Listen to you kissing up."

"I was just being polite."

"You were flirting shamelessly!"

"I was not."

"Yes you were. Look at you. You're positively glowing. And so was he, for that matter."

"Oh, come on. He'd never notice a nobody like me."

"Seems to me he already did notice you."

"You're crazy." But I noticed, as I headed to the elevator, that I enjoyed hearing her say that a bit too much.

Six

"Thanks for the flowers," I said, for the third or fourth time.

"You're welcome."

The bouquet of two dozen yellow roses was sitting on the dining room table. "They're beautiful." Charlie had also bought the glass vase to put them in, since we didn't have one big enough. The note had said, *With All My Love, from your Fiancé.*

"So I spoke to my parents," Charlie said, plopping down next to me on the couch. "My grandmother found a condo in Delray."

"That was fast."

He got a stack of papers out of his backpack to correct. "She's going to talk to her lawyer about drawing up some papers for the house."

"Okay." I reached for the remote. That sounded official.

"So you're feeling good about the move?"

I zapped to *E!*, but it was a rerun of a profile on Reese Witherspoon, so I made my way down to the networks, stopping on a *Seinfeld* along the way. I was biding my time until *Survivor* came on. "I'm feeling like it's probably the right thing to do."

"I know it's scary," he said. "I get freaked out when I think about it too."

"You do? Good." I actually found that reassuring.

"My mom, by the way, she has some ideas about the wedding."

"Surprise, surprise."

"She wants to look into doing it in Westchester. It's up to you, we all agree, so you have to be honest about what you want."

"Does she have a place in mind?"

"I think, you know, if you were open to it, she was going to

call around to some hotels and see what was available. Evident
people plan so far ahead of time . . . We could be talking nex
year. But it would be nice to do it this summer. Does that give
you enough time?"

"To get used to the idea?"

He gave me an odd look. "To plan it."

Whoops. "Yes, sure. Definitely. Sounds great." I glanced at the
clock. Three minutes until the hour. "Hey, did you ever send Gordon Fineberg your script?"

"Yeah. That was a waste of postage."

"That's the spirit." I punched in Channel 2. Almost mentioned
about Jonathan Hill coming in to the museum, but didn't. After
all, Charlie didn't like *Supermodels* and considered the guy a major
sellout.

"So you're okay with the idea of Westchester?" Charlie asked.

"I guess. But we've been living together for so long . . . it's not
like we need some big elaborate thing." Truth was, I hated the idea
of a big wedding. All that planning. Smiling till your mouth is
sore. Coming up with a clever speech before cutting the cake.
Dancing to the "Electric Slide" in front of your relatives. Apolo-
gizing to your relatives for not calling since your parents' funeral . . . "Maybe," I said, as *Survivor* started and the remaining
players confided their strategies to the camera, "we could just do
it on some tropical island."

"How about the traffic island on Sixth Avenue?"

"That's a possibility," I said, and to tell the truth, I sorta liked
the idea. It would certainly reflect something of my real life. But
we'd probably be encouraging rubbernecking and cause an acci-
dent. "If your mother wants it in Westchester, that's fine. Most of
the guests are going to be from your side of the family. And it's got
to be a lot cheaper than the city."

"But it has to be your decision," he said. "You're the bride."

"The bride. Wow." I nudged him. "That makes you the groom."

I watched the show for awhile while Charlie corrected papers.
It was raining outside, and I was happy to be in my comfy apart-

.ent with my "fiancé" while these poor contestants were fighting
.t out on an island. The "reward challenge" involved pulling heavy
pipes through the water and up on the sand to make a tower. It
didn't seem right the women had to do this in skimpy bikinis
while worrying if their boobs were gonna spill out. After the challenge, the winners got to eat a huge feast of beer, cheese, and
crackers. They looked so happy stuffing themselves. Then they had
to do the "immunity challenge." It was some kind of memory trick
puzzle.

Charlie put a score on top of one of his papers and turned to
me. "Have you told your sister yet?"

"What?"

"That we're getting married?"

"Um, not exactly."

"You did see her recently, didn't you?"

"Yeah. Max is taking her to Monte Carlo."

"So you saw her but you didn't tell her about us?"

"I know it's really stupid and ridiculous but . . ." I screwed up
my face in some attempt to show him how messed-up I knew this
was. "I'm afraid to tell her."

"You have to tell her, Daphne."

"I know." One of the women finished her puzzle, but Jeff told
her she'd done it wrong, and she had to try again.

"You're building it up inside your head. She can handle it.
She'll be happy for you."

He didn't even know how much Billie disapproved of him.
"You're totally right."

He stacked his papers and put them back in the duffel bag.
"You can't put your life on hold for her. She can deal with it. And
you'll feel better once you tell her."

"I will. Next time I see her. I promise." No one had managed to
finish the puzzle.

He put his papers aside and edged close to me. "I was sitting
on the train today, just sitting there, feeling happy about us getting married, thinking how pretty you are. . . ."

He was looking at me, so full of love. "You're pretty cute yourself."

He reached over and stroked my hair. "We should get the ring this weekend, don't you think?"

"That sounds like fun." I glanced at the screen. One of the men thought he was done with the puzzle, but Jeff said it was wrong. No one could get the puzzle right! I turned back to Charlie.

"You're like a flower in bloom," he said, "and when I look at you and see how beautiful you are, I can think, you know, life is indeed short, and I'm happy to be alive."

I could hear Jeff announcing that someone had solved the puzzle, and they went to a commercial. "That's such a sweet thing to say."

He leaned over and gave me a kiss on my hair, my ear, my cheek. That's when I heard her voice. Billie's voice. Her limo ad. "For quick service to the airport call 777-7777 . . ." I didn't look. Not that I would need to. I, along with the rest of New York, had seen it so many times it was like a collective childhood memory. "So next time you need to get somewhere . . ."

I looked into Charlie's hazel eyes. "Should we turn it off?"

"I beg of you."

I aimed the remote, hesitating for a moment. ". . . and we'll pick you up in style, so just call 777-7777 and . . ." I pressed the button. Bye-bye, Billie. I glanced at my yellow roses. So long, *Survivor*. We went into the bedroom. No Tribal Council tonight. Charlie's arms came around me. We pressed up against each other. I melted into his kisses. As he pulled off his T-shirt and I pulled off mine, I told myself not to worry. In the morning, I could see who was eliminated when they did the recap on *The Early Show*.

Seven

"So I'm thinking of doing something on women comedians," I said, sitting across the desk from Simon.

"That sounds good," he said, cleaning the lenses of his glasses with a small blue cloth.

"But I'm not sure how to narrow it down." His office was truly his home away from home. There was a comfy old brown tweed easy chair by the window. A gold wool rug. A framed poster of the *Honeymooners* cast next to the window.

"Are you thinking women in sitcoms? Or women who do stand-up?"

"Or women who did both? I don't know. I have to figure it out. I need an angle. If you can recommend any books . . ."

"I'll think about it."

Simon's walls had floor-to-ceiling shelves crammed with books on the history of television. And since the shelves were full, he also had piles of books by the window. And his house was most certainly filled with them too, not that I'd ever been there. His collection had to be better than the city library. No one in the museum knew more about TV than he did. "Thanks. I appreciate it."

"For you? Anything." He folded his hands on his desk, assuming our meeting was over. But I still had the second part of my mission to complete. Before I had a chance, the phone rang. He picked up. "Hello." He glanced at me—embarrassed? One book title on his shelf caught my eye: *Television and Everyday Life.* I pointed at it and mouthed, "Could I see that?"

He handed it to me.

The cover had an old ad photo of a 1940s family gathered around a television with a teensy twelve-inch screen. I opened to the first chapter and skimmed. I never tired of reading about the beginnings of television. This book talked about how people started out with one set for the whole household. Everyone would watch together. Sometimes neighbors who didn't own a set came over. It was much more social. In those days, the companies who owned the products that were advertised on the shows were also the producers. They had to try to make the shows be something the entire family could sit through. Young and old. Male and female. Liberal and conservative.

"Don't worry, Mom," Simon said into the phone, "I didn't forget. *Mr. Peepers.* Sure."

I looked up, our eyes met, and we shook our heads together in a show of unity. His mother was always bugging him at work and asking him to bring her copies of tapes. I went back to the book. By the sixties, families might have two or three sets, so now everyone was in separate rooms watching their own shows. This meant different shows could be geared toward different demographics. It was a whole new ball game. Narrowcasting, they called it. And now, with cable, we were down to "slivercasting." It always amazed me how things like this actually affected what was made. It was so easy to forget that television existed because of the advertising that paid for it—not the other way around.

"Okay. I'll talk to you later." He hung up. "I feel bad for her. Home alone all day. I really wish she'd get out more."

"You're her only child, right?"

"Yup."

"I bet she'd *love* it if you got married again."

"Yup."

At least I'd found the segue way to my real reason for coming down here. "Simon. Are you aware of the fact that there might be someone on your staff who has some romantic feelings toward you?"

"Yes, actually," he said slowly. "I am. But . . . " He shook his head.

"She likes you. And you like her. And you would make such a good couple. I have this feeling about you two."

"Taffy is a very nice girl," he said. "I'm not saying she isn't."

"You should ask her out. Seriously. I mean, really. She would be so thrilled. Why not?"

He stood. "It wouldn't be right to get involved with someone on my staff."

"She'd probably quit if that's the only thing holding you back." I slid the book back into its place on the shelf.

"I don't want her to quit."

"Then maybe you should reconsider." I paused at the door. "Just think. If Mr. Sheffield had that policy, he never would've let himself marry Fran." I was referring to *The Nanny*, a sitcom that helped get me through my most miserable teen years.

"I never liked that show after they were married," he said.

I shook my head and left. What could I say? He was right. It never was as good.

Eight

"So you never told me," Charlie said. "Is your sister taking it well?" He was sitting on the edge of his bed, unlacing his Converse sneakers.

"Taking what well?" I was stalling. I knew exactly what he meant.

"Us."

"Actually, I still haven't exactly told her yet."

"Daphne . . ."

"I'll call her tonight. After I've had dinner."

"You'll feel better once you get it over with." He gave me a kiss on the cheek. "I'm gonna take a shower."

He went into the bathroom. I decided dinner could wait. I'd tell her now. It was my big chance for privacy. The last thing I wanted was for him to listen in while I confessed. Who knows how it would come out? I was bound to say something stupid. The spray of water on the other side of the bathroom door gave me the extra layer of soundproofing I needed.

I sat cross-legged on the bed and put the phone in front of me. This really didn't have to be such a big deal. It wasn't so much that she disliked him as an individual; it was more that she didn't like sharing me with him. The problem was most noticeable on holidays. Times when it was important to have family around. At least it wasn't anywhere near Thanksgiving. Thanksgivings were always hard.

The first year Charlie and I were dating, he went to have turkey dinner up in Westchester with his family. I had potluck in the city with Billie and an assortment of our friends who were also "relative-free." We'd done this for years, and as far as we were conrned, our Thanksgivings were more fun than most people's, with better food, too.

The second year Charlie and I were dating, I had Thanksgiving dinner with his family. That was at his grandma's house in New Rochelle. Our future home. By that time, we were officially "a couple" and living together. I was hungry to be a part of his family's holiday celebration—it was the closest I'd get to what I'd experienced vicariously year after year on *All My Children* watching incredibly heartwarming Martin family dinners. But I wasn't really gung ho on inviting Billie out there too. I was nervous about making an impression, and didn't want her presence to overwhelm the situation or add to my anxiety.

Plus, I figured the last thing she wanted to be was the "older sister appendage" at a dull holiday dinner in the suburbs with a bunch of strangers.

Technically speaking, I did extend the invitation. I believe the way I put it was, "You don't want to come, do you?" I'm pretty sure my face was contorted into a grimace. Yes . . . that was rather ungracious. But I was pretty sure she'd turn me down, so I was feeling defensive.

Her response: "Are you insane? Why would I want to do that?"

The third year Charlie and I were together, I did feel ready to introduce Billie to Charlie's family, and I was intending on delivering a sincere invitation. One chilly night in early November, the three of us went out for Japanese food. We did things like that occasionally. Billie and Charlie did not love each other at that point—she thought he was boring, he thought she was erratic—but they tolerated each other and pretended to get along.

Somewhere after the miso soup and before the chicken teriyaki, Billie described her setup with Max. "It's perfect. I get money and independence; he gets to enjoy my marvelous company and dazzling sexual skills."

Charlie, who perhaps had drunk too much sake, said, "So you're like a hooker."

Billie, who had definitely drunk too much sake, said, "Fuck you."

Charlie broke his chopsticks apart. "I'm just saying, what ab● *your* sexual needs?"

Billie broke her chopsticks apart. "What about my *sister's* sexual needs?"

My eyes bugged out. "Billie!" I took a big sip of sake even though it tasted like gasoline, because at this point I definitely needed to be drunk.

"What do you mean by that?" Charlie asked.

"I hear you're a lousy lover."

Charlie looked at me as if I'd shown her his drawer full of rejection letters. "You said this?"

I wanted to respond, but my mouth was basically paralyzed. The thing was—I *had* said it. I'd complained to her, very early on, way back when we were first dating, in a moment of weakness. I figured if she knew he wasn't so good in bed, she wouldn't have to feel jealous about the fact that I was entering into a happy and secure monogamous relationship.

Billie took a sip of sake then licked her lips. "Daphne is too self-sacrificing to let you know your skills suck."

He continued to stare at me. "Is this true?"

The irony here was that she'd actually helped to improve our sex life. When I'd made my complaint, I'd told her he was pretty much only into missionary sex, and it was hard for me to have an orgasm that way. She'd advised me on training him to use his fingers to stimulate my clitoris while we had intercourse. Voilà, problem solved. Wasn't it wonderful to have an older sister?

She had to understand I simply could not let him know the truth here. I took a sip of sake, transmitted a brief but intense signal to her over the top rim of my cup, then looked straight into Charlie's eyes. "It's not true."

"Are you calling me a liar?" she asked.

I looked at her with pleading eyes. "Billie . . ."

"Screw this bullshit. I'm not hungry." She stood up. "Happy holidays."

She walked off. Left us with the bill, two hangovers, and three ntrées.

Thanksgiving that year? Forget about it.

Not surprisingly, I never confided in her about our sex life again. Charlie let it pass, but I felt bad that I'd betrayed him. And I couldn't take her disapproval. Billie could not relate to the concept of compromising in the bedroom. I was willing to because, well, hey, I wasn't the most adventuresome lover in the world. And he gave me other things.

When this past year's holiday season rolled around, I was seriously considering inviting her up to New Rochelle. She and Charlie were on civil terms—mainly because they never saw each other. His parents were dying to meet her, and, well, it seemed time to present some family of my own. So when she was complaining that Max was going to be with his brood and was blowing her off for the entire Thanksgiving weekend, I asked if she wanted to come have dinner with us.

"Are you inviting me out of pity?"

"No! I want you to be there. I want you to meet his parents. And they want to meet you."

"Sorry," she said. "I made other plans."

This was getting ridiculous. What would happen next Thanksgiving? She'd finally come meet his parents, and they'd be going on about how lovely the wedding was, and I'd have to say, *oh, yeah, sorry, I forgot to mention, Charlie and I got married!*

I picked up the phone and dialed. She answered after one ring. "Darling! What an unexpected pleasure!" Billie liked to guilt-trip me about how I never called. Which of course made me avoid calling her even more. "To what do I owe the honor?"

"I just felt like saying hello. . . . " I turned on the TV. "And I do have some news."

"Is something wrong?" she asked.

"No." I tried to formulate my sentence. *So . . . I do actually have some really good news . . . Charlie asked me to get married. Charlie and I are getting married. I'm marrying Charlie.*

"You sound like something bad happened. Are you ill?"

"It's *good* news," I said, trying to pitch my voice into a more cheerful mode, but it came out sounding defensive.

"Marvelous. I could use some good news. Because I've had the worst fucking day of my life."

"Why?"

"Let's not get into it."

"What happened?"

"I'm so depressed."

"Billie . . ."

"I don't want to talk about it."

"Tell me."

"Alright. But you have to promise you won't rub my face in this. Do you promise?"

"I promise."

"Max is postponing the trip."

"I'm sorry." Damn. Max was letting us all down. "Why?"

"I don't know. He's on his way over. He said he wanted to explain in person."

Oh, god, he was probably calling it off completely, but wanted to let her down gradually. Maybe he was breaking up with her altogether. "I'm sure he's as disappointed as you are. I bet there's a good reason. Did he set another date?"

"He said we'll talk about it."

"Right. Well . . ." I changed the channel, not really taking in what I saw. The important thing was to go from show to show. I had a habit of doing this while on the phone with her. It just relaxed me. Or made me more agitated. I wasn't sure which. There wasn't anything good on. Not until Letterman. He was interviewing Natalie Portman. I loved Natalie Portman, and really wanted to see it. Letterman could be such a flirt. In an interview he once admitted that when he had starlets on, it was like having a date.

"So!" she said brightly. "What's your good news?"

I certainly couldn't tell her about Charlie *now*. I searched my brain for some other "less good" news. "Guess who came to the museum the other day. Jonathan Hill!"

"Did you tell him his show stinks?"

Billie didn't like *Supermodels*. She was always comparing it to the "reality" of being a model. As if a TV show had any obligation to deliver truth and not ratings.

"No." I looked at the door to the bathroom, reassuring myself that Charlie couldn't hear anything. Not that I was saying anything that would incriminate myself. As if I'd *done* anything to incriminate myself. "He was looking for old shows about models. I turned him on to some old *Paper Dolls*. Remember that? I think he's run out of ideas. I was trying to figure out some way I could get him to read one of Charlie's scripts."

I paused on VH-1. They were doing *Love Songs of 2005*. Mariah Carey began to sing "We Belong Together." I zapped down the dial.

"I thought Charlie gave up writing."

"He has. Sort of."

"He misses it, right? And he'll always blame you for making him stop."

"I didn't make him stop."

"But he'll see it that way in retrospect."

The neon numbers flashed 22, 21, 20, 19, 18. . . . It wasn't important to hear what they were saying on each channel, just to have the noise, one voice after another, the procession of never-ending disjointed snippets of stories. A crowd of people to choose from. The illusion they were all there for you. Someone was always there for you out there, on one channel if not the other. Yes, it kept me grounded.

"Charlie has different priorities now. He wants a family, kids . . ."

"Oh, please. When are you going to leave him? It's such a trap to live with a guy. You're using up all your good years on him, you realize that, don't you?"

She was the one using up her "good years." And what a way to think about it!

"I've gotta go," she said. "Max is at the door. And before I give him what he wants, I'm gonna give him hell."

"Good luck." We said our good-byes and hung up. Not that she needed luck. Hell and blow jobs. Those were two things she was good at giving.

I stopped changing channels and watched an ad for ketchup. Charlie would be coming out of the shower soon. Not only had I totally failed in my mission, she had actually told me to leave him. Now I felt even less inclined to tell her my news. Well. Maybe I couldn't turn Charlie into a successful television writer, but I could help him become a better lover. And I could certainly improve there too. We didn't have to be zeros in bed.

I got out my laptop, settled back on the bed, got online, logged on to Amazon, and typed in "sex." A list of hundreds of books appeared. This was too overwhelming. And then it occurred to me that there had to be scads of Web sites on the subject. It's not like this was rocket science. (No tacky imagery intended.) I didn't need to buy a book, just get a few pointers. So to speak.

I looked at the bathroom door. Charlie's electric shaver was buzzing away. Good. That gave me a few minutes.

I did a google on "sex tips," and low and behold, there were a zillion entries. Where to begin? I tried one, and it was just a gross porn site with—I'm sorry—huge, thick, wet, intimidating penises. I wanted something woman-friendly here. It didn't take long before I landed on a "sex positive" site with pink and purple cartoony graphics and all sorts of articles intended to help nice girls spice up their sex lives.

At first I was wary. It started out insisting that we realize blow jobs are fun for both giver and receiver. Hah. If it was so fun, why did they have to *tell* me it was fun? No one needed to tell me eating ice cream was fun. I skimmed down the list of techniques and saw I already knew and used most of them, though one description of "deep-throating" made me squeamish. It said to relax your jaw and throat so you didn't gag. No thanks. I bet Billie was proficient—not that I wanted to think about that.

The next topic listed was on "How to go down on her." Now *that* could be useful. Just then Charlie emerged from the bathroom all nice and clean and naked, with just a towel around his waist.

"So did you tell her?" he asked.

"What?"

"Did you tell Billie about us?"

I closed the window and powered off. To be investigated later. "It wasn't a good time. Max postponed their trip."

He sat on the edge of the bed. "You've gotta get it over with. You're torturing yourself, and I hate seeing it make you so unhappy."

"Sometimes she's in an up mood. I'm just waiting for one of her up moods."

He sighed and went to his bureau to get a pair of boxers to sleep in.

"I don't suppose," I said in a suggestive voice, "you're in an 'up' mood?"

He caught my drift, closed the drawer, and let the towel drop to the floor. Charlie did have a great body—slim but muscular. He kept in shape playing basketball with his students after school. "I could be in an 'up' mood," he said.

Within moments, he was next to me on the bed. I made my offer that I knew he wouldn't refuse, and went all out, making sure to hit all the suggestions from the Web site, except the deep-throating, that is. And he was loving it, that was for sure. And as I labored away, I gave myself a pep talk that I was *having fun*. And telling myself that with a small hint from me, *maybe he would return the favor*.

I pulled away just as he was ejaculating and let it land on his tummy. Now was my moment to make my request. But. He was obviously exhausted and totally ready to drift off into a nice, happy sleep. Okay. That was fine. To be expected. No surprise. I could make my request later. It wouldn't look good to make it seem like a tit for tat kind of thing. Plus, I was still hoping to catch Natalie Portman on Letterman.

"That was really nice," he said, getting a tissue from his night-stand to clean himself off.

"Thanks." I relaxed against my pillow and enjoyed my sex kitten status. "I'm glad you enjoyed it."

He gave me a soft kiss on the lips. "I think I'm gonna fall asleep. Do you mind?"

"Of course not."

"I love you."

"Love you."

Within one minute, no exaggeration, he was snoring.

I turned on the TV and caught the end of Letterman's monologue. Then Natalie Portman came on. She had such a beautiful mouth. Her smile was mesmerizing. And he was totally into her. Natalie's dress was totally low-cut, and she wore no bra. From his angle, he could almost certainly see her nipples. Was she attracted to him? He kept complimenting her, and she kept giggling. Would they see each other later? He broke for the commercial. "Don't go away," he said reassuringly to the camera, "we'll be right back." Then he turned back to Natalie and whispered something in her ear. Something we, the viewing audience, were not privy to. An ad for Tic Tacs came on. I decided not to switch channels. Watching David and Natalie flirt—that was enough oral sex for me.

Nine

"So I've been brainstorming some ideas," I said, standing in the doorway to Ben's office, "and I wanted to run it past you because it's just not jelling."

"I'm all ears. Take a seat."

"I'd love to do something on Valerie Harper. Or Lisa Kudrow. Or Kirstie Allie. Or maybe all three. Something about how they were all in those ensemble megahits, but then when they tried to do their own shows, they flopped."

Ben seemed unimpressed. "That doesn't just happen to women."

"True." Was I being too female-oriented?

"What else?" he asked.

"Well . . . I've been thinking a lot about TV and families," I said. "How when television began, people had one set and everyone would watch it together. But then people got televisions for each room, and everyone liked to watch by themselves. I mean, it's so ironic that television has brought about this alienation within the family. Think about how these days, people even eat meals with their TVs instead of with each other. But at the same time, because it portrays all these idealized versions of families, it's raised our expectations of what real families can be. In a way, TV families have become replacements for the viewer's family." He was staring at me, and I suddenly felt totally insecure, as if I'd just shown him my underwear. "Don't you think?"

"That's interesting, but rather general. What specific shows would you focus on?"

"Well . . . *Boomers*, for example. *Family Ties* and *Full House* and *Thirtysomething*. *Everybody Loves Raymond* . . ." There were too many to choose from.

"Yes, but what's your theme?"

My theme? "I'm not sure yet."

"You need to narrow it down. Be more specific."

"Right. Maybe just dramas? Or just sitcoms? I don't know. I'll keep brainstorming."

"You'll get there," he said.

As I went back to my desk, I felt mad at myself. Why couldn't I just do something totally obvious and simple, like quiz show scandals? My phone rang. I picked up. "He's back!" It was Taffy.

"Who?"

"Jonathan Hill. And this time, he's with his daughter. He wants you to come down and help her find something to watch."

"Are you kidding? Why me?"

"I guess he's still angry with you," she teased, "for not letting him take these tapes home."

I took the elevator down. God. Jonathan Hill had asked for me! I took some deep breaths. Tried to will myself to stop trembling. I was really getting overly excited about this. He obviously just thought he was too good for letting the people who were supposed to help him help him. He needed to have special treatment—especially, no doubt, for his precious daughter. Silly to read anything more into this than there was.

I pushed open the glass door. He was at the same computer we'd used last time. His daughter sat next to him. She was very pretty, like her mom, the actress Lee Harrington, who'd played Lisa on *Boomers*. (She and Jonathan divorced after the show was canceled.) The girl wore a lilac top with the head of a white horse on it and a denim skirt. I was never around kids and wasn't good at guessing ages. Eight? Nine? Twelve? "You're back," I said.

"I couldn't wait to see more *Paper Dolls*," he said grimly. Then he smiled, and I wondered why those crinkly laugh lines that made Billie want to inject toxins into her skin made him look so goddamn sexy.

"That bad?"

"Maybe Andy Warhol could glean some deeper meaning. So I

was wondering if you could suggest something for my daughter to watch."

"Well, you know actually Taffy might be more helpful." I glanced at his daughter, who had her arms crossed over her chest and was staring at me with a very sour face. "We get kids here all the time and she knows what they like."

"I don't think so," he said. "I trust your judgment."

"Okay." I turned to the girl. "What's your name?"

"Lily."

"That's a pretty name. And how old are you?"

"Ten." She turned to her father. "I want to go to Jekyll and Hyde! I'm hungry!"

Jekyll and Hyde was a nearby overpriced tourist-trap theme restaurant you'd never go into if you lived in the city . . . unless you had a kid.

"Shhhh," he said. "You have to be quiet here."

"I'm starving!"

"You just had breakfast."

"I want to go to Jekyll and Hyde! You promised!"

I sat down next to her. "What's Jekyll and Hyde?"

"It's like a haunted restaurant that has scary butlers and stuff." She glared at Jonathan. "My mom took me."

"That sounds cool," I said.

"And they bring a live Frankenstein and then they have to kill Mr. Hyde. Mr. Hyde is the bad guy, right?"

"I think so. I always get them confused."

"And when you go in," Lily was saying, "there's a little, like, little, like . . . *opening.*" Her eyes widened. "I was too scared to see what was actually happening, but it was like the walls were closing in . . ."

"And then?"

"There was a mirror and the skeleton face appeared and it says you were brave so you get to eat in the restaurant."

"That sounds like fun. I hope I can go there someday. But for now, why don't you watch a show? You can pick out any one you want to see. Have you ever watched *The Twilight Zone?*" I figured if she was into horror . . .

"Mmmm . . . I don't think so," Jonathan Hill said.

"Sorry."

Of course, now she was totally interested. "What's *The Twilight Zone?*"

"Maybe you wouldn't like it. From the sixties. Black and white."

"I like black and white."

"Maybe something from the 70s . . ."

"I want to see *The Twilight Zone.*"

"How about *The Brady Bunch?*"

"Blech. I want *The Twilight Zone.*"

"Or something from the eighties . . ." I tried to think of something that was in reruns she would know. "*Full House?*"

"The Olsen Twins? Puke."

"Or . . . there's your Dad's old show. *Boomers.*"

"Boring."

"Did you ever see the one where the mom gives birth to her baby girl?"

"No."

"It's very sweet."

She sniffed.

"It was a good show, really. All about the struggle to be a mom and have a career too. Your dad even won an Emmy for it."

Jonathan Hill looked at me for a moment, then back at his screen. I noticed he was doing a search on himself. "Hope you find something you like," I ribbed him.

"There are so many good ones," he said. "How late do you stay open?"

"I want to go to Jekyll and Hyde!"

I decided to take a different approach. "I know, Lily. How about one of the very first television shows that ever existed. In the 1940s. That's from before your dad was even born."

"Wow," Jonathan Hill said, "did they have TV way back then?"

"Of course they did, Daddy."

"And we still have copies of some of those shows even though they were done live and VCRs hadn't been invented."

"How?"

"Kinescopes. Machines that were cameras that filmed the show right off a television screen while it was broadcasting. The copies are kind of fuzzy, but we're lucky to have even those. No one thought TV shows were worth saving back then."

"Then why did they?"

"Because all the shows were shot in New York in those days and the broadcast signals didn't go far. Just like how most radio stations still broadcast locally, right? So if someone in California wanted to see a TV show, someone in New York had to mail them a kinescope."

"That's so dumb!"

"That's how it was."

"Can I see a really old show from back then?"

"Sure. Let's move over here to our own computer." Now I just had to think of one she'd like. "Have you ever heard of *Howdy Doody*?" She was probably too old, but maybe . . .

"What's that?"

"It's the first kid show, and it was really, really popular. There's a cowboy marionette puppet and a clown named Clarabell who never speaks. . . ."

Interesting trivia: Clarabell was played by Bob Keeshan, the man who would later be known as Captain Kangaroo.

"I don't like clowns. They give me nightmares."

"Me too, actually. Let's see . . ." So much for that idea. "I know. One of my favorites is a show called *The Goldbergs*. It's from 1949, and it's about a family of immigrants in the Bronx with a teenage girl named Rosalie. In one episode she wants to cut her hair and wear lipstick, and she invites a boy over when she's babysitting and gets into big trouble. . . . Oh, and there's one about when she wanted to get a nose job."

"Wow. I want to see them!"

"And they even have the original advertising," I said, as I typed in the requests. "The commercials were written right into the shows back then. So the actress who plays the mom—Gertrude Berg, who also wrote and produced the show, by the way—she looks out her kitchen window, talks right into the camera, and tells us to buy Sanka."

"What's Sanka?"

"Um, freeze-dried decaf coffee. And you know what? All the stores in New York sold incredible amounts of Sanka because of her. That's when people began to realize the power of television advertising."

"Hurry up, Daddy, so I can watch."

"Hold your horses. I have to find what I need." He gave me a grateful "Thanks."

"Glad to be of service." I turned to Lily. "I hope you enjoy them. Remember, they're from kinescopes, so the pictures aren't as sharp as you're used to."

As I walked away, I could hear her say, "This is gonna be so cool."

A few minutes later they came up to the desk to wait for the shows to be ready. "I couldn't help but notice," Jonathan Hill said, "you don't have many *Boomers*. And there aren't any *Katie McCalls*."

"Some of the networks are better than others about donating shows. If you have any you'd like to contribute, we'd be happy to add them to our collection."

"I don't know if there's much point."

"It's part of the history. They should be here."

"I look at them now, and they just seem pretentious."

"Are you kidding? *Boomers* was brilliant. The way the characters were all so articulate. That whole struggle to reconcile the idealism of youth with adult desires for material success." Here I was again, sounding like I'd written a Master's thesis on him.

"Wow," he said. "I'm impressed."

"Your shows are ready," Taffy said. She handed him his slip.

"So why," I asked, "are you looking at all these old *Paper Dolls*?"

"You want to know the truth?"

I raised my eyebrows and tried to look casual, but it was blowing my mind that he was talking to me about his work.

"I'm looking for inspiration," he said. "I don't like the direction the show is taking, but I'm not sure where to go with it."

"Don't you work with a staff of writers?"

"Sure, but the really elusive thing for all of us," he said, "is a good idea. I would kill if someone would come up with a really great idea. And I'm not feeling very creative these days. My well has run dry. You see? 'My well has run dry' — I'm even speaking in clichés."

Well, my boyfriend has this wonderful pilot. . . .

"Everything's been done," he went on. "There's nothing new to say."

Not that we're serious, my boyfriend and I.

"Daddy," Lily tugged on his jacket, "let's go!"

Okay, well, we're engaged, actually. But you really should read his stuff.

"Anyway, thanks for these. Let's go, Lily."

"Have fun," I said.

They went down to the console room. It was too frustrating. Would I ever see Jonathan Hill again? I turned to Taffy. "Am I insane, or is he being friendly with me for no discernable reason."

"Why shouldn't he be friendly? You're pretty, smart, and good at your job, which happens to involve honoring the work of people like him. He's probably sick of flighty model and actress types, and wants to find someone down-to-earth to be the future mother of his child."

"You," I said, heading toward the door, "have an excellent imagination. And I'm going back to work."

Ten

I met Billie in the swimsuit department at Saks. Found her searching through a rack of bikinis.

"There you are! Let me show you my favorites. What do you think of this one?" In one hand, she held up a leopard-skin halter-top. "Dolce & Gabbana. $300."

"Sexy."

In the other, a flimsy little pastel polka dot number. "Moschino. $175."

"Cute."

"How can I possibly choose?"

I shrugged. "Get both."

"You're a genius! Let me go try them on."

Max had rescheduled the trip for a month later. He said it was because of some business obligation. Max was a high-powered real estate agent/mogul–type person. Neither of us really knew exactly what he did. This was reminiscent of our own father. We'd never been quite sure how he'd made his money, but we did know he'd started with next to nothing. And you didn't make a lot of money by being a total nice guy, either.

Max owned a lot of property in New York. Among his possessions was the apartment Billie lived in. He'd bought it for her when they started their "relationship." His wife didn't know about the apartment, or so he claimed. Did she know about Billie? We had no idea.

"So," I said, as I followed her to the dressing rooms. It was not the optimal context, but I was ready. "Guess what."

She stopped to take a sundress off a rack and hold it up to herself.

"That looks nice . . ."

"With my coloring?" She wrinkled her nose and put it back. "So what am I guessing?"

I blurted it out. "Charlie and I are getting married."

She turned. Looked at me. Blinked. She wasn't smiling. "What?"

"Charlie asked me to marry him. And I said yes."

"Oh." I watched her process the news. It took about seven seconds. Which doesn't sound like a lot of time, but it sure felt like it. At first she wasn't smiling. But then her smile was so big and fake, she could've been doing a toothpaste ad. "That's great. Congratulations."

"You mean it?" I anticipated the "but." *He's not good enough for you. Don't sell yourself short. You could do better.*

"Of course I mean it."

"You're not going to try to talk me out of it?"

"Why should I do that?"

I wondered if that smile was making her mouth sore. "Because you were never that excited about Charlie."

"But I'm excited for you! So did he give you a ring?"

"Not yet. We're going to go to the Diamond District and pick one out together."

"How sweet."

"The other thing is . . ." I paused before continuing my sentence, aware that perhaps I was about to say what I was going to say because I wanted to give her a big reason not to feel jealous. Not that she would be jealous of Charlie, just the marriage concept. "He wants us to move to New Rochelle."

Her face immediately brightened. She compensated by furrowing her brow. "That's horrifying."

"His grandmother will sell us her house cheap, and then Charlie would have a really short commute." I didn't add that it would provide a room for a baby.

"Sounds dreadful."

Good. The balance of nature was somewhat restored. She

could remain superior. Thank god we were moving to New Rochelle. "It's a drag. But we have to be practical. I mean, it'll be good to have the space."

"Space to mope around in." I followed her to the entrance to the dressing rooms. There was no attendant. She looked both ways and said loudly, "Is anyone working here? Don't they want people to try things on?" Then she said to me, "We'll have to go upstairs and find you a wedding gown."

"That would be fun." In a nightmarish sort of way. "So you'll be my maid of honor, right?"

"Of course! If you want me to be."

"Of course I want you to be. So we'll need to find you a dress too."

"Hmmm. What color are we thinking?"

The dressing room attendant appeared and told us a room would be free soon.

"I hadn't even thought about a color. How can there be so much to think about?"

"You have to pick a color for your wedding."

"It seems like such a pain to have to plan it all."

"Are you crazy? That's the fun of it! There are all sorts of incredible spaces you can rent. I had a friend who got this rooftop in Tribeca with fantastic views. . . ."

"His parents want to do it in a hotel in Westchester."

"Daphne, you cannot let them bully you into anything you don't want to do. If they want to pay, fine. But have the wedding you want. For god's sakes, they have money. Make them give you a great big beautiful wedding in Manhattan."

Some people finally left and the attendant let us into a room. I followed Billie in and sat on a short stool in the corner.

"I wouldn't even know where to have it in Manhattan. And I don't have so many people to invite. The whole thing boggles my mind."

"Don't worry, Kitten. I'll help you." My father used to call me Kitten and her Princess. The same nicknames the two daughters had on *Father Knows Best*. She too must've been thinking of mom and dad. How they were the ones who would've given me the wedding. Should've been. It was too depressing to mention, and too obvious.

Luckily she was pulling off the top and couldn't see me tear up. "That would be nice," I said.

"You must let me take you downtown. There's a fantastic little shop. Celia Wing. Just your style, and quite reasonable. We'll be able to get you something for a couple thousand dollars."

"I don't need to spend that much."

"You can get a sample for around a thousand—maybe even less, if you insist."

"Why does it sound like you've already researched this?"

"Because I have, Darling. Thoroughly. But when Max proposes, I'm getting myself a $40,000 Badgley Mischka. Okay? So live a little. My treat."

"Really? You sure?"

"Of course I'm sure."

I diverted my eyes while she took off her underwear—not that she had a shred of modesty. "Thank you." Maybe I'd been underestimating Billie. Maybe she really would be able to be happy for me, and she'd actually be able to help look out for me and make this fun. Was it possible?

She had the bottoms on, and we both observed her in the mirror. She asked me her favorite question.

"How do I look?"

"Totally hot." Her body still did look great, but I knew she'd been having some spider veins lasered out, and there was a bit of cellulite rippling on her thighs even though they were skinny. Luckily she wasn't focusing on that right then, and god knows I wasn't going to point it out. "You look incredible."

"If anything is gonna make Max leave his wife, this little number will. Don't you think?"

"Do you think he's seriously considering that?"

"He says he needs to make some changes in his life. Big changes."

"Wow." Maybe he was serious.

"And he's been particularly sweet to me lately." Billie put her face right up to the mirror. "Oh, god. My face. Look at these shadows under my eyes! And my worry lines!" She rubbed the space between her brows with her finger. "I have got to get an injection this afternoon. Do you mind if we save your wedding dress for another day?"

"Of course not. We haven't even set a date yet. No rush."

Thank god. A reprieve. That adventure would have to wait.

Eleven

I was in the living room reading a book I'd borrowed from Simon, watching Spring Break trash on MTV, and munching on peanuts. Even though it was depressing to watch drunk girls in bikinis making out with random drunk boys, I was also able to vicariously enjoy the Florida sun and beach settings.

Charlie was at his computer running Spybot. It was a Saturday afternoon. Too bad we weren't prancing around on a sun-drenched beach. But, on the other hand, the book I was reading was fascinating me. It was a series of profiles on various television producers.

I told myself I was doing research to help me come up with an idea. But the only subject I was researching right then was Jonathan Hill. He was there along with Steven Bochco, Dick Wolf, and David E. Kelley. The author was observing how many of the episodes of *Boomers* concerned the sex lives of the married couples. The wife played by Jonathan's ex-wife Lee Harrington was often too tired to make love because of their newborn baby. She refused to give it the bottle. The husband had his own issues, most notably a problem with premature ejaculation. Addressing that was considered daring at the time. One thing the author did not reveal, no doubt because he didn't know: Did Jonathan Hill have a problem with premature ejaculation? A powerful and successful man like him? Couldn't be. He must've made that up for the script. He was probably substituting it for something else, like an unquenchable sex drive.

"Have you ever heard that joke?" Charlie asked.

"Which one?"

"There are three reasons why I became a teacher."

I waited for the punch line.

"June, July, and August."

"Ha-ha."

"Just twenty-six more teaching days and I'm free."

"You've almost made it."

I took some more peanuts and went back to my book. And that's when it occurred to me. My idea for a seminar was staring me in the face. I could do a tribute to the works of Jonathan Hill. And I could ask him to make a guest appearance.

"Are you really watching that?" Charlie asked.

I looked back at the screen. Some implant-laden coeds were now cavorting in a swimming pool with a midget. Charlie hated stuff like this more than anything. To him it was evidence of the downfall of civilization and, worse yet, a big reason lots of TV writers were out of work. "You want me to watch in the bedroom?"

"That's okay. I should get outside. It's nice out."

"Maybe you'll have a chance to write something new over the summer."

"Why bother?"

"It's the process that counts," I said. "Not outward success."

"In our society? Outward success is everything."

"Speaking of . . . you know who came into the museum the other day? Jonathan Hill." I said it as if it had been the first time.

"*Supermodels?*" Charlie said.

"And *Katie McCall, M.D., Boomers* . . ."

"Now there's an example of someone who's sacrificed his talent for pandering to the market." Charlie marked up a paper in green pen. "He'll never do anything good again."

I shrugged and took another peanut. How much did a person need to accomplish? The man could retire and live out his days drinking apple martinis by the pool and feel like he'd done more than enough to prove himself. Charlie was just jealous, and who could blame him. "You know what? It's about time you follow up with that agent guy."

"Gordon Fineberg?"

"You have nothing to lose and everything to gain."

"Jesus," Charlie said, looking at his computer screen. I went to peek over his shoulder. The files were finished being scanned. He had three hundred and seventy-two "critical objects." They were like mosquitos in a swamp. No matter how many times you shook them off, they immediately landed on you all over again. "No wonder this has been running slow."

I handed him the phone. "I want you to call right now."

He clicked on the box to erase the files. "That's okay."

"He's just a person," I said, "not a god." I pictured Gordon's huge forehead. The cracker crumbs escaping from his mouth. "Call him."

"He would've contacted me if he'd read them."

"He probably needs to be nudged." Honestly, this whole negative attitude—understandable as it was—did not make Charlie seem attractive. At times like this, I understood why Billie thought he wasn't . . . well . . . no. Of course he was good enough. Ridiculous to even think that way. "At least email him."

"Email is for cowards."

"Then call him. Or I will."

"Don't be ridiculous."

"I will!"

I put the jar of peanuts away and, while Charlie stared at me with disbelief, I looked up William Morris in the yellow pages, dialed, got an operator, asked for Gordon, prayed to get his voice mail or an assistant, and tried my best to ignore the fact that I'd just broken out in a sweat. I didn't want to speak directly to him even though the whole point was to speak directly to him, so I was glad to get voice mail. I waited for the beep. "Hello . . . This is Daphne Wells. . . . We met at a party a couple months ago and I sent you a script written by my friend—the one who was traveling in Spain, but he's about to return—so I just wanted to make sure you received it and, if you did, I just wanted to check and see if you had a chance to look it over. So, thanks very much." I left our phone number and hung up.

"I can't believe you did that," Charlie said.

"Was it too long?"

"No."

"Too aggressive?"

"I wish I *had* been traveling in Spain."

"So what's my reward?"

"What do you want?" He logged on and checked his email. Hmmmm. "Maybe you'd like to reciprocate . . . what I gave you . . . the last time we made love?"

Now he was the one hypnotized by a screen. "Reciprocate?"

"Yeah. You know . . ." I was going to have to be blunt. "You could go down on me."

That got him to look up from his in-box.

I grinned, raised my eyebrows up and down, felt rather foolish.

"Now?" he asked.

He looked like I'd asked him to clean the toilet. Okay, maybe I'm exaggerating, but he wasn't exactly jumping up and down. Not that I'd want him to do that either. "Don't look so thrilled," I said.

"Okay," he said, perhaps realizing that his manhood was to some extent on the line here. "Let's do it."

While he finished checking his email, I went into the bedroom, lowered the shades, and turned out the lights. Then we each took turns using the bathroom, and rendezvoused in bed with our clothes off. It all felt so dutiful. Like it was an arranged marriage and this was our first time.

"This isn't very spontaneous," I said, pulling the sheet over my naked chest, "is it."

"That's okay."

"You sure?"

"Let's get to it."

I wished he hadn't put it like that.

He pulled the sheet off me and went down between my legs, and I felt as naked as I was. And then he started in . . . and it felt . . . totally . . . wrong. Sort of like there was a puppy dog lapping away down there.

Where was the passion? Where was the mystery? Where was the . . . technique?

"You know what?" I said. "Maybe we should do this later."

"Why?"

"For some reason it's just not working. But you know what?" I said it as if I was just thinking of it. "I could print out this thing I happened to see on this Web site that has some good tips. And we'll try again sometime."

"Okay."

"Okay."

We snuggled together under the sheet. Should we make love? Wasn't this sort of thing supposed to be spontaneous? Of course, if it was spontaneous, people wouldn't need all those books and "how-to" articles. Right? It didn't come naturally to everyone. So maybe we weren't so pitiful. But, still. It was scary not knowing if we would ever work this out, or if we were doomed to have a mediocre sex life.

Charlie interrupted my worries with the nicest offer. "You want to go to Silver Moon?"

The Silver Moon was the best bakery in the neighborhood. "That sounds nice." Charlie didn't really have much of a sweet tooth, so I knew he was suggesting this to please me.

As I put my clothes back on, I felt bad for doubting him. Next time we'd both have a glass of wine, relax, be mentally prepared. I was getting all troubled and anxious for nothing. He certainly didn't seem to be worried.

"And maybe when we're there," he said, "we could ask about wedding cakes."

"Definitely. They have the best cakes. That's a good idea."

So we strolled hand in hand down Broadway and got a table on the sidewalk out front. He had tea and I had coffee, and we shared a chocolate cupcake and watched the people go by. Before leaving, I spoke with the woman behind the counter about our options. She had plump red cheeks and a messy bun of brown hair.

"How many guests are you planning to have?" she asked.

"I don't know."

"And where will it be?"

"We haven't figured that out yet. But we know we want the cake made here."

"Well," she laughed, "glad to know you have your priorities straight."

Twelve

I was at my desk reading a book called *Feminism on Primetime* that examined shows like *Cagney and Lacey*, *Designing Women*, *Murphy Brown*, and there was an entire chapter devoted to *Boomers*. The author was raving about the complexity of the women characters. It did strike me as curious that Jonathan Hill was now writing stock-character soap opera like *Supermodels*. Why the change? My phone rang.

"He just got on the elevator," Taffy said. "On his way to the library."

"Great."

Phase one of my scheme was on. I'd alerted Taffy to let me know when he was back to watch the last four *Paper Dolls*. My plan was to station myself in the console room, so when we went there to view the shows, I'd have a chance to chat with him and then ask—as if it just happened to occur to me—if he might be interested in letting the museum do a tribute to his work.

I called the desk in the library and asked them to queue in an episode of *Murphy Brown* for me. It wasn't a total ruse—maybe I'd get an idea for a seminar. Something on when characters get pregnant? The taboo of abortion? Single moms?

Admittedly, I could've simply called him at his office and asked, but he would be more likely to be open to the idea if he got to know me a little. At least, that's what I told myself. Now I just had to make sure I was charming and engaging. I rode the elevator down. I wasn't trembling like last time. I was nearly having a seizure.

Teddy, a student from NYU, was working behind the counter in the console room. I said hello and took the first viewing station by the door. That way I could keep my eye out, and "coincidently" look up just in time to see Jonathan Hill when he came in.

The console room was dark and dull, with no ornamentation—only rows of cubbies with little TV screens. I put on headphones and punched in the number for my show. As it started up, I began to fear my plan was totally obvious. He would know I'd stationed myself here. This was idiotic. Why couldn't I simply call him and ask in a businesslike manner if he'd be interested in a retrospective?

I pretended to watch the *Murphy Brown*. Told my heart to stop pounding, already. Questioned the decision of my thyroid gland to produce hormones that were generating a rush of adrenalin that was definitely not necessary at the moment. My mind reeled as if on fast forward, ready to make conversation. *Were your shows helpful last time? Did you go to Jekyll and Hyde? How's the writing going?* I reminded myself to breathe. Exhale. Why be so nervous? I was engaged. I was part of a couple. It didn't matter what he thought of me personally—this was professional. Even if he didn't want this kind of attention, he'd be flattered by the request, and the worst he could do was say "no."

Someone walked in. Oh, my god. Was that him? Without moving my head, I looked out of the corner of my eyes. Yes! So I casually took off my headphones and stretched my neck back and rolled my shoulders as if I'd been working there for hours and, just as I'd rehearsed in my mind, "happened to" look toward the front counter and pretended to be *totally* surprised to see him. "Hi!"

It was annoying that he was so attractive in his green khakis and black polo shirt. Men that successful didn't *need* to be so good-looking to get their way.

"Daphne Wells." He walked over to me. "Hello. How are you?"

"Great. How are you?"

He leaned against the top ledge of my cubbie. "Overextended, under pressure, and up for a vacation."

"You poor thing," I said, trying not to be sarcastic about it. He really did seem stressed out. "How's your daughter? Did she like her shows?"

"She loved them. She wants to come back."

"I've corrupted her."

"You were great with her, thanks."

"You're welcome." I grinned. He grinned back. I panicked. It seemed too abrupt to suggest the tribute. But how long could I keep him standing there? Conversation was not really encouraged in the console room, but you could get away with it as long as you kept your voice low. Many people came to see sitcoms, so the general quiet was laced with steady but intermittent laughter, as if there was a laugh track supplied by a small but appreciative audience. Since people were there to get some chuckles, there was generally a good vibe in the room.

"So are you watching the last four *Paper Dolls?*"

"Actually, no," he said. "You've got me addicted to these old shows."

"Really?"

"Last time I was here, I ended up watching *The Goldbergs* with Lily. It was amazing. That's real history. So today I picked out episodes of *Your Show of Shows. The Ernie Kovacs Show. Texaco Star Theater.* I still have some vague childhood memory of seeing Milton Berle in a sequined gown. . . ."

"Mr. Television. He was the reason people turned off their radios and bought television sets."

"Can't deny the attraction of seeing a man in a dress."

I laughed. "So are you giving up on *Paper Dolls?*"

"It wasn't really helping. The truth is, I'm sick of *Supermodels.* I have no interest in those people anymore."

Hmmm. Maybe it was because Jessica Cox left the show. It was no secret they'd been having an affair. "Don't you get spec scripts for *Supermodels* all the time?"

"Sure."

"Can't you just use those?"

He snorted.

"*None* of them are good?"

"There might be something in there, but you'd have to wade through too much junk. Most people don't know the show well enough."

I knew every episode of *Supermodels*, probably as well as he did. I could come up with lots of ideas based on Billie. She'd had some pretty dramatic stories to tell through the years. Should I enlighten him? It was tempting. But I didn't have any fully formed to toss off, plus people were paid for these ideas, you didn't just give them away. "Well," I said, "I'm sure something will come to you."

"I can hire writers. People I've worked with before. The first year is done; I can step back from it. It shouldn't bother me, but I'm a control freak."

"Maybe you want to do a sitcom for a change."

"Sitcoms?" He frowned. "Not my thing."

"People need to laugh."

"But why are there so few good ones?"

"It needs that magic combination of people."

"And how do you find that magic combination?"

"It's all in the voice. The creator. That's why your shows are so good. You can tell there's an individual behind them as opposed to being some assembly-line show."

I wished everything I said didn't sound like I was just trying to suck up. I really meant it.

"At this point, I don't have an original thought in my head," he said. "Maybe no one does."

"Oh, since you're blocked, then everyone else must be too?" I was teasing—sort of—then regretted it, because I saw him flinch.

"I didn't mean it like that. Everyone's been corrupted from growing up on TV. No one's actually experienced anything but what they've seen on the screen. We don't need reality anymore, we have reality TV.

"You do need a vacation."

"Everything," he said, "is a knockoff of something else. At this point we're getting knockoffs of knockoffs of knockoffs."

"You should go lie on a beach somewhere and drink banana daiquiris."

"It's true. I've lost my spark. I need to be around someone who still has enthusiasm. Someone who isn't totally cynical. Someone who still has ideals." He stared straight into my eyes. "Like you."

Was he, like, asking me out on a date? No. Of course not. He just meant . . . What did he mean? "Hey," I said. "I just had an idea."

"Yes?" He was leaning on the top edge of my cubby, looking straight at me. Closing the space between us. I mean, what was going on here? I panicked. Nothing going on. Nothing but a common interest in television programming.

"Would you be interested in letting the museum do a tribute to your work?"

He straightened up. "A tribute?"

"A retrospective. I could put together a clip of highlights. Write up something about your development as a writer and producer and what you've contributed over the years."

"I don't know. . . ."

"It would be great to look back and see what you've accomplished."

"I'm very flattered, but . . ." He shook his head.

"Don't answer me now." I had to stop him from saying no.

He shrugged. "I don't—"

"Just think about it. Here's my card." I pulled one out of my back pocket. "Call or email if you want to discuss it further."

"Okay." He put my card in his back pocket. "I'll think about it."

"He said he'd think about it."

Taffy and I were taking lunch together across the street. We had to stand in line for soup and salad. It got so crowded, what with eight million offices in midtown and everyone spilling out at the same time to eat. But every place within walking distance was swarming, so you just dealt with it.

"Do you think he will?"

"It's hard to say." We moved up to first in line. I called out my order. "Gotham Salad, blue cheese on the side!" They were incredibly efficient. I had my food within thirty seconds. Taffy, right behind me, had a bowl of split pea. We took our trays to a cramped table next to the condiment bar, and I waited until we'd had a chance to intake some food before changing the subject. "So," I said innocently, "has Simon said anything to you?"

"About what?" She took a spoonful of soup and blew on it.

"About . . . you know . . ." I foraged for a piece of bacon in my salad.

"You didn't say anything to him about me, did you?"

My cell phone rang. I checked the caller ID. "Billie." I hesitated. Didn't like wasting my short lunch break when there was barely time to eat. But maybe she was still in her good mood. "I'll make it quick."

"I'm not dropping this."

"Hello?"

She had to get it out between sobs. "Can you come over tonight?"

"What's wrong?"

"Everything."

Damn. Had to be Max. He let her down. "I guess I could come after work. Six-thirty?"

"I'll make dinner. What do you want?"

"Whatever you want to make."

"Fish?"

"Except fish."

"Steak?"

"Or steak."

"Chicken?"

"I'm sick of chicken."

"Daphne!" Her voice was sharp. "Just tell me what you want."

I panicked. "I don't know what I want. I'm eating lunch. I can't think about dinner."

"I'll make osso buco."

"You don't have to go to that much trouble."

"I have nothing to do. It will keep my mind off my shit life."

"Okay, then. Sounds good. See you later." God, we were so neurotic. I closed my phone.

"I'm guessing she's not in a good mood anymore?" Taffy said.

"Max broke up with her."

"Really?"

"She didn't say so. Not in so many words. But I'll bet you anything he did."

"You know Billie. He probably just postponed their trip again."

I searched for a piece of lettuce that would fit into my mouth. "Maybe."

"So what did he say?"

"Who?"

"Don't play dumb. What did Simon say when you totally humiliated me and told him how I feel?"

I crunched on my lettuce, debating whether it was a good idea to fess up. I decided it couldn't hurt. "He seems to have a problem with the concept of dating someone who works under him."

"Do you think he means it? Or was it just an excuse?"

"I'm not sure what goes on in Simon's head. He did say you're a very nice girl."

"Yuck. Maybe that's the problem. Maybe I should come to work in black leather boots and a dog collar like Emma Peel. Wouldn't that be cool?"

She was referring to a sixties show imported from England called *The Avengers*. We'd recently done a special screening of one especially notable episode where Emma was kidnapped, drugged, and dressed to look like a dominatrix. "But Simon is so timid. That might scare him away."

"You have to watch out for the timid ones," Taffy said, scooping up the last spoonful of her soup. "Sometimes they're the ones with the voracious appetites."

I looked at her skeptically as I dipped a piece of carrot into the blue cheese dressing. Simon? Voracious? Right.

Thirteen

"**M**ax broke up with me."

"He did?"

"Well, not in so many words."

"In fewer words?"

"He canceled our trip."

"You mean he postponed again?"

"Canceled."

"I'm sorry."

Billie had not made the osso buco. She'd barely gotten out of bed. At least five more packages had joined the box of *Seventeens* by the door, and the kitchen was filthy with grimy pans and dirty dishes. Most disconcerting, though, was her appearance. Her nails had leftover patches of pink polish. Her highlights had grown out. Her face was broken out and splotchy.

"I hate my life," she said. We sat on the couch. *Entertainment Tonight* was on. We looked at the TV instead of each other.

"Did he say why?"

"Guess."

"He didn't want to miss his psychiatry appointments?"

"You're closer than you think. He decided to go to a couple's therapy weekend retreat with his wife."

"He actually admitted to that?"

"Yes!"

Sounded like, in so many words, he was breaking up with her.

"He says he really wants to leave his wife, but when push comes to shove, he can't. He's worried about the kids. Can you believe it? His daughter is practically in college already! What does she care? He actually—get this—had the gall to say he needs to improve his relationship with his wife."

"That scumbag!" I was being sarcastic. Billie chose not to notice, which was probably just as well. No need to tell her this was the most human Max had seemed to me yet.

"So," she said, getting some wine from the refrigerator, "if he thinks I'm going to waste more time on him, forget it."

I followed her into the kitchen. "You're ending things with him?" I seriously doubted that. How would she pay the rent?

She poured us each a glass. "I've got to do something. I can't live like this."

"Okay." I'd been telling her this for years. She'd always said this was the way she wanted to live her life, and I should stop judging, and there were no good alternatives. "So what are you going to do?" I opened the refrigerator. I'd been expecting dinner, after all. "Is there something to eat in here?"

"Cheese? Crackers?"

"Sound perfect." It sounded good, actually.

"Sorry, I never made it to the grocery store. Tell you the truth, I haven't been outside in three days."

"Really?" I took out a hunk of Muenster. "Does it matter if there's mold on one side?"

"Cut it off." She grabbed a knife from the drawer. "So what do you think I should do?"

"Hmmmm." I paused, as if I was taking a moment to rack my brains. "Get a job?"

"I have a job."

"A regular, steady job."

She turned toward me, seemingly unaware that the ten-inch serrated knife was pointing straight at me. "Doing what?"

I decided not to joke that she should sign up with an escort service. For one thing, she might not find it amusing; for another, she might just do it. And then they'd probably want someone younger, and she'd have another reason to feel depressed. "I know someone who got training to be a bookkeeper, and it didn't even take her that long. She's making like forty dollars an hour."

"A bookkeeper? *Me?* Please." Billie sliced up the cheese and arranged it on a plate.

I looked for crackers in the cupboard. "I know it's not glamorous"—I reached for a box of low-fat Wheat Thins—"but maybe it's time to get practical." I had a sudden horrible vision of Billie moving in with me and Charlie in New Rochelle. "So what do *you* think you should do?"

She tore a slice of cheese into four pieces and put the small bits on half a cracker. "Get new head shots. Look for more acting work."

"Billie, actresses in their late thirties who have no credits other than a voice-over for a limo service don't rely on acting for their money job." I put a piece of cheese on a cracker. "They need a money job to support their acting." I ate it. "You know that." It was stale.

"You're in a bad mood."

"I'm worried about you."

"It's obvious what I should do."

"What?" I took a piece of cheese but left the cracker. *Please let this be something reasonable.*

She reclined luxuriously and crossed her legs. "Find a rich husband."

"Okay, that's an idea. But maybe you have to make some compromises."

"Such as?"

I took a good gulp of wine. "Does he need to be good-looking?"

She thrust out her chest, all indignant. "I should hope so."

"That will make it a lot harder." Especially, I was thinking (but would not under any circumstances say out loud), because of the fact that she couldn't have kids. About five years earlier the doctors had found some irregular cells in her uterus and suggested she should consider having a hysterectomy as a preventative measure. She did it without hesitation. There'd been a good chance she wouldn't have had kids anyway. She was not the maternal sort. I could still remember her looking down at her crotch and saying, "Uterus? It's been good having you around, but it's over." And then she added, like that MC on *The Weakest Link*, "Good-bye." I couldn't really blame her. She'd just started getting serious with Max. He took care of the hospital bills. That had seemingly bonded them in some way I didn't really want to think about.

But the bond was unglued and—unsavory as it sounds—her value in the marketplace was not what it used to be. Sure, it was possible that she'd find a wonderful, handsome, rich guy who would fall in love with her despite the fact that she was losing her looks, couldn't reproduce, would not intake nutrients, only wanted to go shopping for things to enhance a gradually declining appearance, was a recovered but at-risk ex-cocaine addict, still somewhat of a pothead, and seemed to be developing a mild agoraphobic condition. But was it likely?

"So," she asked, taking another sip of wine, her crackers untouched, "what do you think I should do?"

"Why don't you work on finding a husband . . . but maybe he doesn't have to be rich and good-looking?"

"Then what's the point?" She wasn't joking. At all.

"Maybe he just earns a living. He doesn't have to be rich."

"Can he still be good-looking?" She still wasn't joking.

"How about mildly good-looking and earns a good living."

"How about broke and ugly but has a big dick."

I decided to ignore that. "Billie, I'm trying to be practical."

"Fine. Rich and ugly, or good-looking and middle-class. I can't tolerate handsome and poor, though. *I* have to be the pretty one."

"Right."

"So how should I find one?"

"Don't act like you haven't lived in this world the past thirty-six years of your life. How do you think?"

She got all offended. "I am not doing the Internet dating thing. I'm sorry. I've heard too many horror stories. You email back and forth, meet for dinner, find out he posted a picture of his cousin and even the cousin lost his hair since the picture was taken."

"How about video dating? There's a bunch of dating Web sites set up for it. You get a Web cam. You talk with each other *and* you see each other before you have a first date."

"I like that. How much does a webcam cost?"

"A hundred dollars or something. Get Max to buy you one. As a consolation prize for the trip."

"That would show him."

"Yeah." My guess was Max would be relieved if she found herself a husband.

"So. Let's not talk about this anymore. It's too depressing. What's new with you? How's the wedding planning?"

"Nothing new to report. Hey, did I tell you Jonathan Hill came to the museum again?"

"Now *he* would be a good catch. Did you get his number?"

"Get real."

"I slept with lots of show business royalty in my day."

I didn't want to say it wasn't "her day" anymore, so I kept my mouth shut. I'd already said too much.

Fourteen

*I*t was late, I wanted to get home, and a taxi would've been so much more pleasant, but the bus was cheaper. Then I spent ten minutes waiting for the bus to come while taxi after taxi sped by. When it finally did come, I could see it was packed. I still got on. After all, I'd waited all that time; I wasn't going to pay up for a cab now.

I held onto my pole and stared at an overhead ad for vodka. It featured a skinny model wearing a red miniskirt. I proceeded to have a mini existential crisis. It was as if my brain was a dial turning to all the same channels over and over again. And this brain didn't have cable, so there were only a few channels with nothing interesting on and a lot of reruns.

Channel one. Why couldn't I be happy about getting married when I was around Billie? It wasn't like pretending that my life was stuck like hers would make her situation any better. Maybe she was fixated on a man who had basically paid her for blow jobs all these years and was now retiring her, but that wasn't a reason for me to feel guilty. It would not kill her to think I was happy.

Switch to channel two. Maybe I wasn't happy. Maybe I didn't want to get married, and not just because I was guilty toward Billie. Maybe Charlie really wasn't the man I was meant to marry.

Switch to channel three. It was silly to think I wasn't "meant to" marry him. You marry the man you're with when it's the right time in your life to get married. Charlie was a good guy. We made a good couple. We could be perfectly happy together. Was I holding out for some fantasy that didn't exist like (god forbid) Billie was doing?

Switch to channel four. On the other hand, what was wrong

with holding out for something better? Maybe I should've been shooting higher. Maybe I was settling on Charlie because at least I was marrying someone who wouldn't make Billie jealous. He didn't make much money, our sex life was uninspired, and I was headed for an isolated bedroom community. She at least would still have her "glamorous" Upper East Side existence, and would probably find some new man to pay her to give him blow jobs.

Switch to channel five. Why was I putting down my future suburban existence? The Petries were perfectly happy on Bonnie Meadow Road. I could keep my job. I could commute into the city every day. I could spend all my income on a babysitter. Maybe Jonathan Hill would let me do the tribute. I'd do a brilliant job and feel my life was worthwhile.

Switch to channel six. Was I just clinging to the museum because it was an institution that was related to the entertainment business? Was I fooling myself that I was doing something creative? Was I wasting my life enabling people to waste their time watching reruns of stupid shows that were produced only to fill in the time between commercials?

Switch to channel seven. Maybe the real problem was that I didn't think I was worthy enough of being one of the creative people, the people who "did" things. The "mover and shaker" type people. I only thought I was worth being a support person, a behind-the-scenes person, a passive person with no voice, just a member of the audience with no "vision" of my own. Unlike Jonathan Hill, who got everything he wanted in this world and then went around feeling sorry for himself.

Back to Channel one. What was I complaining about? I had a job I liked. I was engaged to be married. I was in good health. Was I just telling myself life was no good so I wouldn't have to feel guilty toward Billie?

Oh, god. It was times like this I wished I had a mother. I would've loved to be able to talk this over with her. My heart burned to have her back.

My nose got itchy and my eyes teared up. I was not going to cry on the bus. I was not going to cry on the bus.

Mom!

It wasn't fair. I hated my father. I hated him for flying that stupid plane. Because he thought he was such big shit for flying his own plane. Stupid! Stupid, stupid, stupid! People were so stupid!

The bus hit West End Avenue. Speaking of stupid. I'd missed my stop. I got off and headed back toward Broadway. Eventually, I would get home. Eventually.

Is it any wonder that all I wanted to do once I got there was get in front of the television set, watch *Law and Order*, and eat a stack of Fig Newtons? But Charlie was in the mood to talk. He was already in bed, in his boxers, reading *The Kite Runner*. As soon as I got comfortable next to him with my cookies and a glass of milk, he put the book down. "I got it today."

"Got what?"

"The rejection. From Gordon Fineberg. He sent the script back with a form letter."

"I'm sorry." Damn. It was one of those days. I gave his hand a squeeze. It was his rejection, but it felt like mine too. Why was the world so hard?

"It's not surprising," he said. "Obviously it wasn't stupid enough."

Pretending to be casual about it didn't keep him from using it as an excuse to complain about his day. "People are more dumbed-down than ever. My students? They don't know how to listen. We started *Romeo and Juliet*. I'm psyched, looking forward to it. Thinking maybe I'll be able to get through to them. But it's impossible. They don't know how to listen! As soon as I start talking, they take that as their cue to start talking with each other. It's impossible. And you know what's ruined them? Television. Passive entertainment. The entire generation is lost."

"Uh-huh." God, I wished he would just let me listen to my show.

"Did you hear me?"

"They don't listen because of television."

He babbled on about how he was endlessly correcting papers, and how his "screenager" students hated to read, couldn't write an essay to save their lives, and wasted all their time on stupid electronic devices. I knew he needed my attention right then, and my support, sympathy, empathy, but I couldn't. I needed to immerse myself into Sam Waterston. Oh, god. He was it for me, my ideal man. Okay, a little old, but I was attracted to unavailable father figures, I have to admit—I mean who isn't—and he was it. So moral, so sensitive, so good-looking in a weathered, WASPY-sort of way. Come to think of it, Jonathan Hill looked a bit like a younger Sam Waterston if you waxed the eyebrows.

"You haven't been listening to a thing I've said!"

"What?" Whoops. "Sorry." If only Gordon Fineberg hadn't let him down. It sucked. He would be a lot happier if he could do what he really wanted to be doing. "I'm sorry you had a bad day."

"Would you turn off the television?"

"I'm watching."

"I'm trying to relate to you."

"I'm tired. My day wasn't so great either. I had dinner with Billie. All I want to do is veg out."

"She made you feel like shit again?"

"Max," I said, my voice tight, "is in the process of dumping her." I wasn't sure I wanted to bring this up. I didn't think I could take it if he started criticizing her, even though I no doubt would agree with him. "She seems not to be useful to him anymore."

"So you feel guilty."

I really didn't want to get into it. We were both sick of my guilt. I was missing a major plot point. What had that character just said? A young girl was on the stand. Sam was cross-examining her. The judge was glaring. "Plus I was already in a bad mood."

"Bad day at work?"

Damn. He was being attentive, thereby making me an even worse person for neglecting him. And it's not like that encounter had actually been bad. Now I'd have to make it sound bad, though. "Jonathan Hill was there again today. I asked him if he'd be interested in the museum doing a tribute, but I don't think he's gonna go for it."

"What did you expect? That guy is a huge success. He's incredibly busy. The museum means nothing to him. You're like a fly flying around his face to be swatted away."

I stared at the TV. My face felt hard. A thick sheet of glass. This was not making me feel better. "We had an interesting conversation the last time he came."

"So you were hoping he was attracted to you?"

"No! God. You make it sound like I have a stupid crush on him."

"Maybe you do."

"Don't be ridiculous. Let's just drop it, okay? I'm trying to watch this."

"Why is it always more important to watch your show than talk to me?"

"If you're just going to insult my intelligence by suggesting I have a crush on Jonathan Hill, I'd rather watch my show."

"Your *shows* insult you. They insult your intelligence. I'm going to sleep. Will you turn out the light?"

"You're going to sleep already?"

"Why do you say that as if you're surprised? I have to get up early in the morning."

Right. How could I forget? I turned out the light.

"And could you turn down the sound?"

I turned down the sound. Even though now I could barely hear.

Within five minutes, Charlie began to snore. I wished I could have the apartment to myself. Then I could blast the TV if I wanted to, and no one could stop me.

But that thought scared me. I didn't want to be alone. TV wasn't really more important than having Charlie there next to me, was it?

Oh, god. I was messing up. I should've suggested making love. That's what normal couples did. That would've fixed both our moods. He could face teaching with renewed vim and vigor. I could forget about Billie. But my eyes were drawn back to Sam Waterston. Who was seemingly giving me what I needed. At least, until the verdict came in. And the credits came on. And I was left with my guilt. Case closed.

Fifteen

I knew I shouldn't have picked up the phone. That's why caller ID was invented. But still, I picked up. You'd think I wanted her to ruin my day.

"It's over."

"What?"

"He broke up with me."

"Really?"

"Fucking bastard."

"Are you sure?"

"I hate him. I want to fry his balls, boil his dick, and . . ."

"Billie!"

"Squirt some Grey Poupon on it, put it in a bun, and—"

"That is so gross."

"Maybe I should just kill him, do you think? Take him to the observation deck of the Empire State Building and—whoops—I don't *know* how he fell over the banister, officer . . ."

I let her go on. I had no idea what to say. Idiotic clichés went through my mind. *It's all for the best. Now you can move on. He's not worth putting your life on hold for.* And then there were the snide comments. *So I guess he's not leaving her for you after all. Congratulations on wasting two years of your life on him. At least he paid the rent.*

"I'm sorry," I said.

"What am I going to do?"

Binge, purge, drink, smoke, snort . . . "You'll manage. You'll be fine."

"I feel like shit. Thank god you're home. I don't think I can survive being alone today. What are you doing?"

"Today?" *Charlie and I were planning on buying my engagement ring.* "Nothing much."

"Do you want to come over?" she asked. "I could use some company."

"Tonight," I said, "would be better."

"Are you sure?"

"I sort of promised to spend the afternoon with Charlie. I think he wanted to go to Central Park and ride bikes or something."

"Ew," she said, as if I was going there to eat bugs. "You don't have a bike, do you?"

"They rent them I think."

"Okay, then, tonight. I'll probably take a valium and sleep off the day."

"Are you sure you're okay?"

Her voice got all haughty. "It's not exactly a surprise."

"Right. Well. At least you can move on now. Right?" I couldn't wait—an evening of plying her with empty encouragement.

"Move on to what?"

"We'll talk tonight. I'll take you out to dinner."

"Let's order in. I can't go out looking like this."

"Okay. That sounds like fun."

A barrel of laughs.

Charlie and I walked up and down 47th Street, the heart of the Diamond District, peering into each store window, searching for just the right place to buy just the right ring. After all, this event would end up being a major memory. One store seemed too gaudy, with mirrors everywhere and bright fluorescent lights. Another had so many trays lined up in the window the rings seemed like rows of identical toys from an assembly line. How was anyone expected to choose one and feel like it was special?

We finally made ourselves venture into a store. A bored, depressed-looking salesman with sparse white hair and sad blue eyes stared at us like we were trespassing. We looked in his showcase, but he offered to show us nothing. We crept out.

In another store, two salespeople were busy shouting at each other about another employee who was constantly coming in late. We left before they noticed us.

Then we went into a very large store where different vendors had their own counters. I began to feel very confused. There was too much choice. Maybe the shape was slightly different, the size bigger or smaller, but really, the "rocks" struck me as alarmingly uniform. The fact that we had a modest budget was not a problem; to my untrained eyes, they all looked more or less the same. A perspiring salesman with acne scars lured us over to his counter near the door and tried to teach us. "You gotta know your four C's," he said in a heavy Brooklyn accent. "Clarity, color, cut, and carat. Clarity. You want the stone to sparkle? Then you don't want any imperfections, no blemishes on the surface."

"But does it really matter?" I asked, trying not to let my eyes linger on the nicks and grooves on his skin. "I mean, if you can only see the difference under the microscope . . ."

He looked at me like I'd spoken blasphemy, then showed us a ring that would've been too gaudy for Cher. "Now this ring . . ."

How could anyone walk around with a rock that huge? Wouldn't it get stolen? They said to turn your ring around on the subway, but who wants to think about that when you're busy nabbing a seat, and who wants to have to distrust every person you come into contact with for the rest of your life? "I think that's a little big for me."

He frowned and put it back. "Color is the next important thing. The closer you can get to colorless, the better. The more yellow in the stone, the worse the quality."

It all seemed so random. Who said a little yellow was bad? I liked yellow. If someone in charge decreed that yellow rings were the most valuable ones, then everyone would raise their prices on the yellow ones.

"You want your ring to sparkle, right?" he said. "You want everyone to notice your ring."

"Not really," I said.

"You don't want them to notice your beautiful ring?" He looked at Charlie for confirmation that the bride was nuts.

I already knew I wasn't buying from this man. He hated me.

Time to move on, but Charlie wanted the rest of his lesson. "And carat?"

"A half a carat is the size of a pea. Richard Burton? He bought Liz Taylor a 69-carat diamond. That's the size of a golf ball."

"We can probably only afford a pea," Charlie said.

"Or half a pea," I said.

Charlie looked wounded, as if I'd insulted him, but what I really meant was that I wouldn't want a stone as big as a pea. Maybe a lentil?

"What can you tell us about the cut?" Charlie asked.

"When light enters the ring," the man said, "it goes in at certain angles. The angles determine how much it will sparkle. But this young lady doesn't want her ring to sparkle."

Now he was getting hostile. I tugged on Charlie's sleeve, but the man was pulling out a tray. "So let me show you what I got. Do you know what you want in the way of setting?" he asked.

I shook my head. Even if I did know, I wouldn't tell him.

"You want it to ride high? Or low? You want a cluster? Solitaire? And then the band. You got your gold, your white gold, your platinum. . . ." He looked at me for an answer. "You gotta decide these things!" He was practically yelling. "You gotta know what you want! Don't just walk into a store having no idea what you're doing! You gotta be informed, or you're gonna get taken!"

I took a step back. "I need to get some air."

Charlie backed up with me. "We have to think some more about this. . . ."

"You don't have to decide now," the man said to us as we continued to smile and nod and back up toward the door. "Look at what I have! You'll be back! No one else has prices like I do. You're lucky you walked in here. I happen to be honest, but there are a lot of people out there who will rip you off!" He was still making the sale as the door closed behind us—"I'm here until six o'clock!"

Charlie and I kept walking. Was I being overly picky? Avoiding buying the ring because I wasn't really ready to? No. We were not going home without a ring.

"You know what?" I said, as we strolled. "Maybe we should forget about diamonds. Maybe that's the problem. Why not get another stone?"

"But don't you want a diamond?"

"Just because everyone says you should have a diamond?"

"I want you to have a diamond."

"Because it will prove something?"

"What do you mean by that?"

Now I'd offended him. "Nothing. I just feel like we're being slaves to the convention. Diamonds all look the same to me. I want something with color. And I want the salesperson to be nice, because I'm always going to remember this."

"I don't know. Let's just keep looking."

In the middle of the block, we turned into another large store that had individual vendors. I saw a gentle-looking elderly man wearing a white shirt and a tweed vest at a booth in the back. I went to him first. He stood silently as I looked in his showcase and saw a tray of beautiful vintage rings that were unlike any others we'd seen. There were rubies and emeralds and all sorts of stones I couldn't begin to identify. One especially called out to me. A beautiful blue stone set in a deco platinum silver band. I didn't know what it cost or what it was. I just knew. . . .

"What kind of stone is that?" I asked, pointing through the glass.

"Sapphire," he said, taking it out. He put on a monocle, wiped the ring clean, and put it on a black velvet tray. "Beautiful color, isn't it? The ancients used to say the sky is a huge blue sapphire stone."

I looked at Charlie before sliding it on. He seemed skeptical. But it happened to fit perfectly. "I didn't know they were such a dark blue."

"You know how the sky can be many different shades?" he

said. "So can the sapphire. Midnight blue, like this one. Or a clear blue, like a summer afternoon. Or a blue-gray, like before a storm shower . . ."

"It's really pretty," I said to Charlie.

"But are you sure . . ."

"I want this one."

"Okay." He still didn't seem convinced, but he turned to the man and asked how much it was.

"Five hundred dollars."

We could've spent much more. And Charlie could've tried bargaining the man down—it was done all the time on this street. But—and maybe this made us foolish—there was something repellent about the idea of haggling over an engagement ring. I was relieved when Charlie simply said, "We'll take it."

The man wrote out a receipt on an old-fashioned pad with a piece of carbon paper.

Charlie said to me, "You're absolutely sure you don't want a diamond?"

I could hear the insecurity in his voice. "It's perfect. I love it. Thank you." I gave him a kiss, and he hugged me. Then he wrote out the check as the man put the ring in a blue velvet box. I stood there thinking: *This is one of the best moments of my life.*

And then it hit me. The surprising thing.

Maybe it actually was.

We went to a restaurant on the corner. I didn't want to eat too much, since I was meeting Billie soon for dinner, but it did seem right to have a celebratory meal over this, and I didn't want my "date" with her to rule that out. They seated us in a comfortable table by the window. Charlie ordered a bottle of wine. I dipped a piece of French bread into a shallow bowl of olive oil, letting the soft whiteness sponge up the thick green liquid. Yum. It was so good. *This is the most you can expect from life. This, here, right now. If only I could tell my parents. If only I could tell them they didn't have to worry. I was going to be just fine.*

Charlie brought the velvet box out of his pocket and put it on the middle of the table. "Are you going to put it on?"

I opened it. There it was. I put the ring on my finger. The stone glistened. My hand became the hand of an engaged person.

"Well, this is starting to seem quite real, isn't it," I said.

"Yep."

"We still need to figure out where we're going to do it. And then we have to think about flowers, a band, invitations . . ."

"A honeymoon . . ."

"Where should we go?"

"Paris? London? The Caribbean?"

"Can you see us on a honeymoon?" I had to laugh. Just like a married couple.

The waiter came with the wine and poured. Charlie swilled it around and tasted it. "Good." The waiter poured mine. Silly rituals. Still, it was nice.

He raised his glass. "To us. And a happy life together."

"To us."

We clinked and took sips. Looked into each other's eyes and smiled. For the first time, I really felt it. We were really going to do this! The waiter brought our menus. I tried not to order too much.

My stomach was quite full when I arrived at Billie's. I hadn't been able to resist ordering an appetizer of duck, and it came with some salad, and that bread was so good in the olive oil. Before going in, I put the ring back in its box and into my purse. I didn't want to show it to her yet. I needed to see how she was holding up. If she was a wreck, this could wait.

There were now six boxes of magazines by the door, and two shopping bags of clothes. No surface was safe from clutter. Clothes and shoes were strewn everywhere.

"Shall we order Chinese food?" she asked. She still hadn't done her hair, and now I noticed stray grays that I never knew she had. But I was really shocked to see she still hadn't done her nails. She never let them go this long.

"That sounds good."

"What would you like?" she asked.

"Hot and sour soup?"

"That's all?"

"You decide."

"Don't make me decide. I don't want to be responsible."

"How about Moo Shu." At least that was mostly lettuce.

"You want the crepes?"

No way I could eat a crepe. "Just one."

She got on the phone and ordered a huge amount of food. I wondered who would eat it all. Certainly not her, unless she was on a bingeing cycle.

We set the table, which required clearing off the table, which required filling garbage bags with old mail and newspapers. The sink was full of dishes. There were garbage bags full of empty two-liter bottles of Diet Pepsi. More stacks of magazines were on the chairs.

"What are you going to do with all these magazines?"

"Read them."

"And then?"

"They're collector's items."

"Maybe you should donate them to the library."

"Who's going to lug them down there?"

I shrugged. Not me. I went to pee. The bathroom counter had various cosmetics sitting in puddles of water. Her shower curtain was hosting a rain forest of mold. The toilet bowl was brown.

I went back out and found Billie in the study, back on the computer. There were so many boxes, you could barely make it to her desk.

"I've decided to start a blog," she said.

"Are you sure that's a good idea?"

"Why do you disapprove of everything I do?"

"I just think the last thing you should be doing now is spending more time in front of a computer."

"How is that any worse than spending all your time in front of the TV?"

"Fine. Do a blog."

"I've been reading one by this woman who writes about dating. She has it on her site: 'Email me if you want to date me.' I could do that. Evidently she has a huge following. And she's always going on dates. You can read all about them."

"Why would I want to?"

"It's very entertaining."

"Billie, let's clean up the apartment. And then we can take a walk. Or go out to a restaurant. Or a play. Or a movie. Anything."

"I don't want to go out."

"Then let me just throw some stuff out."

"Are you insane? You have no idea what's important!"

I peeked inside an open box. "What about these old *Vogues*? What are you going to do with all these?" They were from the seventies. Kind of cool, actually. Covers with Margaux Hemingway, Marisa Berenson, Farrah Fawcett, Janice Dickinson . . .

"I enjoy reading about people with high hopes. People who were being hyped. People who thought they were successful and now they're old and ugly and forgotten."

"Or dead."

"Reduced to being in an old magazine in a box."

"You don't find it depressing?" After all, the same could be said for her and her glamorous old spreads.

"It's reassuring."

The buzzer rang. Our food had arrived. She went down to the lobby to pick it up. I took her seat at the computer and checked my email.

There was something from *JH@BoomerangProductions.com*.

He'd written to me!

I clicked on it and read.

So I've been thinking about your proposition. Still not convinced. But I'd be happy to donate some episodes to the museum. I have all the DVDs. Do you want to come by the office and pick them up? Or I could just mail them. Let me know, J.

I saved the email. I wouldn't write him back until I'd decided exactly how to word my response. Of course he could've just mailed them. That was easiest. He had assistants to do things like that. Was he inviting me to the office to give me a chance to convince him to do the tribute? Maybe. It often took a few tries to get people to agree. I would go there. I just had to think of something to say that would sell him on the idea.

Which reminded me . . . I had another idea to sell. I went back to that girl-friendly Web site where I'd found the sex tips and found the page for "How to go down on a woman" and copied the link into an email. For the subject line I put "Some informative reading" and sent it off to Charlie.

"I'm back!" Billie said, poking her head in. "Come eat before I inhale it all."

I joined her at the sofa. We put the food out on the coffee table. I reached for a container, doing my best to ignore my full stomach.

"All I really want is my fortune cookie," she said, cracking one open. "Aha. Listen to this. 'A handsome and successful man will change your life.' " She smoothed it out on the table.

Jonathan Hill was a handsome and successful man. Could he change her life? I unfolded a crepe. She had slept with lots of show business royalty in her day. Maybe it wasn't a bad idea.

Sixteen

*J*onathan Hill's production office was in the Mandarin Oriental Hotel, which was part of the Time Warner Center on Columbus Circle. I'd occasionally been to the mall that was part of that complex. It wasn't far from the museum, and there was a huge Whole Foods and a good Borders there. But most of the stores were out of my price range. As far as I was concerned, Coach, Cole Haan, and Tourneau were just taking up valuable space.

The building had been under construction in September 2001, and I remembered wondering if anyone would want to buy in. It was two towers . . . taller than any other building around. Wouldn't a person feel vulnerable? Evidently not. I'd read in the *Times* that apartments were selling for double-digit millions to Saudi Arabian princes, Asian bankers, and, well, television producers. Maybe if you're that wealthy, you just don't feel vulnerable.

The lobby was a fusion of oriental and sleek hip, with a marble floor of golden brown hues radiating from the middle. A man behind an intimidating thick counter phoned up and nodded me in.

I stepped onto an elevator that barely seemed to move but almost immediately opened its doors to the seventy-second floor. On the last door at the end of the hall, a small gold plaque said BOOMERANG PRODUCTIONS. I rang the bell and was buzzed in. A brunette receptionist sat behind a blond wood desk in the entrance hall. A framed 1994 American Film Institute Award for *Boomers* was on the wall behind her. Next to that was a framed promo poster of *Supermodels* with all the models posed in front of a pagoda from when they shot two episodes in Japan.

"Hi. Jonathan Hill is expecting me."

She blinked at me from behind trendy black rectangular glasses. "One sec." She picked up the phone and punched in his extension. There were piles of scripts on her desk, and she had one open in front of her. "I have a . . ." She raised her eyebrows at me.

"Daphne Wells."

"Daphne Wells here to see you." She hung up. "He'll be a minute. You can take a seat." She nodded toward three cushy coffee-colored sofas arranged in a U shape around a white shaggy rug and a low wood table. The sofas were oriented toward a gigantic television screen against the wall. The tones in the room were all subdued creamy yellows and tans. A staircase, a real honey-oak staircase—such a rarity in Manhattan apartments—went up to the next floor.

She saw me looking. "Yeah, he lives upstairs."

"Nice commute," I said, but her smile was token, and I had the feeling she'd heard that one before.

I sat on a sofa and stared at the flat screen. It was one of those big ones I'd had the pleasure of watching when cruising Circuit City. Even the museum screening rooms all had crap equipment. No money to upgrade. They'd been working on going digital for years, but it was taking forever.

I didn't see a remote, just a laptop computer sitting on the coffee table. I inched forward on my seat and took a closer look. I realized this was actually the remote—with a laptop as an added accessory. A totally sleek and elegant gadget with a touch-panel display. Maybe it wasn't good form to watch TV right then, but this was, after all, a television production office, and how could they leave this out here as a temptation without expecting people to succumb? I found the power button and turned it on. Ellen was interviewing Scarlett Johansson, and they were flirting like crazy.

"Is that the only thing on?"

I looked up. It was Jonathan Hill. "Oh, sorry," I said, nodding toward the TV. "I couldn't resist." I turned off the power then stood.

"Cool, isn't it? Fifty-inch high definition flat screen. It displays 1080-resolution broadcasts in all their glory."

"Wow," I said as I followed him into his office. God, why did this feel so awkward? Not that we knew each other so well, but seeing him outside the museum made me feel like I didn't know him at all.

His office was light and airy. But the astounding thing was the floor-to-ceiling corner windows with a northeastern view of the city that showed off Central Park in all its glory. It was almost like looking out the window of an airplane. I didn't want to seem overly in awe, though, so I didn't let my eyes dwell on what was out there or even say anything about it. Piles of scripts and books were on a couch and on the floor. A treadmill was positioned in front of a television set. On the TV, a Steve Urkel doll was propped up next to Maxwell Smart. Next to him was Herman Munster.

"I like your doll collection," I said, as I sat down on the edge of a high-tech black mesh chair opposite his desk.

"Thanks. I'm looking for a Lily Munster. Herman seems kind of lonely."

"I bet you could find her on eBay," I said, wondering if he was aware of any double meaning behind his comment, if he'd meant one, if I was totally reading in. . . .

"So I had Martha scrounge up copies of all my shows," he said. "My entire body of work fits inside this shopping bag." He moved a small Hugo Boss shopping bag toward my feet. "Isn't that sad?"

"Heartbreaking." I spied an invitation for a movie premiere propped open on his desk. There was a glamour shot of Jessica Cox on the front. Would he go? It would've been so fun to just come right out and ask if he was upset when she left the show and what he planned to do with her character Mirage, but no way I was going to ask.

He leaned back in his chair. Folded his arms behind his head. "How are things at the museum?"

"I'm gearing up for a seminar this week on *Days of Our Lives*.

That show premiered in 1965, which makes it the longest-running scripted program in NBC's history."

"So what, you have members of the cast coming?"

A framed photograph was on the wall behind him. He was standing next to Christina Applegate in front of a Broadway theater. Probably from when she was doing *Sweet Charity*. His arm was around her. Had they dated?

"And the creators behind it. Everyone will sit around and reminisce. I'm an *All My Children* person, myself. How's your writing going?"

He groaned. "Maybe I should just retire."

"You're too young to retire." A script titled *Honeymoon Without Runways* was in front of me on his desk. My heart raced and my thoughts sped as if to keep up. This could be a moment to mention Charlie. His script. But no, it felt wrong. And I needed to convince him to do the seminar. "And your work really deserves some attention."

"That's not true."

"It is. Your work not only reflects society, it's actually changed society. In *Boomers* and *Katie McCall* you had characters who pushed the boundaries. These shows truly changed what women have been able to imagine for themselves. That's so important!"

"I did all that?"

"You're too modest."

I didn't say anything about how *Supermodels* set women back another ten years.

It would be so interesting to know, how *did* he feel about producing *Supermodels*? It was certainly fun, but he obviously wasn't getting much out of it. Maybe he wasn't using his own relationships for material anymore.

But I couldn't go there. He'd find that insulting. Or naive. *Supermodels* was a big hit. And why should his personal life be material? Worse thought: Maybe it still was—and he was now totally into dating models. Better thought: This would mean he'd be totally into Billie.

His phone rang. "Sorry," he said as he picked up.

I looked at his bulletin board. There was a letter tacked on. "Jonathan, The honesty and humility in your speech was touching, and your talents are a gift for everyone. Love, David E. Kelley." It was sobering to realize, no matter how high up the food chain, you still needed reassurance.

"Listen," he said into the phone, "I can't talk to him right now, just take a message. Thanks." He hung up. "I don't know," he said to me. "I think you're trying to flatter me into doing this event."

"But it's all true."

The receptionist came to the door. "Hi, sorry, excuse me? Your brother-in-law wants to know if he can send you his script."

"Oh. Yeah. Tell him sure. And when we get it, skim it and give me the CliffsNotes."

"I can't wait," she said.

After she left, I asked if his brother-in-law was a writer.

"He's a dermatologist."

"Oh." I gritted my teeth in sympathy.

"Exactly."

"It must be awkward when it's a member of your family."

"Even my own mother has pitched ideas to me."

"You're kidding."

"I had to reject my own mother!"

"Ouch."

"She didn't speak to me for a year."

"Really?"

"I'm exaggerating . . . sort of. She still holds it against me."

"Wow."

"It's incredibly aggravating. People only look at me to see how they can use me."

"That sucks."

"That's what I like about you," he said.

"Me?"

"You don't have these pretensions. You're perfectly happy to be a member of the audience. It's great. No inflated ego. Do you know how rare that is?"

"There are a lot of people out there with talent."

"Do you really think so? Not to be arrogant, but talent used to be something we considered a special gift. Now everyone likes to think they have it. If they're not famous, it's because no one's given them a chance."

I frowned and shook my head to convey I agreed. People were such fools, and of course I would never imagine that I, or anyone I knew—such as my own boyfriend—had talent.

He stood. "I have to get back to work. Or should I say not working. Time to torture myself through another script. Let me pay for your cab. I don't want you to have to carry those."

"Don't be ridiculous, it's nothing. I'm only going a few blocks."

He held out a twenty, but I picked up the bag and shook my head.

"Please?"

"No way. Thank you for donating them. After we make copies, I'll get them back to you. And think about the seminar."

"I will."

I wished he would say something more definite than that. Would this be the last time I'd ever see him? "And don't forget to bring Lily back. I'll continue her history lesson."

"Sounds good."

I left his office with regret. I hadn't even fixed him up with Billie or told him about Charlie's scripts. Seemed like Jonathan Hill had the power to solve everyone's problems. I nodded to Martha on the way out. Judging by the constant ringing of his phone, a lot of other people felt that way too.

"Guess what!" Taffy said as I entered the lobby.

I went to the counter. She leaned close and whispered in my ear so Melvin the security guard couldn't hear. "Simon is taking me to dinner."

"Yay! What do you think finally made him . . . ?" I didn't finish the sentence. She was not wearing her usual blue blazer and sensible skirt. Today her white T-shirt was low-cut, tight, and practically transparent. "Don't tell me it was flashing your boobs that made the difference."

"The difference was . . . I asked him. That's right. And you're the one who inspired me. Really. I've been observing you. When you want something? You ask for it."

Only to Taffy could I seem to be aggressive.

"So," she went on, "I took the direct approach. 'Would you like to have dinner with me sometime?' And he said yes! He barely hesitated. No lectures on boundaries and employee relations."

"That's great."

"And the top one size smaller than I usually wear probably didn't hurt. Now we have a date. But the moral of the story? Ask and you shall receive."

"It's kind of scary how that works, isn't it?"

"Terrifying."

Seventeen

There was a large ad right in front of us. A woman in a bikini with one of those perfect hourglass figures. She was relaxing on a beach in Jamaica.

Charlie and I were on the train going to Tarrytown. We were meeting his parents at the station. From there, we were driving to a hotel to check it out for our wedding.

I stared at the flat belly in the ad and wondered: If I didn't eat one muffin all summer, could I look that good for my honeymoon? I had no memory of my belly ever being that flat.

Charlie's mom, Kay, had done some phoning around, and evidently things got booked up like a year ahead of time. When she found out the Pearl River Hilton had a cancellation and a date was open in August, she was pumped to nab it even though it was actually in Rockland County, across the river from Westchester. So she'd summoned us to meet with the wedding planner. I'd never been to the hotel, but I definitely had my preconceived ideas. I have nothing against the Hilton hotel chain, and I enjoyed many seasons of *The Simple Life*. But Hilton hotels—even Paris would have to admit—were so not hot.

But, on the other hand, maybe it would be fun to have a big, conventional, suburban wedding. Too bad I had hardly anyone to invite. Billie and I had not kept up with the extended family like we should've, and since neither of our parents had originally been from the city, relatives were scattered all over the place. They would've come in handy now. We'd have to look in the guest book from the funeral service to track them down. Not a pleasant thought. At least Charlie had enough family for both of us.

I tore my eyes away from the bellybutton. Charlie was reading

To Kill a Mockingbird for his class. I opened a *Time Out* magazine I'd grabbed at the newsstand. It had an article on places in the city to have an unconventional wedding, and I was curious to see what they listed.

First they had the Brooklyn Bridge. Evidently it was perfectly legal to do it there—you just had to get a permit if you wanted to film it. They advised checking with the city to make sure they weren't doing major work there on your big day. Somehow the idea of hundreds of cars whizzing by as I said my vows was not attractive.

Then there was Bowlmor Lanes. They let you reserve as many alleys as you needed, had a full bar and a catering service. A DJ would provide dance music. I envisioned myself on a lane wearing white bowling shoes, a long, white wedding gown with a veil trailing after me, throwing strike after strike. My guests would nibble on chicken fingers, drink beer, and bowl to their hearts' content. The noise from pins crashing and "Rock Around the Clock" would drive Kay to the VIP lounge, where she'd spend the evening popping Motrins.

Next suggestion: Trinity Cemetery, the only remaining active cemetery in Manhattan. Overlooking the Hudson River, it boasted giant oaks, grassy knolls, and manicured walkways. You could say your nuptials in the company of some eminent past New Yorkers like John James Audubon and John Jacob Astor.

I looked up at the belly button. Hmmm . . . My parents' ashes were interred in a cemetery up in Westchester. It was actually quite pretty there, in a bucolic sort of way, with rolling green lawns and swans walking around, or maybe geese, or was it ducks? I couldn't remember. Billie and I were due for a visit.

Call me morbid, but I could see a certain twisted logic to getting married around dead people. Maybe not random dead people. But dead parents? Yes. This appealed to me. It was the only way to get married and have them be there—sort of.

Of course, Kay would probably have a stroke just considering the notion. Even though it was one of the most exclusive cemeteries in Westchester—ha-ha. I snuck a look toward Charlie—still immersed in his book—and turned the page.

I have to say, Charlie's parents were really nice people, and he had a great relationship with them, which gave me a nice feeling of security. They were standing in front of their shiny blue Volvo when we stepped off the train. When I saw them waiting for us with big smiles, a definite part of me wished I'd forget about my emotional ties to the city and just give myself over to this happy picture.

His father, Richard, was still a good-looking guy (which boded well for Charlie), with brown hair that he wore in a side part. He reminded me of Robert Wagner back when he was on *Hart to Hart*. He wore tan khakis and a lemon yellow polo shirt and loafers with tassels (yuck). As soon as we were all done kissing cheeks, father and son got into their favorite topic. "The Yankee pitching is good this year," Charlie said.

"Can you believe that play in the ninth last night?"

"They're only three games back. . . ."

Kay had prematurely white hair that, in a rebellious sort of way, she refused to dye, so when you glanced at her you thought she was older than she really was. She wore it in a straight page-boy, had thin, round black-rimmed glasses, and matched her husband with tan khakis and a pink polo shirt and loafers, but without the tassels. "I hear you two got a ring," she said.

I held out my hand.

"Beautiful. So *clever* of you to get a sapphire. What's the big deal about diamonds, anyway?"

She was really good. I mean, I had no idea if she was coddling me or really meant it. "Thanks."

I felt wonderfully comforted in my leather seat as we drove down tree-lined streets past upscale strip malls and fast-food places. Living in Manhattan, I sometimes felt distant from the way the rest of America lived. It was almost like being a tourist just to be in the burbs. I enjoyed looking out the window and phasing out of the conversation while Kay talked with Charlie about a band someone had recommended, the guest list, floral arrangements, a place to rent a tux. . . . I felt my reticence melt away. Charlie was their only son. I could understand this was important to them. If they all really wanted a magazine-style wedding, well, I could go with it. Why not?

We pulled into the lot of the hotel. This particular Hilton had a whimsical pseudo French château look to it that I found ridiculous right here in the midst of Middle America. Kay remarked on how lovely it was. Richard agreed. I nodded and tried to look pleased. They were kind people. Good people. And I was impressed with the longevity of their marriage. They really seemed to like each other. How rare was that?

We walked inside the lobby. Muzak was playing. Colleen, a young woman in her thirties with a bouffant hairdo that made her look like she was in her fifties came to give us the grand tour. "This is the conservatory," she was saying. "Don't you just love how romantic it is with the hand-painted clouds on the ceiling? Le Jardin is a delightful glass-enclosed room that looks out over our gardens. We pride ourselves on having one of the best golf courses in Westchester and seventeen acres of grounds." She led us to a pretty white trestle on the lawn behind the restaurant. I did manage to conjure up a sweet picture of Charlie and me standing under it.

Then she led us back inside, down a long hallway through some double doors with gold trim. "This is the Westchester Ballroom. It's one of the largest banquet rooms in the area. We find it's a good idea to have the ceremony outside and serve the food inside. That way, if it happens to rain—which, of course, we all hope and pray doesn't happen—we have our bases covered."

"That makes sense," Charlie's dad said, perhaps appreciating the baseball allusion.

I finally had to speak up. "I don't think we'll need this gigantic space." I was planning on inviting about three people.

"Actually," Kay said, "if all our friends and family decide to show up, we might be able to make use of it."

Our tour guide took us back to her office and gave Charlie's parents some brochures and price lists that I did not get a chance to look at. "If you'd like to think about it, that's fine. Why don't you have some lunch at La Maisonnette—as our guests—and you can all talk it over. If you have any questions, I'll be in my office."

We moseyed over to the entrance of the restaurant and let the hostess seat us at a round, glass-covered table that had a view of the golf course. I sunk into my cushioned wicker chair.

"I think it's just lovely here," Kay said. "And we're so lucky the date opened up."

"I'm a little worried about the cost," I couldn't resist saying.

"We don't want you to worry about that," Richard said. "No problem at all. We just want you two to be happy and have a wedding you'll always look back on with joy."

"This place is pretty nice," Charlie said.

"More than just nice," Kay said.

They all looked at me. It was my moment. My moment to proclaim that I loved the Pearl River Hilton and we should definitely put down a deposit. "If you'll excuse me, I'm just going to run to the bathroom."

I was hoping to get a moment to myself, but Kay said she needed to go too. We found the restroom off the lobby. After peeing next to each other in adjoining booths, we washed hands in adjoining sinks. "I just wanted to tell you, I'm so happy you and Charlie are finally getting married."

"Thank you," I said, drying my hand on a paper towel. "That's sweet of you to say. Thank you."

"Sometimes you see couples living together, and they never take that next step. Not that I'm against it. Richard and I lived together for a year before we got married."

"I don't know how people get married when they haven't lived together first."

She put her paper towel in the garbage then took both my

hands in hers. "I want you to know, Daphne. I never had a daughter—always wished I did. I'm very thrilled to have you as a daughter-in-law."

"Thank you."

"And . . ." She still held my hands. I hoped I'd washed them well. "I know this must be hard for you, what with your parents gone. So I want you to know that I hope you will think of me as a mother, and come to me with any concerns."

"Thank you," I repeated. Tears came to my eyes. "That's so sweet of you. Thank you."

She opened her arms. I stepped into her hug. She was being so nice! I tried to hold back the tears, but they trickled down the sides of my face. The back of my throat felt hot and I could feel myself start to heave, but I didn't want to sob. I made a concerted effort not to. My lungs ached, but still I did not let those sobs rise from up out of my chest, because if they came, I would turn into a blubbering idiot and make a fool out of myself in the women's bathroom at the Pearl River Hilton. She released me and I stepped back and quickly wiped the tears off my cheek. "Thank you."

"Of course," she said, rubbing my back. "Of course."

I followed her back to the table, wiping off more tears, desperate to look composed by the time we reached the boys. Here it was. I could finally have a family. A normal, regular family just like everyone in America wanted. I could fit in. Be safe. Be normal. Be loved. We sat back down. Ordered our food. Charlie and his dad argued about a recent trade they made on the Yankees. Then they agreed to disagree. And everyone turned toward me.

"So what do you think, Daphne?" Richard asked. "Would you like to have your wedding here?"

"It's lovely." I glanced at Charlie, Richard, and Kay. They waited for me to say more. I was ready to give up my resistance, embrace it, come what may. But Kay's eyes met mine, and she must've seen the confusion on my face.

"Think about. Think about it, and let us know."

"Thanks."

Charlie raised his eyebrows at me. I smiled pleasantly. And was grateful the waitress came with our drinks.

After the hotel, we drove to New Rochelle to look at the house. I peeked out the window alert with expectation. Reality was finally setting in. The neighborhood was perfectly pleasant. There were trees. Idyllic-looking houses with windows and shutters. No sidewalk, for some reason. What if you wanted to take a walk? I was going to have to take driving lessons so I could get myself to a sidewalk somewhere.

We pulled into the driveway of the brown shingled house. The lawn was more brown than green, and some bushes were looking quite scraggly. A narrow, curvy cement path led to the front door. We walked inside. His grandmother had already moved a lot of her things out. (Though the aqua carpet was still there.) It was up to us to make it a home. Our home. With children. A family. This was for real.

The walls were talking to me. Feed me, they were saying. Clean me. Give me paint. Furniture. Rugs. Light fixtures. Devote your life to me.

Kay walked into the center of the living room. "You can start thinking about what kind of color scheme you'd like, and where to get your new furniture. I'd be happy to go looking with you. And I definitely think you should put in a new kitchen. We'll help, of course. I have my eye on one of those gorgeous stainless-steel refrigerators."

"That sounds like fun," I said. And there was a definite appeal to hitting one of those huge stores, walking the aisles, choosing appliances as if I'd just won a game show. On the other hand, I felt quite attached to my junky old fridge. Of course, all my major kitchen appliances (such as they were) had come with the apartment and weren't really mine. I decided it was not the right time to ask if we could keep my place as a pied-à-terre.

When we were done walking through the empty rooms, Kay

invited us over for a light dinner. Part of me would've liked to let her feed and pamper me. But I was mentally exhausted and wanted to catch the train and get back home. "That's okay," I said. "We don't want to be a bother."

"It's no problem," she said. "I made finger sandwiches for everyone this morning."

"Did you make me a thumb?" Charlie asked. "You know those are my favorite."

"They aren't nearly as good as her pinkies," Richard said.

I smiled at Richard to let him know I appreciated the joke, then gave Charlie a look. He picked up on it. "You know, I think we'll head back home, Mom. Thanks anyway. This was great."

They dropped us off at the station, and we waited on the platform, where there were all these poster ads for Broadway musicals. Charlie and I never went to plays. Who wanted to pay a hundred dollars for a ticket? Suburban commuters, evidently.

When the train came, we took our seats. The car was air-conditioned even though it wasn't hot. I complained, and Charlie gave me his sweater out of his backpack. I snuggled up to him, and he put his arm around me. "I know the Hilton isn't your first choice," he said to me.

"It's fine."

He kissed my hair. "My parents really like you."

"And I like them."

That same ad with the belly button was in front of us again. But I felt like a changed person since that morning. I saw it much more clearly now. I, Daphne Wells, was entering the twilight zone.

Eighteen

"I thought you might find this interesting," Simon said, handing me a thick paperback book. "I found it at a garage sale."

It was a collection of actual scripts from *Boomers*. "This is great. Thanks!" I couldn't wait to delve in.

Taffy was watching us from behind the desk. No one knew they were dating. I wasn't even sure *Simon* knew they were dating. He treated Taffy no differently from before. If anything, he gave her less attention. She, on the other hand, was constantly blushing and stammering around him.

When he walked past her to get to his office, he said hello to her in his quiet, formal way.

"I had a nice time the other night," she said, her cheeks flushed.

"I'm glad."

After he was gone, I joined her at the desk. "So how's it going with you two?"

Her face again turned so red, I wanted to find the knob to adjust her blood pressure. "We went out to dinner again."

"In the city this time?"

"I went to his place and then took the train home."

"Why does it always have to be up at his place? Why can't he come into the city to see you?" I was surprised to hear myself disapproving, and only vaguely aware that I was projecting my own suburban angst onto her.

"He has to commute in every day."

"But still."

"And I like his place. It's very comfortable. And I don't want him to have to come over to my place—not with my parents right downstairs."

"True . . ."

Taffy leaned over on the counter and whispered. "I'm fairly sure that he has strong feelings for me."

For Taffy, this was an extremely bold statement. "Has he said something?"

"It's just the way he treats me. You know that big mall up there? We went this weekend."

"How exciting."

"No, really, it was fun. You should see the way he opened the door for me. You'd think we were entering a palace. Then we strolled around, checked out the One Dollar store. Can you believe they only stock things that don't cost more than a dollar?"

"Amazing."

"And then there's the gag shop, which has all this fun stuff like soap that turns your hand black, and fake barf."

What was happening to her? Or should I too have been imagining the suburbs as some exotic, life-altering adventure.

"Then we went to TGIF. He got the ribs. I got the nachos. And then we went up to this bar that had pinball and video games and played Nok Hockey. I was pretty good at it, you know."

"Really."

"Then we went to Cinnabon. I love the smell of their cinnamon rolls, don't you? It's making my mouth water just to think of them. Then we went home, turned the lights down low, and settled in on the couch."

"And . . . ?"

"Watched TV."

"Is that all?"

The girl was blushing again. "None of your business."

I'd never seen her so happy.

Charlie was watching the Yankees while correcting papers. I was reading a *Boomers* script. It must've been so exhilarating for

Jonathan Hill to write these and then get to see them acted out and filmed and broadcast to millions of people. My job was so passive compared to what he did.

I closed the book. I felt bad for Charlie. He'd put in so many years writing scripts and never got to see one made. But I also felt disappointed for myself. The truth was, I'd invested quite a bit of my own creative energies in his work. He'd always given me drafts of his scripts to read and asked for my feedback. It was something that had brought us close, and I missed it.

"Get a hit, you bum!" he yelled at the screen. "You're way overdue!"

The guy struck out. Charlie groaned. An ad came on—some girl in a bikini with rednecks drinking beer. He went to the kitchen, came back a minute later with a can of soda and some baby carrots in a bowl, and returned to his papers with a groan. "You know what the biggest problem with my students is? Attention span. The kids complain I take too long to get to my point. They want it faster, edited down. They want the spin."

"Well," I said, "you've gotta compete with what's out there."

"Are you serious? They need to learn to listen and think. It's ruining the entire generation."

I tried to think of something to say that would cheer him up. "You know what? I'm going to pass *Sitting Comics* on to Jonathan Hill."

"Really?"

"You understand I can't do it right away. It would feel crass. I have to wait for the right moment."

"Sure, whatever."

I understood his nonchalance. God knows, the last thing he wanted to do was grovel to me. What a weird thought.

"I just want to build up a relationship first."

He crunched on a carrot. "Relationship?"

"A professional relationship."

He narrowed his eyes. "Right."

"What?"

"Nothing. So did you come to a decision about Pearl River?"

I crunched on a carrot. "Not really."

"Mom called. She's freaking out. If we don't put down a deposit, we'll lose the date."

"Well, is that what you want?"

"Is that what *you* want?"

"I don't know what I want."

"Do you want me to make the decision?"

I screwed up my face with confusion, as if all the opposing forces were pulling on my mouth and cheeks and eyebrows, turning my face into a rubbery mask. "I can't decide."

"You can't decide if you want me to decide?"

The carrot made me thirsty. "I'll be right back."

I went to the refrigerator. Orange juice? Soda? Iced tea? I pushed them all aside, but there was nothing good hiding in the back. If my mom was here, we'd be planning this together. She'd make sure I was getting what I wanted. Maybe I'd *know* what I wanted.

I went back to the bedroom. "Okay, I've decided. I want you to decide if I should decide if you should decide."

"Okay," he said. "I'll decide that I should decide."

"Okay. Let me know what you decide."

I went back to the kitchen. Tea sounded good. Charlie followed me in. I put the kettle on.

"Okay," he said, leaning against the cabinet next to the fridge. "Let's go for it."

He waited for me to agree or disagree. Now I really had to decide!

I opened the refrigerator again and let the cool air bathe my face. If only my mother could somehow telepathically give me some sort of message. She'd never go for the cemetery idea. At least, not if she were alive. Of course, then I wouldn't need to do it. But if she knew she and dad were dead, would she want . . . Okay, I had to stop. I had to focus on this experience, the one that was happening here and now with these people around me. I grabbed the milk.

"Yes," I said, letting the refrigerator door shut. "Let's do it." I turned to look at him.

"You're sure?" he asked.

"Uh-huh," I said with uncertainty.

He looked at me with suspicion. "Really?"

I tried to sound convincing. "Really."

"Okay. Good. I'll tell my parents."

"Good." I put a tea bag in a mug. At least a decision had been made. And at least he was getting his wish. Would this make him more open to satisfying a wish of mine? I remembered Taffy's triumphant lesson of the week that she'd supposedly learned from me: Ask and you shall receive. Maybe it was time for me to do a little more asking. "So, did you ever get that email I sent?" He'd never said anything about it.

"Which one?"

"You know, with the tips?"

"Oh. Yeah, I got it."

"Did you read it?"

"Not yet. I will. But thanks for sending it."

"You're welcome."

Even if he *was* thanking me, was this really an area where politeness was called for? Why wasn't he printing it out and insisting we go down that list (or should I say "on me") right that second? I considered being outright pushy about it. *Demand* and you shall receive. But I held back. I wanted him to step up to the plate. But he went back to the bedroom to watch the rest of the Yankees. And I stayed in the kitchen to drink my tea.

Nineteen

Manhattan's East Village seemed to function without any adults present. A constant influx of twenty-year-olds from everywhere in the world moved there to live out their free-spirited years of sex, drugs, and California rolls. Even the grown-ups in the mix seemed to be people who should've moved on a long time ago but were clinging to their youth. Was there such a thing as an *in*grown-up? Maybe since I lacked parents, the atmosphere reminded me too much of my own life. So I tended to avoid going down there. But Billie was insistent that I'd like the dresses in this little shop on 9th Street. And she also insisted that she was up for it.

"I'm obviously never going to get married," she said, as we pushed open the door to the shop, "so I might as well enjoy *your* wedding."

The owner was a tiny Asian woman named Celia Wing. She had an angular, asymmetrical haircut, a tight asymmetrical black dress, and huge red earrings that looked like luggage tags. She'd designed every single gown in the small, narrow shop, and as soon as we walked in, she swooped over us, lathering me with compliments on what a lovely bride I would make and how lovely it was for my sister to help me pick out a dress. But when I reached out to take a look at one on the rack, she yapped like a dog whose paw's been stepped on. "No!"

I stepped back.

"Don't touch, please! I will show you!"

It turned out she was the Soup Nazi of wedding gowns. There was only the one rack, and it only had about fifteen dresses on it. I was anxious to actually *look* through them so I could consider each one. But Celia wouldn't let me.

"I know what is right for you," she said. "I will pick."

I was soon made to feel like I knew nothing about fabric, cut, design, cloth, buttons, thread, shoes, hats, veils, gloves, necklaces, shoes, bras, underwear, or how to breathe air. My opinion? "Extraneous" would be one way of putting it. "Wrong" would be the other.

I learned that I had an unflattering haircut, bad posture, did not look good in nature colors or pastels or primaries (what did that leave?), and that the length between my feet and my knees was too short in proportion to the length between my knee and my panty line—something of which I'd managed to be ignorant for the first 29 years of my life.

I was half expecting her to tell me I wasn't good enough for her dresses and kick me out of the shop. But there were two on the rack that she deemed suitable for me. "And I have one more in the back."

She disappeared behind a thick white curtain. I stepped toward the rack to sneak a look at the others. After all, we'd come all the way down here. Couldn't I just see what else was there?

"Daphne," Billie said. "Don't you dare touch those."

"But maybe there's something I like." My hand was itching to slide each dress down the rack. I reached out, but was afraid to actually touch them.

"Celia knows what's right for your body. What's that?"

"This?" I withdrew my hand. "Oh," I said casually, "it's my engagement ring."

"When did you get it?"

"Recently. I decided to get a sapphire. It's pretty, isn't it?"

"What's the deal? You don't rate a diamond?"

"It was my choice. I think it's pretty."

"It's very pretty. It just isn't a diamond. Don't you want everyone to know you're engaged?"

Celia returned with the third dress. I knew, immediately, it was way too much dress for me. We're talking $5,000 worth of satin ballgown with an embroidered tight bodice and a flouncy tulle skirt. I refused to try it on, much to their chagrin. (I do have my ways of getting revenge.)

Compared to that dress, the two from the rack were bargains. Especially one. It was $400. I tried it on first. It was a simple silk sheath dress, with a long, clean line, no frills, a low V-neck, with an Empire waist. It fit me perfectly, and that made me feel at ease.

"Boring," Billie said.

"Comfortable," I said.

"Irrelevant," Billie said.

"It is very simple but elegant," Celia said. "To tell you the truth, it usually sells as a bridesmaid dress."

Billie rolled her eyes and groaned. But I didn't care.

"A good dress," Celia added, "to wear to city hall and elope in."

Now that was an idea.

"This other one I picked for you makes much more of a statement."

The third dress was $1500. It was an ivory silk gown with spaghetti straps, a low sweetheart neckline with floral detailing, and more floral detailing on the rather full skirt. I slipped it on. The waist didn't hit me right. Celia tugged on it, mumbling that she'd need to take it in. "I love it," Billie said. "This one is lovely."

It was true that this dress did something the other one didn't. It was very feminine and made me look more like the doll you see on top of the cake. While looking at myself in the three-way mirror, turning from side to side, I imagined all eyes on me. I would satisfy everyone's expectations of "bride." Celia started pinning the seam in so I could see how it would look after alterations. I willed myself to fall in love with it.

Billie sat on a low white sofa and watched. I felt for her. She looked really depressed. "Anything new with Max?" I asked.

"He says I have three months to move out."

"Bummer." I stood very still so Celia wouldn't stick me with a pin.

"I think he should let me stay, don't you? It's only fair."

"You mean like as a settlement?"

"That would be the decent thing to do."

"Could you even a[fford] around $2000 a mont[h] (minus Max) for the past y[ear] than a few months.

"I could start looking for m[en] that anyway. Or find a husband fa[st]

"Right."

We were silent until Celia was do[ne] pulled my hair up into a chignon. Celia p[ut on] the dress. Billie and matching pearl earrings. It felt good to time they were done, I looked like a *bride*. [ironed] over. By the

Billie gazed at me. Her face looked pained. W[as she] despairing over her own wedding, the one she might never ha[ve] if she thought she wanted to be married, I had a hard tim[e imag]ining her actually living with someone. She liked having her [ap]artment to herself. Everything was just as she wanted it. Wherea[s] in a way, Charlie and I were already married. This whole thing [w]as for show. I had nothing to prove. Or did I? Maybe I wanted to [p]rove I had nothing to prove.

"Beautiful," Celia said. "You will be a lovely bride." I coul[d] see her tasting the sale on her tongue, could see Billie congratula[t]ing herself on transforming me.

"I like the other one," I said.

"But this one is much prettier," Billie said.

"This one," Celia said, "makes much more of a statement."

"It's so frilly, though, don't you think?"

"The other one is very nice too," Celia said, "but . . ."

"You're insane." Billie stood and opened her purse. "But do what you want. I'm dying for a cup of coffee."

Aha. She gave in easily. Was she relieved? "It's just . . . I feel more comfortable in the simple one."

"Fine," she said, taking out her wallet.

"I know it's not as fancy. . . ."

"I can't stand listening to you! Just get the one you want! I really need a cup of coffee."

I clamped my m...
ture my skin. Well,
out of there. So i...
I almost called ;
out of it so Bill
annoy her fur...
"Excellen
it up."

sharp tongue seemed to punc-
...up of coffee. And I wanted to get
We'll take the simpler one," I said.
maid dress." Wanted to make a joke
...ax, but I knew it would probably only
...elia said, with an efficient smile. "I'll wrap

We went...his,
with me
"It was...
wasn'...
unpla...
We...
...ee shop on the corner. "Thank you for coming
...his," I said, hoping to butter her up for the meal.
...nice of you to pay." She'd used Max's credit card. I
...how I felt about that, but it didn't seem worth more
...tness to question it, so I let it go.
...ttled in at a table by the window with a good view of people w...ing by on Ninth Street. "I'm happy to help. I just got hungry. I...ve the worst headache. Do you have any aspirin?"

"I."

...ut the thick glossy white paper bag with a gold rope handle
und.r the table by my feet. At least I'd found something without
dragging the search out into a huge ordeal.

"You have to admit," Billie said, "she has lovely designs. And they do happen to work for you."

"Yes, you spared me a long and arduous search."

"As if you would've bothered. I'm surprised you didn't order a dress from Penney's."

"Do they do wedding dresses?"

"A hundred-percent polyester wash 'n' wear."

"Thanks for telling me now that it's too late." I opened my menu. Part of me just wanted a blueberry muffin I'd seen in the window. Part of me wanted to get something with more sustenance. "I'm sorry it's such bad timing, with the Max stuff happening."

"Don't be ridiculous. You're helping me get my mind off my miserable life. I just really need an aspirin."

"Maybe the waitress has one."

We both looked at the waitress. [...] was rushing around like crazy.

"You do like the dress, though, right[...]ew she liked the other one better, and I should've stopped [...]g it up, but now I needed her to lie and reassure me. "Even[...]

"Everything Celia makes is gorgeous, [...]s for bridesmaids?" the waitress. "You can't go wrong." [...]said, trying to flag

"Of course, you would never have picked th[...]ne for yourself," I said, wanting to give her a chance to vent her [...]approval.

"For my wedding? Never. But I do like it, or I [...]ldn't have let you buy it." The waitress passed by without mak[...]eye contact. "Is she ignoring us on purpose?"

"And it's good that it doesn't have to be taken in, [...]ght?"

"Daphne, for god's sake, can't you enjoy this?"

"Sorry."

"Stop torturing yourself."

"You're right. It's just . . . it's such a big decision."

"The dress?"

"The whole thing."

The waitress finally came to us. Billie asked her if she had an aspirin. She said she would check in the back. Then Billie ordered a cheese blintz with cherry topping, which totally shocked me. Well, I had to join her. So I got mine with blueberries on top. This would be better than a muffin. I felt better. If we could splurge on calories together, maybe this could be a bonding experience. "What the hell," Billie said, attempting some festivity. "It's not every day you buy a wedding dress with your little sister, right?"

Things were looking up. The waitress returned quickly with our coffee, but she could find no aspirin.

"I'll run to a pharmacy if you want," I said. Anything but sit through this meal with her in pain.

"Never mind." Billie rubbed her temples. "Max says he's going to sell the apartment because he needs the money, but I bet he just wants to give it to the next girlfriend."

"Does he have a riend?"

"Do you think he me if he did?" she snapped. "What am I going to do?"

I reminded my at this was not my fault, I did not create the situation, so it appeared that she was angry with me, she was not ang th me, she was angry with Max, not me. "I don't know."

We both to ps of coffee and then sat there a minute not saying anythi couldn't believe how exhausted I felt. Finally Billie asked, cting false levity into her voice, "So how are the rest of the v ding plans going? Have you decided on a venue?"

Yay. An er unpleasant subject. "I agreed on the Pearl River Hilton."

"Why dn't you tell me?"

"Bec se I know you're going to disapprove."

"Be use it's horribly dull."

"It's not that bad. There's a pretty lawn with a trellis. And it's not cheap. There's nothing wrong with it. I *should* like it."

"No you shouldn't."

"Charlie's mother is really into it."

"It's your wedding."

"But they're paying."

"If they're gracious enough to pay, they should be gracious enough to let it be what you want."

"He's their only child. It's the only wedding she'll have."

"She had her wedding. This is yours!"

I did feel Billie was basically in the right, except . . . "I want to make her happy. She's so nice to me, and maybe I'm being ridiculous for not appreciating it. I mean, she seems to care more than I do."

"I don't get it. You're so passive about the whole thing."

"I'm compromising. That's what you need to do in these situations. That's what marriage is all about on some level, you know."

"Compromise?" She looked at me with horror.

"Yes! That's what people do." Not that I meant to be snotty

about it. But wasn't that why Billie had never been able to live with a guy? Because she had to have everything her own way?

She glowered at me.

"I do hope, at the very least, Charlie has improved in bed."

"He doesn't hog the blanket, if that's what you mean."

"You're so funny I forgot to laugh."

"And he's excellent at lying parallel to the edge of the mattress."

"So the sex is still lousy?"

Why, oh, why couldn't I be a good liar? I took another sip of coffee. "The sex is great." I blinked. That kind of blink where you're totally aware you're blinking.

"Is he sensual?"

"Can we change the subject?"

"Willing to try new things?"

"You're embarrassing me."

"How often do you do it?"

"None of your business."

"Meaning not as often as you'd like?"

"For awhile we were doing it a lot. But gradually . . ."

"You've lost interest."

"It's different when you live with someone. Before, there was always the mystery of when we'd get together. Now there's always the mystery of when we'll be apart."

"That's horrible!"

"Charlie and I have been together four years. It's not like we're still in the throes of passion."

"Were you ever? Don't answer that. What you need to do is get high before you have sex. Believe me, a little pot works wonders."

"Thanks for the advice," I said. Now I was getting a headache. "A good sex life, I might remind you, is not everything. It certainly doesn't always lead to a good, stable relationship. Charlie is dependable and hardworking, and he's going to make a good father."

"Charlie is one big compromise for you!" She was practically shouting. "He's lousy in bed, has a low-paying job, and wants to drag you to the suburbs to pop out his offspring!"

"Can you say that a little louder? I think a man in the bathroom missed that last part."

"No wonder you're ambivalent."

"I'm not. I'm just having a hard time . . . making some decisions."

Billie narrowed her eyes at me.

"He loves me," I said. "And I love him."

"If you insist."

"Why are you doing this?"

"Because you let people push you around."

"People like you?"

"What?"

"I know it must be hard for you to go through this right now," I said, frantically trying to come up with a way to smooth the comment over but feeling dreadfully sure I was only making it worse, "with everything going sour with Max."

"I'm glad you're getting married," she said, her voice taut. "I want you to be happy. I know you think I don't, but I am not an evil person."

I was afraid to look at her, but made myself. Her nostrils were literally flaring. "I just know this is unpleasant for you."

"Pleeease. I would never want to marry Charlie," she said, quite obviously enjoying her words, "or someone even vaguely *like* Charlie."

My words came out like a gust of wind. "But you hate the fact that I'm the one who's getting married first!"

There. I'd said it. Thank god. It was such a relief, yet so horrible—victory and defeat at the same moment.

She wiped her hand across the table so her spoon went clanging onto the floor. "Shut up," she said. "Just shut the fuck up!"

She did not say that under her breath. That was on top of her breath—way on top. I didn't dare look around. I felt sure the entire restaurant was looking at us, but on the other hand, people seemed to be chattering on in the background like nothing had occurred. "Billie," I said, this idiot smile on my face, "I was just—"

"I spent the morning watching you try on fucking wedding dresses. I paid for your dress with my own goddamn money!"

Max's money, actually—

"I've been trying to *help* you! If you don't want my help, then do it on your own. But don't you *dare* insult me like that."

I swallowed. Idiot smile gone. Tried not to cry. Stared down at the table. Getting married. It wasn't worth it. It just wasn't worth it.

She grabbed her purse. "I can't do this."

Our waitress, who was of course arriving with our blintzes, stood there and held our plates, not knowing what to do.

Billie threw twenty dollars on the table and walked out.

The waitress set the food down.

"Um. Thanks," I said. "Maybe you should just pack it all up?"

"Are you sure?"

I looked at the huge plates laden with steaming hot, greasy blintzes, the glistening fruit toppings, the huge dollops of sour cream. It occurred to me that Billie had engineered this fight so she wouldn't have to eat her blintz, but that was ridiculous. "Yes, I'm sorry." I couldn't bring myself to leave it all there.

I paid the bill and left a tip, and put on a face as if everything was perfectly normal, not one of the most depressing days of my life. I was grateful this wasn't my neighborhood and I could leave and never have to come back. It wasn't until I got to the subway station that I realized I'd left the dress in the glossy white bag on the floor under the table.

Damn.

I ran all the way back. *Please, god, don't let it be gone. Don't let it be gone.*

Even though in a way, I wanted it to be gone. That's why I left it there, wasn't it?

I ran in past the hostess. Yes, me again. Thought you'd seen the last of me, didn't you, but here I am!

At our table—the scene of the crime—there was a man with a bushy beard reading the *Village Voice*. I looked underneath. It was there. Thank god. "I'm sorry," I said. "I left a bag down there."

Just my wedding dress, which is a bridesmaid dress, actually, nothing important.

"Oh!" He smiled and handed it to me. "I didn't even notice."

"Thanks." I took it from him and walked back to the subway, wondering if I would ever be able to put it on.

When I got home, I was relieved Charlie wasn't there. I needed time by myself to decompress. I put the blintzes in the refrigerator, then stared inside. *Hi, Mom. Well, this was bound to happen, right? Par for the course. The blintzes? I know, I'm not going to eat them, but I just can't bear to throw them out. Yet. I will in a few days.*

This was getting to be a weird habit—relating to my mother as if she was inside the refrigerator. Enough already. I took some milk and let the door shut. After wolfing down two bowls of Honey Bunches of Oats, I changed into my pajamas and got into bed. Didn't even turn on the TV. Just fell right to sleep. That's how zonked I was.

Twenty

"*I*n the second half of the 1950s, domesticoms were really popular."

"Domestiwhats?" Lily wrinkled her nose. Jonathan had brought her by, and I was setting them up at a console.

"Sitcoms that idealized the nuclear family. And made it appear that everyone in the United States was white, middle-class, well-behaved, moral. . . ." (And never seemed to actually have sex.) "Have you ever seen *Father Knows Best*?"

"No."

"It's sort of like *Everybody Loves Raymond*. Of course, now we know that father doesn't really know best—"

Jonathan said, "Huh?" with mock disbelief, while Lily said, "That's for sure!"

"How can you say that?" He made a big show of looking offended.

"You don't know anything about anything!" She turned to me. "Did you know someone in *Entertainment Weekly* called *Super-models* a dumb show?"

"They were too dumb to get its satirical edge," Jonathan said.

I couldn't help but laugh. Considering my ongoing intimidation factor, it was amusing to see him disdained by—who else—his own child.

"Your dad is very successful at what he does, Lily, don't you know that? *Boomers* won an Emmy, and that's the highest honor a show can have."

"Yeah, but that's forever ago, and it was only good because my mom starred."

"Who told you that?" Jonathan's eyes were wide with hurt that was not totally mock.

"She did."

"Oh, really . . ."

"On *Father Knows Best*," I said, steering the conversation to safer ground, "the dad liked to call his younger daughter 'Kitten.' My dad called me Kitten sometimes, because I was his little girl."

Interesting trivia: Lauren Chapin, who played Kathy/Kitten, went on to become a prostitute with a drug habit and then a born-again Christian Evangelist.

I started Lily on the episode from *Father Knows Best* when Kathy goes to summer camp and rebels against her counselor, who keeps pushing her to do better. Her counselor happens to be Betty, her older sister. I'd also picked episodes from *The Adventures of Ozzie and Harriet* and *The Donna Reed Show*. "These will totally fill you in on the fifties sitcom state of mind."

"Will you watch with me?" she asked.

"I should get back to work. But maybe the first one. I haven't seen it in awhile."

Lily pulled on his sleeve. "Daddy, will you call me Kitten?"

"How about Wildebeest."

"That's ugly."

"Just kidding."

She stuck her tongue out at him and put her headphones on.

"So," I said, before putting my own headphones on, "maybe you want us to do that tribute. At the very least, it would impress Lily."

"Ah, very clever of you," he said. "But I don't think so."

"You will still think about it, won't you?"

"I promise to consider it further," he said, "if you come to this thing."

"Thing?"

"A premiere. This Friday night. At the Paris Theater."

I gulped so hard I could've swallowed my own throat. "The new Jessica Cox movie?"

"Would you like to go? She's gonna be there doing the whole red carpet insanity. . . ."

Was this, like, a date? No, it was professional. Of course. He may not have even meant with him. He was probably busy, and he had the invitation, so someone might as well use it. Or maybe he was Jessica's escort. Whatever it was, I felt compelled to avoid the situation. Seemed the safest thing to do.

"No thanks."

"Are you sure?"

"*Supermodels* is on. How can I miss that?" I hoped he could perceive the elements of both sarcasm and sincerity in my voice.

"Escaping real life for the safe and predictable world of television?"

"Said the drug dealer to the addict."

"You should come. I'd like to know what you think of it."

He was interested in my opinion! And he could've asked anyone. "I guess I could tape *Supermodels*."

"Then it's a date."

A date?

"Oh, you know what?"—he turned to me—"Just remembered. The nanny is taking that day off. I'll have to meet you there after I pick Lily up from school. But I'll email you the details."

"No problem," I said as casually as I could.

I put on my headphones. But I didn't hear anything but my own panic. He would be there too! I had to tell him I had a boyfriend. Not that he could possibly be thinking about me that way. It was too terrifying to imagine. *Our shoulders accidentally brushing as we settled into our seats. Our hands accidentally bumping while reaching for popcorn. Me accidentally ending up in his apartment with my clothes off. Him accidentally kissing me passionately, leading to lovemaking that would have to be done with an extremely high level of expertise because, god knows, a man like him was used to women who were total sexual animals in bed.* How could I allow myself to be so vulnerable in front of a powerful man like him? Forget it. That was a job for Billie. Yes. SuperBillie. She could rescue me, and I could rescue her.

After *Father Knows Best* ended, I stood up and took my head-phones off. He took off his headphones to say good-bye.

"By the way," I said, "can my sister come to that premiere too? I've been wanting to introduce you. She's a model, and she's had lots of bizarre experiences. She could be an incredible resource for you."

He looked surprised for about a millisecond, but then said, "Sure. Bring the sister."

Twenty One

When I got home, I considered calling Billie to tell her about the screening. If she was feeling miserable, this was just the thing that would bring her out of it. Not that I thought she'd gone on some kind of binge or drug fest or anything. And if she had, well, it could wait a half hour. I was starving. Or was it anxiety that drove me to the refrigerator? Front and center was the white Styrofoam container of blintzes. One of those would taste really good. But I couldn't quite bring myself to consume them. There was still a residue of bad taste in my mouth from the other day.

I reached for a canister of whipped cream and squirted some directly into my mouth. The sweet, creamy air melted on my tongue. It just wasn't right that I had to go to my sister for wedding help. That's what mothers were for. I took one more squirt. The problem here was that I'd done such a good job downplaying the whole thing, I'd succeeded in making Billie doubt the entire venture. I had to stop doing that. One more last squirt. My last, last one. Yum. I had to show her this was what I really wanted, this was going to make me happy. Then she'd be supportive.

One more last, last, last squirt and I put the canister back. There was that blueberry blintz. I took it out, peeked inside—didn't look too bad considering what it had been through—and put it in the toaster oven. While it was heating up, I called Billie. "Hi."

"Hi."

"Are you okay?"

"I'm fine."

"I've been worried," I said, then waited for her to speak so I

.ld tell from the sound of her voice if she was sober, suffering,
.gh, perfectly okay.

"You don't know," she said, "how hard it was to leave my blintz
behind."

Good. She didn't sound too upset. Maybe it had been worse
for me than her. I was about to ask if I could give the blintz to
Charlie. Then I decided not to. Then I was about to say she never
intended to consume all those calories. Then I was about to start
my apology. She beat me to it.

"I'm sorry I was a bitch."

"It's not your fault."

"I overreacted and ruined your day."

"I realized something," I said. "I've been going around feeling
guilty because you're going through this breakup with Max, and it
must be hard for you, so I've been pretending to be less excited
than I am so you wouldn't have to feel jealous—even though I
know you aren't jealous, but you know what I mean—so I know
it's ridiculous, and I finally realized that, and so I want to tell you
I'm not going to do that anymore."

Phew.

"Well," she said, "I'm glad. But still. Forget about me, and
whatever you think I'm thinking, because it really doesn't matter.
Are you sure you want to marry Charlie?"

I said it as confidently as I could. "Yes."

"Okay. Fine. Then I'll stop bugging you."

"Thanks."

"You know I'm just trying to look out for you. You're my baby
sister, and I love you."

"I love you too."

I took a deep breath. The blintz was making the apartment
smell really good. "So guess what," I said. "Jonathan Hill invited
me to a screening, and I asked if you could come too, and he said
yes." I felt like I was giving her a gift. An expensive one. It had the
desired effect.

"Why didn't you say so? Good work, little sister. This is the best news I've had in weeks. Jesus, I'd better make a hair appointment. I look like shit."

After we went over the details, I hung up feeling almost light-hearted. Order had been restored. I took my blintz out of the toaster oven and laced it with the last of the whipped cream. Now I could *really* enjoy it. I got out a biography of *Roseanne* I'd bought used from the library and savored the pleasure of reading about her roller-coaster life while I ate. Charlie would be home soon. In the meanwhile, it was nice having the apartment to myself.

Twenty Two

I undressed as Charlie sat in bed and read the sports section. He didn't look up or notice I was naked. Of course, it wasn't exactly a special event after living together for three years. But still. Couldn't he notice just a little?

When I came out of the shower (still) naked with just a towel around me, Charlie was folding his laundry. I dropped the towel, and Charlie (still) did not bother to look up. As I got dressed in my pajamas, he paired up his socks. I got into bed. He got his backpack and pulled out some papers. Okay, maybe the exact same thing happened all the time and I was just noticing it now, making something out of nothing by letting it annoy me. But it would've been nice if he'd said something about how he had so much work to do but I was so luscious he couldn't stand it, so let's forget about any silly tensions between us and make love right now this very minute.

"Someone has to pay the bills tonight," he said, tossing a bundle of envelopes near me on the bed. "I have finals to correct, and it's gonna take all week, so it would be really good if you could handle that."

"I'll do it later," I said, turning on the TV.

"We're gonna be late on the Visa."

"I'll do it before I go to sleep, I promise."

I channel-surfed for awhile and settled on *Oprah After the Show*.

"I thought he was so hot when we started dating," a woman was saying. "But now that we've been married ten years, it's more like we're brother and sister. It's really hard to keep that passion alive."

Hmmm. Were Charlie and I headed in this direction? W
already there? Was he listening? If he was, would he even co
any of this to us?

I glanced over at him, but he was getting out a huge stack
papers to correct.

"A lot of married couples have the same problem," Oprah said.
"Believe me, you aren't alone."

The woman's husband went on to describe this place they
went to—a retreat for married couples. A team of therapists had
taught them how to communicate with each other. I wondered if
that's where Max was going with his wife.

"First we took a kissing workshop," the paunchy, balding husband said. "It was amazing. We spent the entire morning talking
about how to kiss and practicing. . . ."

There was a lot of giggling and shaking of heads in the audience. But according to these people, after a four-day program,
their sex life was totally hot. Paunch and baldness notwithstand-
ing.

"Do you hear this?" I asked Charlie.

"What a bunch of idiots." He was circling a run-on. "Can you
change the station?"

"It's interesting. You should pay attention. We might learn
something."

"From a bunch of losers on *Oprah*? Why do they talk about all
these personal things on national television?"

"Sometimes people reveal more when the camera's on them
than when they're in private. And they aren't losers." As a matter
of fact, they were making me feel like a loser. One man was complaining that his wife would only have sex three times a week; he
wanted it every day. If Charlie and I did it three times a week, I'd
feel like a porn star.

Next up was a couple who hadn't made love in a year. Even
Charlie looked up as a guest sex therapist made them sit across
from each other and hold hands and stare into each other's eyes.

erapist called it *"soul gazing."* This simple thing, she said,
help bring them closer.

Okay, this was on television with millions of people watching.
ow could you call that intimate? But still. When I imagined
oing that with Charlie, it made me nervous. What if we stared
into each other with as much intensity as I was staring, right now,
into the television screen?

Would that be too intimate?

And we hadn't even been married for years, like this couple.
But we were together so much. It was no surprise we needed to
find ways to separate off and retreat into our separate mental
worlds. Maybe our close quarters made it impossible to crave in-
timacy. Maybe living in that big house in New Rochelle would help
us seek each other out again. I looked over at Charlie, hoping he
was still interested, but he was back to reading a paper. "I think
you should listen to this with me. Some of this really applies to us,
you know."

"Didn't we just make love?"

"Not since I gave you that blow job."

"Ah, yes," he said, happily reminiscing. He gave my hand a pat.
"And it was very nice."

Ooooh. That was annoying. There was something so patroniz-
ing about a pat. So grandmotherly. I wanted him to grab me. I
wanted him to put his arms around me, pull me to him, press up
against me, and smother me with hard, passionate kisses that
didn't necessarily stay confined to above the waist. . . .

A shampoo commercial came on. I glared at the screen as I
watched the woman lather up. I was totally on the verge of asking
if he'd read the sex tips yet. But at this point, why couldn't he
bring it up? Call me romantic, but a woman shouldn't have to beg
a guy to go down on her.

An ad for razor blades came on. I watched as a patch of animated hairs were sheared off a shin. Was he *ever* going to say
something about the sex tips? I was yelling it in my head. DON'T
YOU WANT TO GO DOWN ON ME? No way I was going to hu-

miliate myself by asking again. Maybe he just really didn
do it. Maybe it disgusted him. Maybe my vagina repelle
Don't they say it smells like fish? God, I was not going to say
What a thought. I was not going to dignify such an insul
thought by saying it out loud.

"Do you think my vagina smells like fish?"

"What?"

Damn. I said it. "Is that why you don't want to do it?"

"No! Is that what this is all about? You gave me that blow job,
so now I owe you?"

"No. It's just . . . it would be nice if you returned the favor."

"And here I thought you did it because you wanted to."

"I did want to. I'm trying to broaden our horizons here. Does
that not interest you?"

Charlie didn't answer. Just sighed. What did that mean? *Oprah*
came back on. One of the husbands complained that his wife had
gained a lot of weight over the years, and he felt like she was
building up a wall.

Hmmm. Maybe I was building some kind of wall without realizing it. Should I get a Brazilian wax? Billie totally believed in
them, but I refused. Maybe it grossed him out. "Is it my pubic
hairs?"

"What?"

"Would it help if I got waxed?"

"No. Please. It's not you, it's me. Really. I just have to get over it."

Charlie was watching now as one of the therapists recommended making "dates" with your partner. "Set up times when
you know you'll be making love." Oprah thought that didn't sound
very romantic, and the therapist agreed. She said you can't expect
it to always be romantic. Sometimes it just needs to be businesslike. You set up an appointment with each other and do it. Not
a big deal. Just part of the routine, like getting your teeth cleaned.

Charlie sighed again. "Look. To tell you the truth, I'm not really
that comfortable with the whole 'going down on you' thing."

"That's why I gave you the tips. So you'd know what to do."

ghed once more. What was with all this sighing? "It's not
⸱e said. "The thing is, it just doesn't really appeal to me."
Oh."

The studio audience applauded a couple who announced that
they went from having sex once a year to once a month. The couple sat there and smiled. I thought that was sorta weird—having
an audience clap for how often you had sex.

"It's not anything having to do with you," Charlie said. "I've
never been into it with any woman."

"Uh-huh."

"Are you mad?"

"Of course not."

I thought of Billie's cold assessment. He didn't make a lot of
money; he wasn't good at sex; he wanted to drag me to the suburbs. Maybe she'd been right all along. Was Charlie one big fat
compromise? "Maybe if you had a drink first or something."

"Maybe."

"I'm not saying right now. I know you have work."

"Okay. Fine. I'll read over that email, and we'll give it a go Friday night."

"So it's a date." Date. Oh, god. I had a "date" Friday night with
Jonathan Hill. Oh, well. Not the time to bring that up. On Friday
I'd let Charlie know I was going to be out a little late. Then I'd give
him the choice of doing it when I got home or postponing until
Saturday. Charlie probably wouldn't care. He'd probably be
relieved.

Oprah finally got to the last couple on the stage. The wife announced that they used to have sex once a month, and now they
had it twice a day. Twice a day? They sat there with these big smiles.

"You're just showing off," Oprah said. The studio audience
laughed.

"Look how smug they are," I said, just to let Charlie know I
wasn't falling for this completely. All the couples were holding
hands and making a big show of exuding sexual satisfaction. It was
annoying. "Do you believe them?"

"No way. As soon as the cameras are off, I bet they'll revert ba
to their old ways. This is all a bunch of hooey."

The credits came on and Oprah plugged the sex therapist's
book one more time, holding it up so we'd all run out and buy
it. Yeah. Probably was a bunch of hooey. But I made a point of
trying to remember the title. Just in case I felt like ordering it
someday.

Twenty Three

It was the big night. My cell phone was ringing. Most likely Billie calling to tell me she was late. I trotted up Fifth Avenue to the Paris Theater while groping in my purse to find my phone. Why didn't I ever seem to put it back in the same place? Just before it went to voice mail, I found it lodged in the bottom of the middle zipper compartment under a pair of sunglasses. As I flipped it open, I saw, yes, it was Billie. "You're late."

"I can't decide what to wear!"

"You aren't even dressed yet?" I stopped short on the curb so a bus wouldn't run me over. "I don't want to stand out front all by myself like some geeky loser fan."

"I put on my gold rayon spaghetti strap—you know the one with the lovely sequined appliqué on the shoulder—and felt over-dressed. So I changed into my silk black bustier dress and felt too slutty. Now I'm in my emerald green slip dress. Is that too much?"

"I don't remember it. Just stop obsessing, go downstairs, and hail a cab, Billie."

"You're no help at all. I'll be there in ten minutes."

"That's impossible." I rounded a corner.

"Fifteen tops."

It would take twenty or thirty depending on whether she could get a cab and how bad traffic was, and that was assuming she didn't change her clothes again. "I'll see you in front of the fountain."

"Don't worry, Darling. I'm on my way!"

She was so excited. Too excited. If Jonathan Hill liked her, I was a genius. If he didn't, I was setting her up for a fall. In any case, she was not going unprepared. The prospect of meeting the

man had been enough to get her out of the apartment and
Bumble and Bumble—courtesy of Max, since he still had not
off the credit card he'd given her "for emergencies." Considerin
how much she'd let herself go in the weeks since the breakup, r
suppose this qualified.

The Paris, one of the few one-screen movie theaters left in
Manhattan, was in a prime location near Central Park, Bergdorf's,
and the Plaza. A quaint marquee with a 1950-ish logo—even the
name of the theater itself—made me nostalgic for an idealized,
cultured New York from my childhood that mostly seemed to exist
now in Woody Allen movies. They often showed foreign films, in-
dependents, and classics. As a matter of fact, I saw a Marx Brothers double feature there with Charlie on one of our very first
dates. I remembered suffering over saying good night to him,
wondering how many days would have to pass before I'd get to see
him again. Was that the last time I'd been there? I bet it was only
a matter of time before it was closed down, bulldozed, and condos
went up.

A small crowd had already gathered on the sidewalk, and there
was a proverbial red carpet leading from the curb to the entrance.
I wore a strapless black dress from Forever21 that made me feel
like Audrey Hepburn in *Breakfast at Tiffany's*. I was pretty sure no
one could tell my black heels were from Payless. I hoped I wasn't
overdressed, which would've been ironic, considering the entire
getup only cost $55. To kill time, I crossed the street and went into
Bergdorf's. They were about to close, and the saleswomen were
happy to ignore me as I wandered around and looked in the glass
cases of jewelry. I needed a necklace for my wedding dress. Billie
did have one of mom's pearl necklaces, but she thought it was the
wrong length. Now I couldn't remember exactly how low the
neckline was. The dress was still in the bag and hidden in my
closet. I could've hung it up, but it was destined to need ironing,
so there was no point taking it out. I seemed to need to keep it
folded up and hidden, as if I was keeping a secret from myself.

At about ten to eight, I went back out and stood in front of the

er. Whether Billie was there or not, I did want to take in some
he scene. Jessica Cox was bound to be arriving, and it would
e fun to catch her entrance.

The crowd had grown larger, and it was easier to blend in.
Photographers were milling around. It all seemed so cheesy. Finally a white stretch limo drove up. A man in a black tuxedo got
out and opened the curbside door. The crowd got all excited as
Jessica Cox's foot, in a six-inch silver sandal, found the curb like
an alien tentacle emerging from a spaceship. Her escort held out
his hand. She took it and seemed to float weightless from the
limo. Her white short dress quivered with frilly fringes. Light-
bulbs exploded as she glided into the theater. What was it like
being better than everyone else?

"Close your mouth or the flies will come home."

Billie had arrived.

"Haven't heard that one in years."

"Have I missed anything?"

She appeared to be an entirely different woman from the last
time I'd seen her. The stray grays were gone and her hair was silky
and lustrous. She'd settled on a red cocktail minidress with extremely pointy red heels that showed off her long, bare, gleaming
sleek legs.

"Jonathan isn't here yet." I loved calling him by his first name,
as if we were buddies. In fact, I'd never actually called him by
name to his face, and I usually still thought of him as "Jonathan
Hill," but maybe it was time to get over that.

A publicist was standing guard at the lobby door with a list.
When I said we were Jonathan Hill's guests, she gave us a glossy
PR booklet listing everyone involved with the movie. As we entered the theater, I felt pretty puffed up. We found seats on the
aisle not too far back. The lights went down and the movie began.
It was something about a bank heist, and Jessica Cox played a
teller who was in on the crime, but I couldn't really concentrate
because of wondering when and if Jonathan was going to arrive.

About ten minutes into it, he appeared in the aisle next to

Billie. We both got up and moved over for him. I whispered ⌐ but there was really no way to talk, so we all settled in to watch movie.

After a moment, Billie whispered into my ear, "I approve. Then she added, "And I'm not talking about the movie."

I whispered back. "Just keep your hands off him." Then I added, "For now."

After it was over (thank god) everyone applauded. Judging by the lack of enthusiasm, I wasn't the only person who thought it was a dud.

"Let me go and congratulate her," Jonathan said, "and let's get out of here."

Billie and I went to the lobby to wait. We could see him by the door talking to Jessica. He looked so, so good in a black suit, black shirt, black tie.

"He could've introduced us," Billie said.

"I guess."

"Are we going out for a drink?"

"I assume."

Finally he joined us, and we went out to the sidewalk. I said the obvious. "So this is my sister, Billie." I did feel proud of how gorgeous she was, even if I couldn't exactly take credit. "Billie, Jonathan."

There. I'd called him by his first name with him present.

"This is a conundrum," he said. "Which one of you is more beautiful?"

Billie beamed. "How sweet of you to say."

I kept myself from saying something asinine, like "She is."

"Would you ladies like to get a bite to eat?"

I wanted to object to being called a "lady," but realized I was channeling "bratty younger sister" and that was not going to be acceptable, so I kept my mouth shut. Billie said, "That would be lovely. I'm ravenous."

He hailed a cab, and I couldn't believe it when he told the driver to take us to the Four Seasons. He was really trying to impress

suddenly felt like my shoes had an orange neon sign on
in flashing PAYLESS.

I held back so Billie could be in the middle seat. We were all
squinched together, and I was hyperaware that they were thigh to
thigh. I searched for something to talk about. The movie? Should
we pretend we liked it? But as soon as we were seated, his cell
phone rang. "Sorry," he said, looking at the caller ID. "I should
take this."

"Go right ahead," Billie said, doing the polite-as–Grace Kelly
act. We listened in to his conversation with fake smiles.

"Conan! How are you! Great! So what's up? Oh, really? Sure!
I'd be happy to. No! I would love to take a look at it. Uh-huh. Uh-
huh. Uh-huh."

He laughed. Glanced at us. We broadened our fake smiles as if
we were in on the joke.

"No," he said, "it sounds intriguing. Absolutely. I look forward
to it. Great! Bye." He hung up. "What a drag."

"Why?" I asked.

"He wrote a script for a pilot and wants to know what I think."

I resisted asking if that was THE Conan. Of course it was. "You
don't want to read it?"

"I don't have the time. And if it's bad, I have to find a way to
tell him without offending him. In this business, people are always
asking you for favors and it's tough to get out of it if it's a well-
known person."

"I can imagine," Billie said, all sympathy and compassion. "It
must be hard."

"It really wears you down. You get successful, and people, they
get like leeches. They want to suck your blood because they think
it will mean they'll have some success too, and it's like, 'Leave Me
Alone!' But you can't say that because then you sound like an un-
grateful asshole. I mean, you want to help, but I have to worry
about my own projects too."

"No one wants to believe it's hard for people who've made it,"
Billie said, "but I've found that no matter where you are in life,

there are challenges. Success just means your old proble.
into new problems."

"It's true," he said. "No one wants to feel sorry for you. Th.
rather be jealous of your success and hate you for it."

"It's not easy," Billie said, leaning into him, her arm against hn.
arm. Hip against his hip. I considered getting out of the cab and
letting them have sex right then and there, but I wanted my expensive dinner, so I stuck it out.

We pulled up to the Seagram Building and entered the elegant
restaurant that I'd never been to, not even as a child. The maître d'
seated us at a table in the Pool Room, so named because there was
a large white marble pool of water in the center. It really was an
amazing totally sixties modern space with walnut paneling,
ceiling-high windows with swags of chains, and a canopy of real
trees.

After perusing the menu (and the prices on the menu) we ordered. Jonathan and Billie both got the sirloin steak ($55) and I
got the rack of lamb ($48), proving yet again that I was a cheap
date. Then Jonathan asked Billie about her modeling. "So Daphne
tells me you're a model."

"Oh, yes, I was with Elite in the early nineties, the waif look,
Kate Moss. You may not believe it looking at me now," she said,
"but in my day I was pulling in $5,000 for a runway show and
doing photo shoots around the world."

"Of course I believe it," he said, his eyes gliding swiftly down
her chest then back up to her face. "Daphne tells me you still
work."

"Mostly hands. I happen to have," she said, picking up the saltshaker, "very expressive hands." She displayed the saltshaker in
her hands as if it was a product.

"Billie gives herself the most amazing manicures, too," I said.
"She knows everything there is to know about taking care of
hands."

"Rule of thumb?" she said, winking. "Always treat your hands
as if your manicure hasn't dried."

love to hear about it sometime. I'm always looking for
story lines." He went on to complain about how hard it was
eep coming up with new material. Billie humored him by nod-
ng and making noises that suggested he was saying very brilliant
nings. I ate half the loaf of bread and olive oil.

"Well," she said, "I have some great stories. You can imagine
the tension when an actress has to have her hands replaced on a
shoot. And then you have to stand behind her with your arms
around her waist slicing a tomato."

As Billie regaled him with stories about how to hold a pen with
grace, cover a bowl of cherries with plastic wrap, and squeeze a
ketchup bottle while writing *anticipation* in perfect script, I finished
off the rest of the loaf. In my defense, it was a relatively small loaf.

"Maybe we can get together for a brainstorming session sometime," Jonathan said. "If you don't mind."

Billie opened her palms in an exaggerated "why not" gesture.
"I'd love to."

I waited to see if he would invite me too, but he didn't, and
why should he? The waiter brought our entrées and his phone
rang again. He looked to see who it was. "Sorry," he said, "I need
to take this."

"I'll be home soon," he said into the phone. "You should go to
sleep, Lily. I'm with Daphne," he said. "You remember, from the
museum? Sure. Hold on."

He handed me the phone. "Hi, Lily."

"Can we do the sixties?"

"Definitely."

"Yay. Can I talk to my daddy again?"

"Here he is." I handed the phone back to him.

"I'll be home soon," he said. "Okay. Sure. Go to sleep."

Almost the same moment he put his phone away, my cell
phone rang. I looked at the caller ID. Charlie. "Hello. I'm coming.
Yes. Don't worry. I won't be long."

I hung up, and Jonathan looked at me with his eyebrows
raised.

"My roommate."

"I didn't know you had one."

"You know how it is, Manhattan rents . . ."

Billie raised her eyebrows so high I was surprised her eyeballs didn't fall out. I smiled as if I had nothing to hide. Under the table, I tucked my thumb on top of the sapphire and spun it around my finger. My new nervous habit.

At the end of the meal, Jonathan insisted on paying. Billie and I put up mild superficial resistance. All of us knew he was going to pay. On the sidewalk out front, she suggested moving on to Employees Only.

"What's that?" Jonathan asked.

"A cocktail bar. Downtown. The best manhattans in Manhattan."

Jonathan said thanks but no thanks, and hailed her a cab to take her uptown.

When we kissed cheeks good night, Billie gave me a penetrating look. "Call me," she said.

Jonathan asked if I wanted a cab or to walk with him a bit. His apartment was just a few blocks away. I got an attack of nerves at the idea of being alone with him, but said that I'd walk him home. As it happened, we were on Fifty-Second Street. The museum was just up the street, and all the storefronts were familiar. Yet because it was night and I was with him, it all seemed new and different. I felt electrified, as if he was a magnet drawing all my energy toward him. This was ridiculous. He was meant for Billie. And I was engaged. My fiancé was scheduled to give me a night of pleasure upon my return. If my fiancé remembered. Or wasn't too tired, seeing as it was almost midnight. Would he be annoyed to have to postpone? Or relieved that he wouldn't have to demonstrate his new skills?

"So Billie's something, isn't she?" I said.

"Oh, yeah. She's a great character. I think she's gonna be a gold mine of material. Look at this. Here we are," he said.

We were passing the museum.

ep. This is my block. You haven't reconsidered the tribute, you?"

"She is persistent," he said.

"I don't mean to bug you. But just tell me—what's the main reason you don't want to do it?"

"I don't think anyone would come."

"Are you kidding? It would sell out for sure. The theater only holds 200 people."

"I'm not even sure I deserve a tribute."

"Of course you do. My god. We've given tributes to *America's Funniest Home Videos* and *SpongeBob SquarePants*."

"Suddenly I don't feel so honored."

"One man's trash is another man's treasure."

"When you put it that way . . ."

"You'll do it?"

He sighed. "I guess."

"Thank you. That's great! I'm so happy."

"Let me know if you need anything."

"I will. At some point, it would be good if I could interview you and get some biographical information."

"Do you like baseball?" he asked.

"Me?" I caught myself from saying my boyfriend did.

"I was invited to this friend's screening. It's a documentary about the history of Yankee Stadium. It's next week. We can meet there and then get some coffee and I'll tell you all about my exciting childhood."

"That sounds like fun." He was asking me out again? Not that he'd asked me out before. Tonight had been professional. And this wouldn't really be out, either. It was just a boring documentary, and then I was interviewing him.

When we reached his building, he hailed me a cab. As I was about to get in, he looked at me in such a way that I thought he might lean over and give me a kiss. This resulted in a wave of panic that made me practically dive into the backseat.

"Thanks for dinner and everything," I said.

"You're welcome."

I barely allowed myself to glance at him as I drove away.

"You were out late."

"Sorry, but he invited us to dinner." I didn't say that we'd gone to one of the most expensive restaurants in the city. Or that we had plans to go out again. Because, after all, it wasn't really going out. "And since I'm trying to get Jonathan together with Billie, we couldn't say no."

"You could've left them together."

"They don't know each other."

"And Billie is so shy."

If he was going to be sarcastic, I could tell him the truth. "We went to the Four Seasons."

"Oh, well."

That silenced him. "They hit it off, by the way."

"I wish him luck."

"God, I'm thirsty. That food must've been really salty." I got a glass from the cabinet. Would Charlie try to get something going with me? Or was he too annoyed? Did he even remember our "date"? The sink was totally full of dishes. He'd been home all evening. Why couldn't he have taken care of that? "Did you leave these for me?" I asked.

"Sorry, I just couldn't face 'em."

I began rinsing. Remembered I had a load of laundry to do. And someone really needed to clean the bathroom. Sure was a comedown after dinner at the Four Seasons. How easy it was to get used to the high life . . . "We need a housewife."

"And a chef," Charlie said, "and a personal assistant."

"Too bad we can't afford even one of those."

He grunted. "So you actually think those two are going to get together?"

"It's possible. Wouldn't that be amazing?"

Charlie muttered something I couldn't understand.

"What?"

ı'm going to sleep," he said.

"I'll just finish up with the dishes."

"I love you," he said.

"Love you."

"Good night."

"Good night."

So. We weren't going to make love. That didn't bother me. But it did bother me that we weren't even going to acknowledge the fact that we weren't going to make love. And the thing that bothered me even more than that? Instead of being disappointed, I was relieved.

Twenty Four

"*I* *must* find myself a new scent."

Billie and I passed a heavily made-up woman in a black smock at the entrance to Sephora.

"Okay." My eyes swept over the incredible array of cosmetics. Billie in Sephora was like me with TiVo on a desert island. Maybe a rescue ship was passing by—who cared. There would be another one along later. That's why I didn't allow myself TiVo.

She was preparing herself for the next phase of the offensive. Jonathan had called and invited her to lunch like he said he would. They were getting together, just the two of them, at Masa, for some famously fantastic Japanese food at a place right down-stairs from his office in the Time Warner building.

I wasn't jealous not to be included. After all, this was the plan that I had set into motion, the plan that would make my life eas-ier. And they weren't actually going to the expensive restaurant part of Masa, where, according to Billie, there was no menu be-cause the chef chose your meal and it cost about $300 per person. They were going to the regular "for civilians" bar area.

So why was I feeling just a bit territorial? Like I should be the one talking about story lines, or at least coming along and getting free *maki* rolls while doing it with her. Ridiculous. "Did he invite you to the Yankee documentary?"

"The what?"

"He asked me to go to this documentary a friend of his made. It's somewhere incredibly inconvenient on the lower, Lower, east, East Side." I wanted to make the venture sound as unattractive as possible so she wouldn't think this was a competition or anything.

"Why did he ask you to that?"

…d him I needed some biographical information for the
…, and he said he'd tell me if I went to this thing with him.
…e he couldn't get anyone else to go."

"Sounds dreadful," she said, picking up a box of Sarah Jessica
…arker's Lovely and spraying some on each of our wrists.

"That's nice," I said.

"Too flowery." She put it back. "I want to find something irresistible."

We sampled. We sprayed. We spritzed. No patch of arm skin
was spared. Nothing seemed just right. Finally, for relief, we in-
haled the aroma of coffee beans that were set out in small bowls.
They supposedly made a clean slate of your nostrils, but after a
good half hour of this, my sense of smell was blown — as was my
capacity to obsess.

But Billie had not yet decided on a scent. She went back to
ones we'd previously rejected. Opium. "Too spicy." Stella. "Too floral." Shalimar. "Too vanilla." When we sampled Paris Hilton's
scent ("too fruity"), I couldn't resist giving her a wedding update.
"So Charlie's parents put down the deposit for Pearl River." Billie
had been very good about not saying anything negative about the
wedding, but it was starting to feel unnatural that we were avoiding the subject completely. I just hoped she wouldn't go back to
discouraging me.

"I'm sure it will be lovely," she said.

This was good. Supportive. I felt encouraged.

"We were going to get a cake from the Silver Moon, but the
hotel works with a bakery out there, so I'm just going with that."
Would she tell me to insist on the Silver Moon?

"That makes sense."

Okay. Hmmm. Maybe I could trust her with my totally inappropriate idea that no one would approve of so there was no need
to mention it but I seemed to need to say it out loud, just to hear
it said, out loud, at the very least. "I know where I'd really like to
have the wedding, but everyone else will think it's crazy."

"Oh, hell." She grabbed a box of Arpege. "It's a clas[.] can't go wrong." I followed her to the cashier.

"It's too bad," I said, as we got in line behind someone [.] "because it would've been almost free."

"The suspense is killing me."

I hesitated. I wasn't sure why I was doing this. Did I want her to convince me to take a stand? I certainly wouldn't be able to without her support. "No one will go for it."

We moved up to the register. "You're the bride. You only have to please yourself."

The cashier gave me a congratulatory smile as she rang up the perfume.

"You're going to think it's weird," I said.

"Just tell me."

"Okay, I'm thinking I'd like to get married at the cemetery."

"What?"

"By Mom and Dad's graves. That way, they can be at the wedding."

The cashier made a sound that was combination snort and chuckle as she put the box into a small black bag. Billie looked at me as if I was insane. "That's the most morbid thought I've ever heard. Who would have their wedding in a cemetery? Anyone would think you equate this marriage with being the end of your life."

"I just want them to be there. What's the point of doing it if they aren't there?"

"The point is to be surrounded by living, breathing people who can witness what should be the happiest day of your life."

Billie handed the cashier Max's Visa gold card. I wondered how long he'd let her keep using it. Maybe, out of guilt, he'd let her go on using it forever. Maybe I'd been wrong to encourage her to leave him. In its odd way, that relationship had anchored her. What if that was all she was capable of having? And the rest of her life would be downhill from here? How did anyone know the best

How did anyone make major life decisions? It was hard
ugh just choosing a scent.

"Have a nice day, ladies," the cashier said. I had the distinct
feeling I'd provided her with her best entertainment all day.

As we walked out of the store, Billie shook her head. "Even
Pearl River is a better idea than that."

Was it such a strange idea? I suppose. But I liked it.

When we were out on the sidewalk, she turned and faced me.
"But you know what? If you want your wedding up at the cemetery, go ahead."

"Really?" I guess she could see I was serious, because her face
softened.

"Don't worry, Kitten. Mom and Dad will be there. Because
we'll bring them with us. They'll be right up front. In our minds.
Right?"

I nodded. She gave me a hug. My eyes stung. As my nose and
cheek nuzzled against her shoulder, I smelled her scent. Her real
one. No perfume could mask it, not from me anyway. She understood like no one else. Because it was just us. It had been just us
for so long. . . . Now it would be us plus Charlie. I couldn't shake
the feeling that it was a rotten thing to do to her. Nothing to
celebrate.

"Maybe we should just elope," I said, as she released me.

"That's an option."

"You wouldn't be mad at me?"

"You do what you need to do."

We walked to the corner. I imagined driving up to Vermont
with Charlie. We could let a justice of the peace in some small
town do the ceremony. His wife would be our witness. She'd be
wearing an apron and granny glasses. An apple pie would be bak-
ing in the kitchen. We could stay in a nearby bed-and-breakfast
and have pancakes and sausage with real maple syrup. There'd be
a TV in the living room and a nice shady porch. Charlie could
spend the time getting back into his writing. I would sit in a rock-
ing chair and read Janice Dickinson's memoir. Sounded perfect.

When we got to Seventy-Second Street, I decided to
bus across town. Time to part ways. "I hope your new scent
its spell on Jonathan."

"If it doesn't," she said with an evil glint, "I'll just have to
my skills to use."

We kissed cheeks. I wondered if she'd get him back to her
apartment and give him a blow job after lunch. On the house, of
course. I swallowed and closed my eyes as if to clear my mind. I
really did not want to think about that.

Twenty Five

"So how's it going with Simon?"

"Very nice."

"Very, *very* nice by the look of those pink cheeks."

"Well," Taffy said, allowing a timid smile, "you have to promise not to tell anyone but . . ." She looked around the lobby. No one was within ear shot.

"Yes . . . ?"

"I stayed over at his house last weekend."

"*Did* you."

"Uh-huh."

They had sex. It was all over her face. "So . . . was he good?"

"Please," she pretended to be offended. "I don't gossip about such things."

"Very funny." I leaned over on the glass case. "Spew."

She leaned over toward me and said in a half whisper, "Simon is an incredible lover."

"Really." Quiet, reserved, shy Simon? "You're kidding."

"Once you get him in the bedroom? Forget about it. Not to mention the hot tub in the backyard."

"I don't believe you!" I squealed softly, letting my enthusiasm mask my jealousy.

"Believe me. He is so sensitive. And sensual. Evidently, he's taken classes in tantric sex. The man knows more about my body than I do."

Gulp. Wow. Simon? "I think this is more than I want to know about my co-worker."

"You asked."

"Jesus. But he hasn't had a girlfriend in years, right?"

"Oh, yes he has. We just never knew about them. [...] discreet."

"I'll say."

I went to the elevator. As I passed Melvin the security guard [...] couldn't help but wonder—how was *he* in bed? I went up the ele-vator with Eleanor from PR (covert sex goddess?) and said good morning to Ben (closet stud?) as I settled in at my desk. Jeez. Maybe everyone was having hot, wild sex and meanwhile Charlie and I were just going through the motions.

I had a tray of frozen eggplant parmigiana cooking in the mi-crowave when Charlie got home. He threw his backpack in the corner, kissed me on the cheek, opened the refrigerator, and pulled out the vegetable bin. "No lettuce or tomatoes. Can't you get to the grocery store more often?" He was only half joking.

"Aisle one, right inside the door, lettuce on your left, tomatoes on your right." I wasn't joking at all.

"I can't face the store after I've been at work all day." Now he wasn't joking either.

"I work too, you know. Just because I don't complain about my job all the time doesn't mean it's not work."

The beeper on the microwave went off. My eggplant was ready.

"Wait!" he said. "Don't eat that!"

"What?"

"I'm sorry. I'm being a jerk. We haven't done anything fun to-gether for awhile. Let's go out to dinner."

I looked down at my eggplant. "Okay." Damn. *Supermodels* was on later, Ashley was getting married, and I really didn't want to miss it. But it would be possible to go out and be back in time. I played it cool. "Sounds nice."

It was hard to decide where to go. We'd been to every restau-rant in the neighborhood a zillion times. When it gets to be that routine, it's almost like not going out. We could've left the neigh-borhood, but the idea of getting in a cab wasn't appealing, and the subway was even less attractive, especially since I didn't want to

...ar or we'd never get back in time for the show. (Not that I
...oned that concern to Charlie.) We decided to walk over to
...mbus Avenue. At least it was out of our normal radius, and
...re was a new Italian place we'd never been to.

It was really nice out, my favorite time of year. The spring air
was clean and crisp, it was warm enough to go without a sweater,
and the whole warm summer was ahead of us. "You know what?"
I said, suddenly feeling lighthearted and optimistic, "Next time I
see him, I'm going to ask Jonathan Hill to read *Sitting Comics*."

"You know what? Don't bother."

"Are you serious?"

"Yeah." We waited for some cars to go by before crossing
against the light.

"You don't want to take advantage of this situation?"

"You know nothing will come of it."

"I don't know that at all."

"I appreciate the impulse, but no thanks." He leaned over and
pecked me on the cheek.

The peck annoyed me. "He respects my opinion. I think he'd
really give it serious consideration."

The light was still red, but nothing was coming, so we crossed.
"I can't get my hopes up again, Daphne, I just can't. I'm putting
all that behind me, and you know what? It's a relief."

"I can't believe you're giving up." I couldn't help it, but that
really turned me off. His dream! How could he let it go? Especially
now, when we had this incredible contact. "Believe it or not, I'm
getting to know Jonathan Hill. This isn't like Gordon Fineberg.
We have a relationship."

"Relationship?"

"Professional relationship."

I rolled my eyes at him. We turned in to the restaurant.

Everything was fine at first. We got a good table by the front
window, the seats were comfortable, the waiter was pleasant. We
both had wine. I ordered some really fattening fettuccini. I was in
the mood to indulge. After half a glass of wine, I was a bit tipsy,

and it was making me feel like there was no reason to worry just needed to communicate better about what we wanted. "know," I blurted out, "maybe we should just elope."

"Are you serious?"

I told him my Vermont fantasy, ending big on the pancakes with real maple syrup part.

"That's sweet, but, you know, my parents. Not to mention the deposit on the hotel."

"I know. . . ." Of course it didn't fly. "But it does sound romantic, doesn't it?"

"We could go there on our honeymoon."

"Vermont isn't special enough for a honeymoon."

"How can it not be special enough for a honeymoon but it is special enough for eloping?"

"I don't know. It just is."

Two waiters arrived in a burst of motion, each carrying a plate. They set them down, offered pepper and Parmesan, bowed slightly, told us to enjoy, and were gone. The smell of the pasta and cream and bacon seemed to go straight to a hungry hole in my gut. I wound a big wad around my fork and took a bite. It was so good.

"Look. It's not just that I don't want to disappoint my mom. The truth is, *I* want a ceremony. I always imagined I'd have one. Eloping is such a nonevent."

"I know. I mean, I can see how you could feel that way." I couldn't really blame the guy for wanting to have a wedding. And the fact that Charlie actually cared what his mother thought and treated her well without being a mamma's boy or anything was a good sign. That's the kind of guy you want to marry, right? Not the ones who hate their mothers and never call them and blame them for everything that ever went wrong in their lives. Eventually they just inserted you into that slot. So I should've been glad he wanted to make his mother happy. And yet . . . "There's such pressure to put all this emphasis on that one day. As if it's the end point."

Or beginning," he said.

"That's true." I dug my fork into the thick pasta. But beginning what? I still couldn't believe that he would actually turn down the chance to have Jonathan Hill read his script. How could he resist the opportunity? Was he being ultrareasonable? Or self-destructive? Some indiscernible combination of both?

After we'd paid our bill and gotten up from the table, he leaned over and gave me a kiss. I wondered if he'd want to make love when we got home. My stomach felt so full. All I wanted to do was get into bed and watch *Supermodels*. We walked back to the apartment holding hands, but it didn't feel so much like we were trying to touch, as we were trying not to let go.

When Charlie went into the bathroom, I turned on the TV. I felt like a drug addict who waits for the chance to shoot up in private. He would be out soon enough, and there would be no hiding it. But at least he wouldn't actually see me turn it on. Maybe he would believe it turned on by itself. Then I couldn't be blamed. And if he made any sort of pass at me, well, if he tempted me enough with his touch, I could always turn it off.

The promo came on.

"You are cordially invited to the exclusive wedding of the most gorgeous supermodel in the world. . . ."

There was a montage of scenes from all season leading up to the marriage, ending with a clip from the previous episode when Mirage arrived late at the rehearsal dinner and promised Ashley she wouldn't do anything to ruin the wedding day. But we all knew there was no way Mirage was going to stand there and watch sweet little Ashley marry the man *she* deserved.

I quickly changed into an old comfy T-shirt I liked to sleep in and got under the covers. Charlie came out of the bathroom and stripped down to his boxers. "This is the big night," I said. "Ashley is marrying Niles."

He glanced at the TV. "Oh."

I had to make him understand the importance of this week's

episode. "Mirage thinks he should marry her, even though s
crack addict."

"Uh-huh."

"Next week is the big season finale. Something drastic is gonr.
happen, but no one knows what. This whole plot development is
because Jessica Cox, you know, the actress who plays Mirage, she
left the show to make that movie I just saw at the Paris. It was so
bad. So for her sake, I hope she isn't killed off."

"Uh-huh." Charlie got next to me in bed.

Ashley was standing in front of the mirror wearing her Christian Dior haute couture dress made from a hundred yards of silk
with a thirteen-foot train. I knew these details because there'd been
a whole article on it in *US Weekly* that I'd caved in and bought.

Charlie scooted closer to me.

The ceremony was about to begin. Ashley's mother told her it
was time to go downstairs. Ashley gave herself one more look in
the mirror. "How do I look?"

"Gorgeous."

Her mother gave her a hug, then held her face in her hands.
"My baby . . . about to get married . . ."

It was idiotic, but my eyes teared up.

"So," Charlie said, "how are you feeling?"

"What?" I'd heard him perfectly well. But Ashley descended
the stairs. All eyes were on her. Niles looked at her with absolute
devotion. She walked down the aisle on the arm of her manager.
Mirage's mouth was twitching. I wondered how hard it was, as an
actress, to force your mouth to twitch.

Charlie ran his hand down my thigh. "Why don't you turn
that off?"

"Can we just wait until this is over?"

"Daphne, come on. I have to get up early tomorrow. Can't you
tape it?"

"They're getting married. Right now."

"How can you find a television show more important than your
own life?"

don't." I smiled at him for a millisecond just so he'd know
much I loved and appreciated him. Ashley took her place
xt to Niles. Mirage stared at them. She now had a big fake smile,
nd there was a crazy look in her eyes. I wondered if she was going
to pull out a gun. "It's just . . . I've been looking forward to this
episode all week. There isn't much more."

"Fine. Good night." He got under the covers and turned away
from me. His voice was icy. "Enjoy your show."

The priest made a little speech.

I hated to continue the argument while this scene was playing
out, but I couldn't resist asking. "Did you ever read those tips?"

"What?"

"The tips I emailed you."

"Yeah, I read them."

"Do you have any thoughts about them?"

"Not really."

I didn't know how to respond. A minute later he was asleep. I
was astounded. That was it? He had nothing else to say?

I watched the rest of the ceremony. They dragged it out as long
as they could, cutting away to a ridiculous subplot that no one
cared about having to do with the caterers being in a panic over
the wedding cake because it had been decorated with pink roses
instead of white. Finally, the priest was just about to pronounce
them man and wife. Mirage stepped forward and yelled, "Stop!
You can't do this!" Niles and Ashley turned toward her. The music
came to a crescendo. . . .

An ad for Ponds antiaging cold cream came on.

All through the commercials, I was hoping there would be
more show. I didn't want to be left alone with my thoughts. But
when *Supermodels* returned, it went directly into the credits. I
turned out the light and tried to get to sleep. But I knew I was in
for a long night. Sleep was the last thing on my mind.

Twenty Six

I walked down a dark and empty street, feeling my way toward the theater. I actually felt nervous—a rare occurrence in this city I knew so well. This area seemed to be a pocket of uncivilization—hard to find in Manhattan these days. I didn't think there were any blocks left I'd never been on, but this was totally unfamiliar. Adding to the sinister atmosphere was a row of abandoned old tenement buildings and an empty lot.

I found the address. It was an old brick building just north of Houston Street. According to a plaque on the wall, it was a courthouse around the turn of the century and had been renovated to the tune of two million dollars as a place to screen artsy and indie films.

I was early, so I decided to leave and hunt down a cup of coffee. It wasn't that I was so interested in drinking the coffee; mostly I just wanted to hold the coffee. Surely, even in this neighborhood, there was a place to buy a cup. I walked in one direction and then the other. There wasn't a Starbucks or even a bodega in sight. I tried the next block. Nothing. Amazing! Unheard of! Was I in a dream? *The Twilight Zone?* Another dimension? Finally I saw the bright glow of a gas station sign. Yes, a gas station. In Manhattan. You never see gas stations in Manhattan. And even stranger, this one had one of those junk food mini-marts. A total rarity. Very strange.

I went in and bought a cup of lukewarm black stuff dispensed from a thermos that had obviously been sitting there for hours waiting for an indiscriminate cabdriver to down it like a drug. No one would buy it for that bitter burnt aftertaste. Yuck. A good dose of half and half and two sugars did nothing to rescue it. Oh, well.

least I could hold it. I carried it back to the theater and stood here.

Holding it.

With a stupid smile on my face.

I really had to stop being so punctual.

There was a table with DVDs of the movie displayed, on sale for ten dollars. Obviously packaged by the filmmakers themselves. I read the blurb. The film was a tribute to the stadium, with interviews from baseball players, old fans, and nearby merchants who were all mourning the fact that it was being knocked down for a new one. My father and I had gone through a phase where he took me to games up there. They were actually some of the few positive memories I had with him. He'd tried to get me interested in sports since Billie had totally rejected anything that involved equipment that was not fashion-oriented. I was in a softball league for a few years in middle school, but even though I was good and basically coordinated, I was never great. I still remembered the best he could do compliment-wise. "You work really hard. Sometimes it pays off." I tried to transpose that in my head to fabulous praise, but it always stopped short. Still, I'd felt a certain contentment on our trips up there, sitting next to each other in the stands, sharing a bag of peanuts and sipping my Coke. I loved waiting for a fly ball to arc way high up in the sky and then drop down near our seats. It made me feel secure to know he'd catch it with his glove before letting it clonk me on the head.

Someone's hand was on my back. I turned around.

Jonathan.

"So are you a Yankee fan?"

"I used to go with my father when I was a kid."

"He dragged you up there?"

He did not remove his hand. He kept it right there, on the small of my back.

"I liked it. Especially the peanuts."

"Shall we go in?"

He gently guided me toward the door to the theater. I clung to

my cup of coffee as if it was keeping me anchored to the g̶
Why was my heart thumping? This was ridiculous.

We took two empty seats on the aisle about halfway back. ̶
springs pushed up against my butt and it was lopsided, but
didn't want to suggest moving, so I decided I would get used to it.
I put the coffee down underneath my chair. He let his long legs
extend out into the aisle. I made some comment about how weird
it was that this theater seemed to be in the middle of nowhere. He
put his arm (*oh*) around my shoulder. . . . (*my god*).

I was tempted to pump him for information about what was
going to happen on the last episode of *Supermodels*. But . . . I had
my pride. "So," I said, "did you have your meeting with Billie?"

She wasn't there to sit between us, but I could still use her to
put some space between us, right?

"Yes."

"Good." *Did she give you a blow job?* "Did she give you some
good material?"

"I've already started writing a script."

"Great. Wow." *So are you in love with her now?* "I'm glad it got
you going."

"And it's all thanks to you."

I smiled pleasantly at him. "And Billie, of course." The lights
went down.

After the movie was over, the filmmaker went up to the front
and made a speech. He was a short guy with straight brown hair
and a bald spot. This was totally not like the HBO screening. In
this case, everyone knew the filmmaker had put his heart and soul
into the project, and it was really kind of touching. He thanked his
family and everyone who had been connected to making it. He
said this night was one of the highlights of his life.

We all filed out, and I sensed a collective feeling of goodwill
over the fact that the guy had struggled to produce this film that
was about something close to his heart (even if it was just a baseball stadium) and maybe art could be a worthwhile thing. Especially since there was now a table set up with desserts in the lobby.

an and I both loaded up our plates with cookies shaped
gloves and round mini cheesecakes decorated with red stitch-
, to look like baseballs. I wondered if we'd still go out after this
r his interview, or if this was going to be it. Jonathan followed
me with two coffees. We nabbed one of the few free tables. Were
we really going to sit there and place food in our mouths and have
a conversation? What would I ask him about his past? Part of me
wanted to make an excuse and run home. Literally. Run all the
way home. And I hate running.

But on the other hand, the cheesecake was yummy. And this
was, after all, part of my work, even if he had touched my lower
back earlier and his arm had stayed behind me for most of the
movie. He had long limbs, and it wasn't his fault he had to find a
way to arrange them. God knows he couldn't possibly be interested in me "that way." He was showing me how grateful he was
for introducing him to my sister. "I'm glad Billie was helpful."

"She's very entertaining."

"Has she hit you up about wanting to act on the show?"

"Not yet, but I'm sure it's coming. You know, I thought her
voice sounded familiar. When she told me she was the woman on
the 777-7777 commercial, I *realized* . . ."

"I know—isn't it funny?"

He paused. Leaned toward me. Got this serious look. "She told
me about your parents."

So she'd gone into that. So it had gotten personal.

"That must've been rough," he said.

I pressed my lips together. Anything you say at moments like
this sounds hopelessly superficial.

"I can see," he said, "that you two are very close."

"Me and Billie?" I gave him my wry smile. "Yes."

"But you're very different."

"My mother once said I make a point of being unlike her.
That's how I assert myself. Of course, since Billie was always so as-
sertive, that meant being unassertive." I took a bite of cheesecake.
"If that makes sense."

"I can see it would be hard to compete with her," he said. "...
you don't seem all that unassertive to me."

"I've been working on trying to get over it," I said, and our eye
met for what felt like a dangerous moment. "To an extent," I added,
lest he think I was trying to compete with her for him. I was so incredibly overdue on telling him about Charlie. And I would, as
soon as I finished my cheesecake. It was so nice and creamy, and
the graham cracker crust was soft and crumbly.

"So I wanted to invite both of you to my house," he said. "In
the Hamptons."

"Really?" To my horror, a blob of cheesecake fell off my fork
and onto the wood-slat floor. I leaned over to wipe it up with a
cocktail napkin, then straightened back up and balled the napkin
inside my fist.

"This weekend," he said. "Can you make it?"

"Umm . . . I think so." Jesus. Had Billie somehow wheedled this
invitation? She loved the Hamptons and had no problem fitting
into that whole scene. I'd been there a few times, but mainly for
the beaches—it really did have great beaches. The stuck-up towns
and snooty party scene I could do without. The last time I'd been
there, it was a long weekend at Gurney's Inn. We'd indulged in fa-
cials and massages that cost Max about $300 per sister. I have to
say I enjoyed every minute of it when I wasn't castigating myself
for not deserving the royal treatment.

"I figure I can pump Billie for some more material."

Yes, Billie must've charmed this invitation out of him, and I
was only there to be her sidekick and chaperone. Now was the moment to ask if my boyfriend could come along too, even though
Charlie hated the Hamptons, and he'd really dislike having to sit
on the train pretending to be civil to Billie in the overly air-
conditioned air.

"We'll take my private helicopter," he said.

"Helicopter?"

"It's great. Ever been on one?"

"No . . ." I still got a woozy feeling in my stomach when I

ught of being up in that tiny plane with my father. I was feel-
g pretty woozy right then. But that was probably due to the caf-
eine and sugar I was pumping into my system, not to mention the
fact that I was being deceptive for no good reason.

"Are you afraid of flying?" he asked. "I didn't even think of that—"

"Whenever I get nervous about flying, I try not to let it take
over, because I don't want it to rule me."

"That's good."

"On the other hand, I've only been on commercial airlines. I'm
not sure about private planes, much less a helicopter."

"I can arrange for you to take a limousine."

I thought of him and Billie alone in the helicopter together. Me
down on the ground, stuck in traffic. "That's okay. It sounds
like . . . an experience. Every time I go up, I become less scared, so
it's good for me."

He broke the thumb of his cookie glove and popped it into his
mouth. "I'd like to bounce some other ideas off you, too. Billie's
full of raw material, but she has no idea how to turn any of it into
a story."

"Great." So this was work. And there was no need to bring up
Charlie. As a matter of fact, it would be inappropriate. My personal
life was none of his business. "I'd love to help."

"My house is right on the beach, so bring a bathing suit."

Bathing suit? Uh-oh. Maybe this was business, but now I was
going to appear almost naked in front of him. Did I have time to
buy a new suit before the weekend?

"And by the way, Lee is bringing Lily. She can't wait to see you
again."

"I'd love to see her too. I've been promising to do the sixties
with her." So it didn't matter what I wore to the beach: I'd be there
as assistant, chaperone, and babysitter so he could brainstorm a
show to lure his ex-girlfriend to work with him again while hanging out with his ex-wife. Maybe he really *should* know about Charlie, just so he didn't think I was some desperate female vying for
his attention. As I was trying to figure out a way to smoothly segue

into my wedding plans, the filmmaker broke away from
crowd that was around him and made his way to Jonathan.
man, thanks so much for coming."

Jonathan stood up, and they patted each other's backs. "
been a long time."

"I was hoping you'd be here."

"It was great."

"You really think so?"

"Yeah, and congratulations on Sundance."

"Thanks, man."

Jonathan introduced me, but the guy didn't even look at me
while saying how nice it was to meet me. "So listen, this is wind-
ing down. You wanna come to Nobu? A bunch of us are gonna get
some grub." He nodded toward a clump of friends that included a
couple of very sexy size-zero twins wearing matching almost see-
through crochet dresses.

"Sure," Jonathan said.

As soon as we were left alone, he apologized. "He's an old
friend. I figure I should hang out with him."

"Of course."

"You should come along."

"Oh, no thanks." No way was I going to spend the evening
watching him flirt. "I should be getting home."

"You sure? I didn't even give you a chance to interview me."

"I'll do it in the Hamptons." But I didn't love the idea of walking outside by myself. "Could you help me get a cab?"

"Of course."

We went out and ended up by the gas station, where we got a
cab after it finished gassing up. Jonathan tried to hand me a
twenty-dollar bill and I refused, even though I had come all the
way down there for that stupid baseball movie and now he was
gonna go off with the twins and stare through their crocheted
dresses. I got in the cab quickly just in case he had some idea in
his head of giving me a good night kiss on the cheek or whatever,
not that he would, but just in case. "Good night."

od night."

the cab pulled into the street, I put on my seat belt and re-
d I was still clutching that balled-up napkin with the blob of
eesecake inside.

Conan was doing his monologue. He was such an odd-looking
person with that big white head and thin lips and orange hair and
those bangs combed to the side like a cartoon character. How did
he get that job? Was he really the best they could find? It was fun
knowing he wanted Jonathan to read his sitcom script, and that
Jonathan didn't want to.

"So we have to decide," Charlie said. "Do we want to look for
a band, or just go with the one the hotel recommends?" He was in
bed next to me reading *A Tale of Two Cities*. It wasn't even for one
of his classes. He was reading it for fun. All eight hundred million
pages of it. We didn't make any mention of our argument the
night before. Had it occurred? Had it seemed worse than it was?
Had it even been an argument?

"Whatever you want," I said.

"Most women are obsessive about this sort of thing."

"I'm not most women."

"Do you still want to cancel it?"

"Charlie, I never said I wanted to cancel the wedding. Just the
Pearl River aspect."

"What's the difference?"

"There's a huge difference." So. He was feeling insecure.
Maybe the argument *had* affected him. "I just like the idea of eloping, that's all. I think it's romantic."

Conan made a joke about Tom Cruise and the studio audience
cracked up.

"Can you turn that off?"

"It's amusing me."

"You have no self-control."

I aimed the remote at him and pretended to zap him with it.

"Not even remotely." I said it with a smile, but one th...
sure: I wasn't amusing him.

"You're having second thoughts," he said. "About us."

"No."

"You're sure?"

"Yes." I looked at him. "Are you having second thoughts?"

"No."

We both looked at the TV. Conan made a joke about Star Jones. The audience cracked up.

"So," Charlie said, "I was thinking we could go to a travel agent this weekend . . ."

"Uh-huh . . ."

"Try to figure out where to honeymoon."

"Sounds like fun." And then I remembered. "Oh, wait. I can't, actually. I'm going to the Hamptons."

"You're what?"

"Jonathan invited us to the Hamptons. Isn't that exciting?"

"You and me?"

"Me and Billie."

"Why?"

"He has a house. On the beach. And he wants to talk about some story lines with Billie, and I still have to interview him for the retrospective. Plus he probably wants to get into her pants."

"Will you turn that off?" he asked.

"He's funny tonight."

"The truth is," he said, "you'd rather watch TV than make love with me."

"Charlie." I sat up on the bed. "Are you jealous of people who don't actually even exist in my life?"

"What about people who *do exist* in your life?"

"What are you talking about?" I suddenly felt like I really needed something to eat.

"You haven't told him about us yet."

onathan?" I got up and went to the kitchen. Charlie

es he even know I exist?"

ot exactly . . ." It wasn't that I was so hungry.

You haven't told him about me at all?"

I needed to put something in my mouth. "Well . . ."

"So he doesn't know you're engaged."

"Not specifically." Maybe I'd have some cereal. Not that I needed the calories, especially considering I was going to have to wear a bathing suit in two days. This was definitely a mental craving, but I was helpless to resist.

"So when are you planning on telling him?"

"I will. Soon," I said, opening the box. "I keep meaning to. There just hasn't been the right moment to mention it. It's really not like he could care less, Charlie."

"Because you couldn't care less."

"What? That's totally and utterly ridiculous." I poured Cheerios into a bowl and then drowned the ringlets with milk. Mostly I just really wanted the milk. The cereal was there to sweeten the milk. I turned on the TV in the living room and sat on the couch and balanced the bowl on my lap. "I'll tell him this weekend." I ate a big spoonful.

Charlie sat down next to me. "I don't believe you."

"How can you say these things? Do you really think Jonathan Hill cares whether I have a boyfriend or not? Billie is the one he wants. You're being totally ridiculous."

The studio audience laughed. Charlie got the remote from the coffee table. "I'm turning that off."

"But he's going to interview Nicollette Sheridan from *Desperate Housewives*." She was like an old friend, from back in our *Knots Landing* days—not to mention she was a model on *Paper Dolls*.

"Your obsession with the television is sick."

"Just leave it on for ten minutes while I have my cereal."

"There's always some excuse, because anything on the more important than relating to me, right?"

"How can you say that? I'm constantly relating to you."

"But you can't do it with the TV off."

"Of course I can."

"Then show me." He handed me the remote.

"Fine." I aimed it at the television. But Conan was in the middle of a joke, so I waited for him to finish.

"Do it."

"I'm just waiting for the punchline." I put my finger over the button.

"Push the button, Daphne."

His doggedness was making me feel all the more stubborn. "After the joke."

"Push it!"

The audience laughed. "Charlie! You made me miss the punchline!"

He sprung up from the couch, reached behind the TV, and disconnected the wires to the cable box. The sound of static filled the room.

"What are you doing?"

"Disconnecting you."

Static. It was the saddest sound in the world. The chaos of the universe.

"You didn't have to do that."

He stared at me. With this look. It scared me.

"You're really being excessive," I said. "Would you put the cable back in?"

He went to the hall closet and got out his duffel bag.

"What are you doing?"

He still didn't answer me. Just went to the bedroom with it. I followed him in. Conan was still on, still doing his monologue. Charlie stuffed his duffel bag with underwear and socks. "Why are you doing that? Charlie? Would you speak to me?"

'll be at my parents' house until I can find my own place."

"What?"

He didn't say anything as he crammed in two pairs of jeans and a pile of T-shirts.

"You're actually doing this?" His extra sneakers. "Charlie?"

He zipped up the bag, got his copy of *Tale of Two Cities*, and stuffed it into his backpack. Then he strode up to the TV and pulled out the cable on that one, too.

"You didn't have to do that."

"Oh, yeah?" He went to the front door. I followed him.

"This is ridiculous. Talk to me. Don't just leave."

He paused, turned around, and looked at me. "Now you know how it feels."

"What?"

"No reception."

Tears started down my cheeks. "I receive you. Of course I receive you. We're getting married."

"You could've fooled me." With that, he opened the door and walked out.

All of a sudden I was alone. In the apartment. With the static.

I ran out into the hallway. He was just stepping onto the elevator. "Charlie, don't leave!" As I ran down the hall, the doors closed.

I went back in and turned off the living room set. Then I went into the bedroom to turn that one off too. But instead, I sat on the edge of the bed for I don't know how long, letting the static fill my brain. At first it resonated with my stunned state of mind. Then it began to bother me. I looked at the back of the set to figure out how to reconnect the cable. I felt quite sure I could figure it out. It was as simple as screwing the wire back in, right? But then I hesitated. I didn't need the TV. I'd be just fine without it. Maybe he wouldn't even know, but I could prove it to myself. So I just left it hanging. And pushed the power button. And the static stopped. And there was silence.

Twenty Seven

The cemetery was almost impossible to get to if you didn't have a car. It involved taking a train from Grand Central to some small town that we could never remember the name of—it basically consisted of an Irish pub—and from there you had to somehow hire a cab to take you to the gate, where you were bound to get lost again, because there never seemed to be anyone around to help, and we could never remember where the family plot was.

I was the one who'd reminded Billie it was the anniversary of our parents' deaths, and maybe it would be a good idea to go up and visit their graves.

"You are so morbid," she said. "And that's one of the things I love about you."

"I'll get the train schedule."

"You know what? This time let's rent a car."

Billie knew how to drive, but her sense of direction was worse than mine. "But we'll get lost."

"Print it out on MapQuest. We'll find it. If we can just remember the name of that town it's in."

We did manage to find our way to the pub. And when we stopped for a beer, we got directions from the potbellied bartender, who tried to hit on Billie, but there was no way she was going to look at him twice. Once inside the cemetery was another story. It took a number of wrong turns until we found the right graves.

After setting down some flowers, we stood there for a few minutes, each of us shedding a few tears. "It's surprisingly pleasant here," I finally said, "don't you think?" There were some gently d picturesque weeping willows. "We really should

wn more often."

now what I like about this place? It's not all crowded

e obnoxious cemeteries in Queens where the graves are

shed together."

That's because it's newer. Eventually this one will be just as

uished."

"Good point."

We both looked at the grass growing where there was room for us.

"Okay, I'm telling you right now," she said. "I'm getting cremated. I want you to scatter me in Central Park or on a beach somewhere, okay?"

"Fine. I don't like the idea of being dispersed, though. I want all my bones staying in one place."

"I suppose you'll end up with Charlie somewhere. Does his family have a plot?"

"I don't know." Telling her about my fight with Charlie would be a risk, and I'd kept my mouth shut about it the whole ride up. It would give her such ammunition against him—especially if we patched things up.

But one thing was becoming clear. I could no longer blame my doubts about Charlie on her, or her meddling, or my guilty conscience when it came to her. My doubts were now disentangled from her doubts. My doubts were my own. "Maybe it's moot at this point."

"Meaning?"

"Charlie got really mad at me last night and stormed out and didn't come back."

"Are you serious?"

I nodded and attempted to laugh as if to communicate that I wasn't freaked out or anything, but it came out more like a twisted squeal.

"Okay. Come here. Sit down."

We wiped some dirt off a marble bench that was near the path. "So how did this happen?"

"He got mad because he wanted to talk about the wedding and I wanted to watch Conan, and he disconnected the TV and walked out. He's staying with his parents."

"I'm sorry."

"And please don't say 'this is for the best.' "

"I'm sure he'll be back."

"Maybe."

"Of course he will. Everyone has these little squabbles while they're going through the whole wedding-planning scenario nightmare."

"I guess. But . . ." I looked at her. Hesitated. Really felt like I should keep my mouth shut, but didn't. "Part of me is relieved he left."

"Hmmmm."

"Charlie makes me feel safe and secure, which has been so good for me the past few years. But maybe that's too much a part of why I hold on to him. I know this might sound ludicrous considering how defensive I've been and everything, but I'm wondering if we really shouldn't be getting married."

"Wow. Okay. I just want you to know—I'm making a valiant effort to stay neutral here."

"And I appreciate that."

"But I will say one thing."

"Yes?"

"You look horrible."

"I haven't been sleeping very well."

"Nightmares?"

I looked at my father's headstone, then my mother's. "I don't remember." At that moment, a dream from the night before popped into my head. "I did have one weird dream. . . ."

"Okay, let's have it."

I paused. "It was my wedding."

"Aha."

"But it was taking place in a doctor's office."

"Yes?"

"But there was no doctor. Just Charlie. He was offering me marijuana, because he said it would ease the pain."

She smiled. "And it does."

"But nothing was hurting."

"Go on."

"So I said I didn't want it."

"Okay . . ."

"But then these policemen started banging on the door, saying I was under arrest. I woke up totally freaked out."

"Wow." She brushed something off her tank top. "Shit."

"A bug?"

"No, your dream. It's brilliant."

"What do you mean?"

She turned toward me and peered straight into my eyes. "Charlie offers you the marijuana because it eases the pain."

"Right."

"But you don't want it."

I squinted. "So?"

"Marijuana," she said slowly. "Marry wanna. You don't want it. You don't wanna marry."

My jaw dropped. "Oh, my god. Do you think that's what it means?"

She shrugged. "It's your dream. You're the only one who can really know."

I looked down at the ground, then back at her. "Wow."

Twenty Eight

Charlie and I were in a café on Seventy-Second Street. It was a neutral place, a place we wouldn't ever need to go back to if this ended up being a really bad memory. "Stand by Me" was playing on the radio. A glass vase filled with thin tree branches was on the counter. Different-colored origami ornaments hung from the branches. They swayed gently from the overhead fans. I couldn't stop staring at them.

"How are you?" he asked.

"Sad," I said.

I tasted my bran muffin. It was disappointing. Too much corn syrup. It didn't matter, because I had no appetite.

I didn't know if he was going to attempt to apologize. Maybe he wanted to return, proceed from where we'd left off, and chalk the whole fight up to nerves. Or maybe he was going to tell me that he felt so relieved to have left me and my television sets. Life had never been so good.

"I'm sorry about the other night," he said.

"Don't apologize. You were right."

"Well," he said, his voice tense, "I'm glad you realize that."

"I've been escaping into the television set. Fuzzing out."

"Because?"

"I guess I was avoiding dealing with us. But it wasn't good for me, and it wasn't fair to you."

"And why do you think you've been doing this?"

I picked a raisin out of my muffin. Was I on trial here? He sounded like an automaton. I knew he was really angry, holding it in. He had to see me as failing him, but he had failed me, too. "Because I was scared, I guess. Scared of letting everything come into focus."

"Is it in focus for you now?"

"I think it's getting there."

"And?"

I was silent. How could I say that the idea of spending the rest of my life with him now seemed . . . dull. I chewed on the raisin and looked at him. Was there hope in his eyes? "You're a good person," I said. "You gave up on your writing so you could have a home and a family. That's so commendable."

"Commendable? Are you giving me a medal?"

"No, it's just, I know your intentions are good."

"But . . . ?"

"I don't know. Maybe it has something to do with the fact that you hate one of the things that drew us together."

"You mean television?" He snorted.

And why shouldn't he snort? I'd let the TV come between us like a lover. An electronic lover that seemed to have more power to seduce than my own human boyfriend. And to make matters worse, it was a lover that had "rejected" him. But how crazy was this? I could love my television, but my television would never love me back. "Maybe we should take some time to figure this out."

"Maybe we don't need to take any more time."

"What do you mean?"

"I don't want to marry someone with so many doubts. So unless you can tell me, right now, that you'll be committed to me forever, that you want to be married to me more than anything else in the world, then . . ."

He looked at me and frowned.

I swallowed. God, I would've done anything not to hurt him. Anything except . . . well . . . marry him. "I *want* to want to, because you're a good person . . . and you're going to make someone very happy . . ."

"But not you."

I looked at him and shook my head. Was this really happening? "I'm sorry."

"Well," he said. "There's nothing else to talk about the
there."

He looked down at my hand. His eyes were on the ring. "D
you want it back?" I asked.

"What would I do with it?"

"I don't know." I didn't want to take it off. "It just doesn't seem
right."

"No," he said, "it doesn't."

"I'm sorry." I slid it off. But it seemed almost cruel to give it to
him, so I held it in my palm and looked at him. I didn't know what
to do. My eyes were pleading but he avoided my gaze. I almost
wished he would yell, scream, plead, make a scene. He stood up,
ignoring the ring. "Good-bye, Daphne."

I watched him leave. The door shut behind him. I put the ring
back on my finger. My eyes were drawn back to the quivering
origami. I felt like I was mourning my unborn child. I apologized
to it in my mind. *I'm sorry. It looks like he's not going to be your daddy
after all.*

Twenty Nine

Considering the family history, you'd think I'd be spooked by landings. But no. It's takeoffs that have a way of scaring me out of my wits. At least landing involves coming closer to the ground, safety, mother earth. Going up into the air? It's not only unnatural, it's just plain wrong.

As the pilot did his preflight routines and I clenched my gut, I remembered how carefully my father used to go through his twenty-point check before takeoff. The way he'd dutifully scream "clear prop!" out the window even though there was obviously no one around the plane in danger of getting sliced open by a propeller. I knew the truth: All those safety procedures were just for show. Every liftoff was a matter of luck. Pilots pretend to have this stuff figured out, and, okay, maybe countless planes have taken off since the Wright brothers condemned us to trust our lives to the skies. But that doesn't mean there's any guarantee the next takeoff will work, or the next one.

Billie and I were strapped into the backseats. Jonathan was up front with the reassuringly stern pilot. We had life vests on and headphones over our ears to lessen the noise. Even though I was using my most concerted telepathic powers to will it to stay on the ground, the helicopter lifted straight up. I felt like a human tea bag. As the ground telescoped away from me and adrenaline shot through my veins, I tried not to think about newscasts I'd seen of helicopters floating sideways in the Hudson River. I will say, that vertical movement was so much more deliberate than the way a plane gradually ascends. There was much less mystery as to whether the thing would actually manage to climb in altitude.

I tried to relax my bones as the pilot steered over Manhattan.

Billie seemed perfectly fine, but she'd smoked pot in [...] room of the terminal to relax, so it wasn't just the altitud[e ...] her high. "This is fucking fantastic," she said. Or at leas[t ...] what I thought she said—most of her voice was getting lost [...] racket.

I didn't attempt to speak, so as not to interfere with my tele[...] pathic powers, which were now concentrated on keeping us aloft. But it was fantastic—a clear, beautiful day and an amazing view. Sunlight reflected off the Time Warner building, and I tried to pinpoint where Jonathan's office was. Out the other window, the downtown cluster of high-rises reminded me of the Emerald City in *The Wizard of Oz*. My eyes searched for the World Trade Center towers, something I could never resist doing when the southern end of the island was in view, as if I needed to confirm yet again that they were really gone.

The pilot handled the helicopter like a sports car. I began to relax. Every movement of the controls had an immediate effect on our motion, and it gave the illusion that we were more than human—we were masters of the sky. Or he was, anyway. This must've been how my father felt flying his plane. Billie smiled at me. Was she thinking of dad too? Or simply enjoying the moment.

I didn't usually like giving credit to men for their accomplish-ments, but the city really was an amazing display of ingenuity. Even though I felt miserable about Charlie, I had no regrets about avoiding New Rochelle. Those streets down there were my back-yard. That feeling of ownership alone seemed to justify my exis-tence, as if the fact that I lived and worked in a couple of those buildings was an accomplishment in itself—enough to qualify my life as well lived.

As we zipped past the Brooklyn Bridge, I wondered what Charlie was doing. Was he incredibly angry with me? Was he walking through the empty rooms of his grandmother's house hating me? After two days, I still had not hooked up the cable. I'd done a lot of reading, baked a lasagna, and appreciated having the apartment to myself. But it was very quiet. And there was no missed having Charlie in bed next to me, and wasn't ly sure if I'd made the biggest mistake of my life. At least distract myself with trying to get Billie and Jonathan to- er. Yes. This was a good weekend to avoid reality as much as ssible.

After we passed the Archie Bunker row houses in Queens, Billie leaned over and said something to me, but I couldn't hear. I shook my head and shrugged. It was useless to attempt conversation. The blades rotating above us were mad noisy—though Jonathan did somehow manage to take a call on his cell phone as we sped over the Long Island Expressway. Down below, on the one ridiculously inadequate road that was the only artery out to the Hamptons, bumper-to-bumper traffic hardly moved. Oh, yes, we were zooming around up here, totally superior, trumping the rich motorists in their Ferraris and Mercedes. I gave Billie a conspiratorial smile and let my gaze slide to Jonathan, as if I was ensnaring them together in a web.

Soon the helicopter swept over the shoreline, and I took in the beautiful blue sea and white sands that stretched out below us. It was odd to have reached nature so soon. The few times I'd been to the Hamptons had involved hours of tedious travel, but here we were. The coup de grâce was when we swung around and descended onto a large square of cement in the middle of a small field right near the ocean. We touched ground—oh, wonderful solid ground—and I unclenched my gut. Once I was out of the helicopter, I looked around at the trees, the beach, a white house. This didn't seem like a heliport. Where were we?

"This way," Jonathan said, as a slightly chubby bearded guy in jeans and a white T-shirt came running up to us and began unloading Billie's Louis Vuitton rolling suitcase and my Gap duffel bag. "Don't worry," Jonathan said, "Sam will bring it all in for us."

Who was Sam? And why weren't we getting into a car so we could drive to his house? And then I realized. The white house *was* Jonathan's house. And Sam was the caretaker. And Jonathan Hill had a friggin' heliport behind his own house.

Billie and I followed him to the front door. I'd feared his place would look like some showcase for an uptight magazine layout, and was glad to see it actually appeared to be lived in. There were walls of bookshelves in the living room and a million framed photos of Lily and Lee and Jonathan. Lily's plastic horse collection was on a coffee table, and her various flip-flops, extra swimsuits, and assorted sunglasses were strewn all over the place. I'd brought some DVDs to watch with Lily, and so was happy to see a comfortable-looking chintz slipcovered couch facing a huge (of course) flat-screen TV.

"The guest bedrooms are up here," Jonathan said, as we took the stairs to the second floor. "You two can fight over which one you want." I took the green and violet room; Billie took the pink and yellow one next to it. It was all very clean and simple and unpretentious. The wonderful thing was the view: Our rooms looked out on the ocean. You could smell the salt of the ocean and hear the waves breaking on the beach. The windows were open wide, and a soft breeze made the sheer curtains billow into the room.

Then Jonathan gave us a tour of the house. We went back downstairs through a door to a one-story wing of the house. We passed by Lily's bedroom, then Lee's, and got to Jonathan's at the end of the hall. There was a king-size bed—I involuntarily swallowed as I looked at it—but we didn't linger there. He took us through a sliding glass door from his bedroom that led out to a huge, white wood patio. There was a set of white lounge chairs, and a white table with white chairs under a white umbrella. The patio was expansive and went right up to some grassy, reedy dunes bordering the sandy beach.

"This is gorgeous," Billie said, as we both made three-hundred-and-sixty-degree turns.

"Beautiful," I agreed.

The "bedroom wing" reminded me of a motel, in a good way. Sliding glass doors also led out from Lily and Lee's rooms. There was something unsettling about the idea of him and Lee still sharing this house even though they were divorced, but I could see it would be hard for either of them to give up. And it was probably good for Lily to be with both of them here. Or maybe it was confusing. Was this another sitcom idea? Anyway, I didn't want to think about that. I turned to look at the ocean. Their own private beach.

"That's where I want to be," I said.

"Me too," Billie said. "My body is craving the sun."

"I'm up for a swim." Jonathan looked at both of us. "You want to change into your suits? Or you want a bite to eat first? We could go into town."

"I am kind of hungry," I said, wanting to stall the moment he would see me in my bathing suit.

"I just want to get as naked as possible and let the rays hit me," Billie said. "That's my total ambition for this weekend."

Jonathan raised his eyebrows. I proposed lunch. "No one else is hungry?"

"You know what? I'll have Sam go into town and bring us some sandwiches, and we can eat out here under the umbrella. How's that?"

"Perfect," Billie said, and I nodded in agreement. I had to give it to him: He'd managed to please both of us at the same time.

"And then we'll take a swim. Just be careful of the riptides," he said, looking at both of us. "You know about swimming parallel to the shore if you start to get carried out, right?"

"I'm not planning on going in," Billie said.

"She never gets wet," I said. "And if I go in, I'm staying where it's shallow. The ocean intimidates me."

We went to unpack our bags, which took me about twenty seconds. I had two suits. My old one—a basic two-piece purple Speedo—and a new black bikini I'd bought in a panic at Macy's the day before. It was as if the ritual of making some sort of purchase—and presenting a new me—would insure that the trip would be a success. Which was ridiculous, since the whole point of the trip was to bring Billie and Jonathan closer. I must've burned hundreds of calories stepping in and out of the bottoms and reaching behind my back to hook the straps.

I put on the new one and looked in the mirror.

Hmmm.

The bottom hit me very low on my stomach. There was a denite convex pouch there. What had I been thinking? That my boc would magically transform overnight to the dimensions required by the suit?

I tried on my old one. Much better. It really sucked that I had to compare myself with Billie all my life. Some would find her too skinny, but really. It was so much easier to present those boy hips and skinny thighs to the world. I could only look forward to when she was eighty and I was still a spry seventy-three.

Before going back down, I had the urge to call Charlie on my cell phone. But what would I say? I'm so sorry. Please don't hate me. I'm suffering too. And, oh, yeah, the helicopter ride was so cool and I'm about to sunbathe on the gorgeous beach at Jonathan's back door. So instead, I practiced holding my stomach in while Billie changed. Finally, she came to my door. "Let's go." She was wearing the cute polka-dot suit she'd bought for the aborted Max trip. The tiny triangle front barely covered her, and the side stringy ties dangled against her hips. Jonathan would probably want to jump her right on the back porch.

As we crossed the patio, Billie called in to the sliding door to Jonathan's room. "We're heading down!" We could see that he was at his laptop. Doing work? Checking email?

"See you down there!" he yelled out.

At least I wouldn't have to walk next to him. I could deal better with him arriving after I was already comfortably arranged on the sand.

The beach was beautiful and empty. I didn't envy the wealthy Hamptonites for driving the horrible traffic on Route 27, jockeying to get into parties, or lining up for expensive restaurants. But this was most definitely to envy.

"I think I'll be more comfortable up on the patio," Billie said. "I'm just going to lay out up there."

kay." I had no memory of Billie ever going in the ocean, not when we were little. "I'm staying on the beach."

She went back up. To nab Jonathan? That was fine with me. All wanted was the sun. I spread my towel out, took off my cover-up, and slathered myself with lotion. Then I lay flat on the sand with my sunglasses on and shut my eyes. When Charlie came into my mind, I made him leave. I didn't want to think miserable thoughts. I wanted to think about nothing. Absolutely nothing. This was perfect. The rhythm of the breaking waves lulled me into a trance. The rays felt so good. I loved the way the heat enveloped me. You couldn't worry about anything inside that warmth. Yes, this was true luxury.

"You look comfortable."

I squeezed open one eye to see his hairy calf. I closed it again. "This is so nice."

He sat down next to me. "Yeah, it's great."

I kept my eyes shut, knowing he was probably looking me over. At least, since I was on my back, my stomach was flat—one of the few times gravity works in your favor.

"You want to take a swim?"

"No thanks." I was too comfortable, for one thing. For another thing, that would involve walking down to the ocean with him.

"Okay . . ." He got up. "But you don't know what you're missing."

After about ten minutes, I lifted my head and leaned back against my elbows. I was hot. My skin was glistening from the lotion. With my sunglasses on, I looked like I had a tan. Jonathan was in the water, swimming parallel to the shore. Maybe it would be nice to get wet. Cool down. Stretch my limbs. Suddenly I had to move.

I took my time wading in. The waves were coming in pretty strong. I let them crash against my legs. Jonathan was still pretty far out there, swimming back and forth. My plan was to stay close to the shore. I didn't like going out farther than I could stand up in. Finally I took the plunge. It was cooler than I would've liked, but the initial shock went away pretty fast, and I began my trusty breast stroke. I was an okay swimmer thanks to years summer camp—had received a yellow chip by the time I was ten Not that I'd had all that much chance to swim since then.

After swimming about twenty seconds, I stopped and looked back at the shore. There were a few houses down the beach, but no one was around other than us. I let myself float on my back a bit, but the waves were pushing me out, so I began to swim against them to get closer to shore. Jonathan saw me, and shouted something, but I couldn't hear. "It's nice!" I yelled, and then made a big show of letting him see what a good swimmer I was.

After a bit, I looked up and treaded water for a second. I really wasn't very far from shore, but those waves were surprisingly strong. I decided to swim back in. A wave pushed me out farther. I swam against it, but realized that the waves were not only stronger than me, they were coming up high. My view of the shore kept getting obscured. I went under and tried to swim toward the shore that way, but when I came up, I actually seemed to be farther out than when I'd started. That's when I panicked. Was this riptide? Or was it undertow? What was the difference? I couldn't remember what he'd told me to do. It was something obvious. Something simple. Don't panic. I tried again to swim toward shore but seemed to be moving in place—no, carried out farther. How could I be so stupid? And how could this be happening so fast?

"Hey!" It was Jonathan. He was swimming toward me, about ten feet away.

"I seem . . ." I tried to keep my voice casual, but I couldn't finish my sentence because a wave splashed into my face. In any case, who wanted to admit to being carried out to sea?

As he got closer, I worried that he'd be swept out, too. Wouldn't that be romantic? We could die together. Great. He extended his arm toward me, and I reached for it. Our hands clasped tight. I felt his strength pull me.

We swam parallel to the shore—*that's* what he'd said to do—for about twenty feet or so. Then we swam in to a point where my

s could touch the ground. The waves were no longer so high,
d there was nothing pushing me out.

"I think you just saved my life!"

"Riptide! That's what I was talking about. . . ."

"I didn't realize—" Another wave hit me in the face. I pushed
my bangs out of my eyes.

We swam to the shore and plopped down on the wet sand. Billie was still up on the patio. "Thank you," I said, breathing deeply
to catch my breath.

"What kind of host would I be if I let you drown?"

For the moment, my relief that I still had a functioning body
actually overtook my self-consciousness over how it looked. That
little swim had totally exhausted me. "Lucky you saw me."

"I had my eye on you."

"I didn't realize how easily . . ."

"You can get pulled out just like that. It happens. Seems like
every summer, you hear some story."

I shivered. "Don't tell Billie, okay? She'll just freak out that I
could've died and then tease me about it without mercy all
weekend."

"Your secret is safe with me."

The three of us went to dinner at this restaurant in town called The
Patio, famous for its crab cakes, though from what I read in the
local paper, it seemed every restaurant in the Hamptons was famous for its crab cakes. We sat on a wraparound porch sipping
white wine, and I tried not to pig out on a basket of salty deep-fried
zucchini. I was trying to think up a topic of conversation when a
woman with short curly blond hair came up to Jonathan to say
hello. "Delphine is hosting a benefit for the Parrish Art Museum
this evening—you must come!"

He told her we'd try to make it.

"You look familiar," she said to Billie, examining her face.

This woman looked familiar to me, actually, and so did her
voice, but I couldn't place it.

"I've done some modeling," Billie said, pretending to be modest.

"You see!" She seemed delighted. "I never forget a face. Do come tonight. Gilles Bensimon will most certainly be there with his wife, Kelly—she's such a dear."

"We wouldn't miss it," Billie said.

"Lovely—that would be divine."

Divine. Did people really use that word? And then it hit me where I knew her. Of course. She reminded me of Thurston Howell's wife on *Gilligan's Island.* What was her name? Lovey. She'd been such a good sport being stuck with the lowbrow castaways rather than mingling with her society friends. "Anyone who thinks money can't buy happiness," Lovey once said, "doesn't know where to shop."

"Do people like that really exist?" I asked after she'd left the table.

"They sure do," Jonathan said.

"And most of them have summer estates within twenty miles of here," Billie added somewhat wistfully.

"They must be all over Manhattan," I said, "but you could live your whole life and never cross paths."

"*You* could," Billie said.

I took another zucchini stick. Billie watched but didn't dare indulge. "It's like they lead parallel existences within the same grid," I said.

Jonathan took one too. "I try to avoid them as much as possible."

"You must like this whole scene," I said to him. "You do have a house here."

"Lee was the one who pushed for it. We bought after Lily was born so we could have a place for her to run around. I've adjusted to it, though. You can't beat the beach."

Billie sipped her wine. "So tell us about that woman whose party we're going to."

"Are we going?" he asked.

"Of course! You want to go, don't you, Daphne?"

"Ugh. You two go ahead."

"I'm really not big on the social scene here," he said.

Billie looked at him with her poor-little-me pouting face. "You don't expect me to go alone, do you?"

He shrugged. "I'll take you, but I may not stay long. I can only relate to those people for so long."

"We don't have to relate to them," she purred. "I'd just love to observe it all, since we're here. And then maybe we can get a drink, and I'll give you more juicy material for your next episode."

"When you put it that way," he said, "I'm all yours."

Ugh. Now they were grinning at each other like a couple of idiots and I had to fight off an urge to say something snide like 'should I leave you two alone?' Which was ridiculous, seeing as the idea was for them to fall in love and get married and live happily ever after—and that would certainly involve them being alone. But did they have to enjoy each other's company? They were only allowed to get married if they hated each other. And loved me best.

I took another zucchini stick. Honestly. I was being such a baby. Had to be fallout from Charlie. It was totally horrifying to think of myself as single again. I really could not take in how drastically my life had now changed. This was the longest I'd gone without speaking to him since we met. "Well, you guys go to the party. I'll hang out at the house." Maybe they would beg me to go with them, tell me not to be alone. I'd refuse, and then maybe they would decide to stay with me and we could all watch one of the DVDs I'd brought with me. It would be fun. Just the three of us.

They dropped me off at the house. It was so quiet. No one else was there. The caretaker guy didn't live on the property. I was all by myself. I went up to my room and sat on the edge of the bed and pushed all thoughts of boogie men, rapists, burglars, and clowns out of my mind. Geez, you'd think I'd never been alone in a house before. Actually, I rarely had been alone in a house.

Was my apartment empty right that minute? Or had Charlie

come back knowing I wouldn't be there? I looked at the phone. I would've been comforting to hear his voice.

No it wouldn't.

I could do this. I could be by myself. I was not going to freak out. This was no big deal. I would be fine. Just because Billie and Jonathan were going out to a fancy schmancy party at some rich socialite's house where there would be a live band and dancing and celebrities and really good food, that didn't mean I was missing anything. And this would give them a chance to bond. And I had come prepared. I'd brought a tape I'd seen years ago, back when I first started at the museum, that I'd been looking forward to seeing again.

I dug it out of my duffel bag, avoiding my phone. Which was still off. Should I check voice mail? No. If Charlie had called, he might've left a message, and I wasn't sure I wanted to hear what he had to say. If he hadn't called, I'd feel insulted over how easily he was going on with his life without needing me. Better not to know.

I went downstairs and popped *When Television Was Young, Part One* into the VCR. Yes, this had been the right decision. No party— no pressure. Let Billie and Jonathan waste their evening making irrelevant small talk. Let them get sore mouths from fake smiling all evening. Let them make out in his car on some deserted road north of the highway. I was perfectly happy curled up on the couch all by myself. This show was entertaining as much for the seventies commercials—like an ad for Schlitz beer with guys sporting handlebar mustaches—as it was for the history. There was a great clip of George Burns and Gracie Allen doing their vaudevillelike routine on their show. Production values were so unsophisticated. You could see the shadow of the microphone on George Burns's face while he did a soft-shoe. For awhile, I forgot about everyone, living in my imagination, high on nostalgia

I'd finished *When Television Was Young, Part Two*. It was almost midnight, and they still weren't home. I tried channel-surfing but got restless. Couldn't resist going to the door and looking for the car o drive up. Nothing. I went back to the TV. Didn't dare turn it off—then I'd really be alone. How dare they leave me vulnerable to boogie men, rapists, burglars, and clowns? They should've seen I didn't really want to be by myself. They should've insisted I come with, or stayed at the house with me. We could've watched the video together. There was some excellent footage on the McCarthy Hearings and the blacklistings. But no, they had to go to a stupid party and leave me alone.

I went out to the patio. It was dark. It never got this dark in the city. Even the white patio was dark. Lots and lots of stars, but no moon to be found. I listened to the faint sound of the ocean in the distance. It was starting to get really depressing and creepy, and the bugs were really annoying. I would've considered going down to the beach and taking a swim and letting a riptide pull me out to sea, and wouldn't *they* be sorry they'd stayed out so late together.

I couldn't believe my own thoughts! Yes, I was down in the dumps because of Charlie, but no need to get melodramatic about it. No way was I going near that beach in the dark and getting back in that cold water. Plus, I had no intention of dying. Not when there was so much good stuff to watch on TV. That's the problem with dying: You don't get to see the next episode. The next season. Okay, maybe life sucks, but there's always free entertainment available twenty-four hours a day.

I went back inside.

If only there was something good on.

If only I didn't keep feeling Jonathan's hand grip mine in the water.

Finally, I heard the car drive up. I listened for the sounds of them flirting. Oh, god, had I stationed myself here just so I could witness them going upstairs together? I wished I could make myself invisible. But then it turned out to be just Jonathan.

"Where's Billie?"

"Last time I saw her, she was in a hot tub with Puffy Combs."

"Oh." Had he been in there with her? His hair looked dry enough.

"That woman likes to party, doesn't she."

"Yep."

"I don't have the energy for all that socializing," he said. ". me it's a party when I finally get to be alone."

"I know what you mean."

He sat down next to me on the couch. My heart was not pumping any differently than usual, I was just hyperaware that it was pumping.

"What are you watching?"

"Nothing right now really, but I *was* watching this great documentary on early television. Look at this."

I rewound to a clip of *See It Now* from 1951 when Edward R. Murrow was reporting on a new network of cables that tied the East Coast and the West Coast together for the first time. One camera showed the Brooklyn Bridge live. Another camera showed the Golden Gate Bridge live.

"We are impressed by a medium," Murrow said, "through which a man sitting in his living room has been able for the first time to look at two oceans at once. . . ."

"And so the monster was born," Jonathan said.

"Monster?"

"The hugest advertising market ever. And the resulting mediocrity because of the networks trying to appeal to as many people as possible."

"They had no idea at the time how pervasive it would become."

"Yeah. It's fascinating."

But so not sexy.

I turned it off.

Not that I was intending to seduce him or anything.

"You want some wine?" he asked.

"Sure." But wasn't it supposed to be Billie having a glass of wine with him on this couch? Why had she let him come back without her?

"So when did your obsession with television begin?" he asked, handing me a glass and then sitting back down next to me.

ve always been this way. But I guess it really became extreme
 my parents died." Billie sure didn't have to worry about me
 a threat. Not considering my expertise at using a depressing or-
han story to make a downer out of a potentially intimate moment. "I moved in with Billie, and she was away working a lot, and,
well, you know . . . the beauty of TV. No matter how lonely you get,
it's always there for you. How about you?"

"I was always a TV watcher too. But, kind of like you, when I
was ten my brother got sick. He was in and out of hospitals.
Leukemia. That's when I got an unhealthy, shall we say, addiction.
And then he died. . . ."

"I'm sorry."

He nodded.

We sat there in silence, sipping our wine. I began to tremble
very slightly. Could he tell? He seemed to be deep in thought. I
cleared my throat just to make some noise. Crossed my legs. Un-
crossed them. Sat forward. Moved one of Lily's plastic horses
aside and picked up a Yahtzee cup filled with dice. I shook it.
Something so satisfying about the sound of dice colliding. "So I
hope Billie's giving you some good material."

"Yes, she's very inspiring."

"Good." I spilled the dice onto the table. Full house.

"And so are you," he said. "In your own way, of course."

I put the dice back in the cup. What did he mean by that?
"You'd better not be thinking of writing something about me."

He rested his arm on the top of the back of the couch. If I
hadn't been sitting forward, my head would've been against his
arm.

"Such as?"

"No comment. I'm not planting any ideas in your head."

"You act like I would write something cruel and insulting."

"No." I spilled the dice out again. "Full house. I got full house
again. What are the odds of that?"

He put the dice back in the cup and placed it out of my reach.
"Why are you trying to fix me up with your sister?"

"I'm not."

"Seems that way."

"No," I said, as if that was the most ridiculous concept in the world. What would happen if I did nestle my head against his shoulder? I stood up. "I'm tired. All that sun. I think I should get to bed."

"Okay." He stood too.

"Good night."

I was standing, facing him. He wasn't going to kiss me, was he? Okay, he did seem to be looking at me that way. Well, if he was, it was just going to be a regular good-night kiss, right? He leaned toward me. Surely he was just aiming for my cheek. No. Help! His mouth was coming straight toward me. Before I could do anything, his lips landed on my lips. This was not right. Billie would not like this. She would be very upset. I had to stop this, but it was just for a moment . . . it was over. That was not a big deal. She really couldn't have a problem with that. Uh, oh. He wasn't done. His lips hovered ever so slightly and then came back in for another one. This time he lingered. His lips were soft. No tongue, just soft gentleness. I wanted more. But no. Billie would kill me. I backed away to safety before he put his arms around me. "Good night," I said.

"Didn't you already say that?"

He was sort of smiling at me. Was I amusing him? I turned my body and started away from him. I wondered if he would turn the TV on after I left. I wondered if anything good was on. At the staircase, I turned around. "Lily is coming tomorrow?"

"Lee is bringing her in the morning."

"Good."

"That reminds me," he said when I was halfway up the stairs. "Would you mind staying with her for a couple hours so we can have some time alone? There are some things I need to discuss with Lee."

"Sure, I'd be happy to." Time alone? For some really hot post-divorce sex?

"You sure you don't mind?" he asked.

"Not at all."

"Thanks. Good night."

"Good night." Good thing I'd cut that whole kissing episode short. I would've felt like a fool if I'd done something stupid like fallen in love with Jonathan Hill. Yessiree. I'd certainly saved myself grief there.

I could not sleep. I was in bed with my eyes wide open for hours, totally aware that he was downstairs. At one point I crept ever so quietly to the top of the staircase and listened. The TV was on but I couldn't figure out what the show was. It was tempting to go back down there and watch with him, but I crept back to my room, closed the door behind me, and got into bed. About an hour later—still wide awake—I went to look again, or should I say listen. The TV was off. He'd turned out the lights. Gone to bed. It was two in the morning. Billie's door was still open. Where was she? I went back to bed. Tried to sleep, but still couldn't, even though I felt exhausted. I noticed I was grinding my teeth and tried to slacken my jaw. Then I noticed my entire spine was tensed. I tried to relax it, but couldn't let go of the tension. It was as if my body was intent on keeping me aloft—safe from sinking into the mattress and drowning in my dreams.

When Billie's door creaked and I heard her heels on the floorboards, I sat up and shout-whispered her name. "Billie!"

She poked her head into my room. "What the hell are you doing up?"

It was four. "I couldn't sleep."

She sat on the edge of my bed, slipped off her shoes, and massaged her arches. "I had the best time."

"Where were you?"

"I met up with Noah Tepperberg, the owner of that nightclub Marquee, and we went out for drinks and lobster rolls with Mandy Moore and Lara Shriftman, this fantastic publicist. Maybe I should hire a publicist."

"For what?"

"We have to think of something. What do you think? A hand bag line? Nail polish? Or maybe my own perfume."

"Do we have to think of it right now?"

"Someone's grouchy."

"It's four in the morning. You were supposed to be here. The whole point of this trip is to hook you up with Jonathan, and you're running around with these people."

"He insisted on leaving. What was I supposed to do, lasso him?"

I couldn't tell her about the kiss. She'd either laugh at me for taking it seriously or resent me for trying to move in on him. "You could've left *with* him."

"I know. You're right. I probably should've. I just couldn't tear myself away. There were so many incredible people there."

"His ex-wife is coming tomorrow. He wants me to babysit so they can have some alone time."

"Ew. Well," she said, getting up off my bed, "I can't think about that now." She did her Scarlett O'Hara imitation as she went to her room. "We'll think about that tomorrow. After all . . ."

We said it together: "Tomorrow is another day."

I tried to get to sleep, but my thoughts kept blathering like an insensitive roommate. I seemed to need to explain to myself over and over why nothing could ever happen between the two of us. And it wasn't just because of Billie: There was the sex to consider. I couldn't possibly "do it" with Jonathan Hill. I wasn't experienced enough. How could I possibly measure up to the women he'd been with? He was probably used to all sorts of fancy techniques and positions. I'd only end up humiliating myself. Best to avoid that entire situation. I finally drifted off explaining to myself how Billie was the one who could satisfy him. Billie would know what to do. Billie would save me.

Thirty

"Sitcoms in the 1960s broke away from portraying idealized families with wise father figures."

"Domesticoms," Lily said triumphantly.

"Right. This was the era of gimmickoms. There was often some outrageous premise that couldn't exist in real life. In *Bewitched* Samantha was a witch. *I Dream of Jeannie* was about a genie who lived in a bottle. *Mr. Ed* had a talking horse. *My Mother the Car* had a talking car. *The Munsters* was a family of monsters."

"I saw those on Nick when I was little."

"They're fun, right?"

"Did you bring *Mr. Ed*?"

"Yep." I'd come prepared with all sorts of DVDs from my own collection. My plan was to give Lily a decade by decade mini survey course on the history of sitcoms. I could still remember the pleasure of learning what each decade was about. It was as if some higher order, and not humans, had organized each decade into some kind of social statement.

"Goodie. I want to see *Mr. Ed*. Which of my horses do you like best?" She'd set out a whole family of horses—one black, one white, one dapple gray, and a brown and white pony.

"Um, well, it's between the pony and the white horse, I think."

"Me too." She took the white horse and held it in her lap.

As I put in the first of two discs from *The Best of Mr. Ed*, Lily told me she was learning to ride. "My mom promised to buy me a horse by my next birthday."

"Wow."

Jonathan and Lee were in town having lunch. Billie was still upstairs sleeping. I was still recovering from meeting Lee. No wonder Jonathan had fallen for her: She had this alabaster skin and white hair and looked so perfect, so marble statue, she didn't seem quite real. At the same time, I felt like I knew her, having watched her in *Boomers*. Of course that wasn't really her, but on the other hand Jonathan had obviously based the character on her, so in a way it was. I had no idea what to say. Not that she was interested in hearing what I had to say. When Jonathan introduced us, she assumed I was a babysitter, and thanked me for being so good with Lily. I didn't bother to correct her, but Jonathan made a point of saying I was a curator at the Museum of Television—not that she could care less.

Three hours later, Lily and I had polished off the disc, but Jonathan and Lee still hadn't returned. It seemed obscene that you could consume so many episodes in one sitting, especially when you consider that when they first came out, people had to wait for it week to week, and each episode seemed precious.

We decided to google the show to find out how they got Mr. Ed to talk. We learned that there was some controversy on this subject. One source said they gave him some peanut butter–type substance that he'd try to work out of his teeth, thus giving the appearance of talking. Another said he was hooked up to nylon strings that someone off camera would pull. Lily and I were about to go back and rewind to look for those strings when Jonathan and Lee returned.

"We watched the entire first season of *Mr. Ed*," Lily said.

"What fun!" Lee gave her a hug. "Would you like to come with me to the polo match?"

I thought she was kidding. Polo? Did that exist outside England?

Lily jumped up and down. "Yes! Yes, yes, yes! Can I put on my Ralph Lauren?"

Lee laughed. "Of course."

Lily ran upstairs and Lee excused herself. Which left me alone with Jonathan. This was the first time since "the kiss." Maybe he wasn't even thinking about "the kiss" or didn't consider it "the kiss" but just "a kiss."

"Thanks again for hanging out with her," he said.

"We had a good time. I hope you had a nice lunch."

"It was okay. . . . Where's Billie?"

"Still asleep."

"Would you like to go for a swim?"

"I'm not really in the mood to drown today."

"How about a drive? I can show you around, and you can interview me."

"That would be great." I went up to my room to get my sandals, but made sure to be extra quiet. I didn't want to risk waking Billie.

As we sped along on the Montauk Highway, I had to wonder if this was really me. Here. In this BMW. With Jonathan Hill. TV producer. It didn't make any sense. And yet . . .

"So where were you born?" I asked.

"Levittown."

"*The* Levittown?" Levittown was the development built in the fifties and famous for its identical houses built on potato fields for returning GIs.

"Yep."

So on some level, he was just a regular guy. "Was it horrible?"

"No, I loved it. There were so many other kids around. It was great. There was always someone to play ball with. Oh, and you'd like this: Our house—all the houses, actually—they came with a hi-fi and TV built into the wall."

"That's so cool."

His car phone rang. "Sorry," he said, "I should take this."

"No problem." He began talking and I realized . . . he was discussing *Supermodels* with the president of ABC.

But maybe I could let go of some of my intimidation here. Levittown? I'd grown up in perhaps the most upper-class neighborhood in the United States. Theoretically, my childhood had been much more "privileged" than his. I mean, okay, maybe he was smarter than most. But let's face it, he wasn't *that* much smarter. Luck had entered into it. Luck and drive. But he was not some

higher form of life, even if he was on his cell phone talking to t．
president of ABC. So what? We were all just people. Skin an．
bones attached to egos. Destined to be a pile of bones with no
skin and no ego.

We passed the town of Southampton, with all the beautiful
people going from shop to shop. Anyone perceiving me sitting in
this car would see me as an object of envy. Even I would see me
as an object of envy—but at the same moment I would disdain
myself. Because it was all trappings. The trap of trappings. My father would certainly approve. He'd owned a BMW too. And I knew
that at one time he'd considered buying a house in the Hamptons.
If he'd gone for that instead of Martha's Vineyard, maybe my parents would be alive. And I could visit them, and introduce them
to Jonathan. But that would never happen. And I could only communicate telepathically. Like on *My Mother the Car*. On that show,
Jerry Van Dyke (Dick Van Dyke's real-life brother) talks to his dead
mother, who's been reincarnated as a jalopy. He was the only one
who could hear her voice. Same way Wilbur was the only one who
could hear Mr. Ed. I spoke silently to the dashboard. *Hi, Mom and
Dad. See me now? In Jonathan Hill's BMW? Aren't you impressed?* If
I were to reincarnate my mother, I wouldn't put her in a car,
though. No way. It would have to be . . . the refrigerator. Yes.
Definitely.

Not a bad idea, actually.

"Sorry," Jonathan said, putting away his phone.

"No problem." A very good idea, actually.

"It never ends," he said. "What are you thinking about so quietly over there?"

"I just had a great idea for a show."

"Really?"

"Yeah. It's sort of inspired by *Mr. Ed*. And you remember *My
Mother the Car*?"

"Sure. So what's the idea?"

"Well. After my parents died . . . ever since . . . you know . . .
the hardest thing has been missing them of course. So I really re-

e to those shows. And it drives me crazy, because sometimes I worry I'm forgetting what they looked like. I have so few images of them in my head except the way they look in photographs I have. But their voices. I can hear their voices in my head exactly. And sometimes I can imagine they're giving me advice. My mom especially. I can imagine what she would say. I'm sorry, I'm not telling this very well . . . it's really not so complicated."

"I'm listening," he said, and gave my knee a little squeeze.

And it was as if he'd set off an electrical charge that surged straight up my leg.

"So," I said, "I have this tendency, I've noticed, when I get upset about something, to stare into the refrigerator. It's that whole thing of feeling empty so you think food will fill you up. So you open the refrigerator and there's already, before you even eat anything, something comforting about it. How that little light goes on, and the motor is running and, well, you know, it's always good inside the refrigerator. It's peaceful in there. A haven. The food seems content. All is well. You know what I'm saying? Maybe men don't feel this way."

"I know what you mean."

"So what I'm imagining is on my show, the mom is dead, and the main character associates the refrigerator with her mom. She looks into the refrigerator, searching for her mom, like she's in there, and then all of a sudden one day—I don't know how it happens, I'd have to figure that out, maybe she has to buy a new refrigerator—she asks for advice from the mom, and the mom talks back to her."

"The refrigerator talks."

"Yes. This refrigerator talks to the daughter, and gives her advice when she needs it. Oh, and I just thought of the perfect title! *My Cool Mom*. Isn't that cute? I could just see it in the line-up. *My Cool Mom*."

"So is the daughter an adult?"

"I'm thinking she's in her twenties."

"Or a teenager."

"Possibly."

"I like it."

"Really?"

"It might be too innocent, though."

"You think?"

"Kind of retro. Even kids are pretty sophisticated these days."

"Yeah . . ."

"But it's a very nice idea."

"Thanks." *Nice*. In today's world, that word was an insult. "Anyway . . ."

"Thanks for bringing those shows for Lily. And watching with her. You're so good with her."

"It's fun," I said, "to have a TV-watching buddy."

"She really likes you."

"Thanks. That's nice to hear." *Nice*. "And I like her." I paused. "You and Lee seem to be getting along really well."

"Where'd you get that idea?"

"Just observing."

"That's just for Lily. Today we had a lot to talk about, that's all. I'm buying her share of the house. Lee's spending more time in L.A. and hardly uses it anymore."

"Oh," I said, telling myself there was no reason to feel relief over that.

"She was trying to convince me to move out there. It would make things easier on Lily, and I am there a lot on business. But I hate it out there."

"Me too. I'd *never* want to live there. My boyfriend—" What did I just say? "*Ex*-boyfriend. He used to live there. He really liked it. But I'm definitely an East Coast person. I don't even know how to drive."

"What did your ex-boyfriend do?"

"Teacher," I said. "High school."

"That's a challenge. He must have a good soul."

"Yes."

We were silent as he pulled into a parking lot.

It was a place called Gosman's Clam Bar at this old pier that had been turned into a bunch of shops. Everything looked very newish with tidy gray shingles. The shoppers all seemed to be wearing Dockers and J. Crew. There was a picturesque view of an inlet. You could feel you were in nature, but you didn't have to actually touch it.

"They have really good crab cakes," Jonathan said, and I giggled.

There was an inside and an outside. Since it was so nice, we decided to rough it on the patio. Jonathan went to a walk-up window and ordered for us. I took a seat at one of the tables with a white umbrella poking up from the middle and looked at the inlet. A sailboat went by. I watched it pass. Seagulls perched nearby. They watched people eat and as soon as anyone left any garbage on a table, they descended on the leftovers. Like vultures.

Jonathan brought over two beers, then came back with two paper plates with huge piles of fish and chips. When he went back to get some napkins, a seagull flew onto the back of the extra chair at our table. I tried to shoo it away, but this bird had the audacity to hop right onto the tabletop. "Hey," I said. Then it walked over to my plate and took a French fry. I stood up and backed away and looked for Jonathan in a panic. I didn't want him to see this. First I almost drown—now I let a bird eat my food. "Go away!" I said to the bird. It took another French fry. Then three more seagulls flew up. It was like something out of Alfred Hitchcock's *The Birds*!

"They're eating my French fries!" I said to Jonathan when he came back. I tried not to sound too hysterical. People were looking. It was odd, because the birds weren't eating anyone else's food.

He laughed. "Aggressive, aren't they?"

"What are we going to do?"

"Let's go eat inside."

"It's as if they know I'm not a nature person," I said, following him in.

We settled in at a table. A waiter came and we ordered again. There was still a nice view of the inlet, but it was through a large window. "Those birds were out to get me, I swear."

Jonathan looked at me with amusement but [...] anything.

"Why do I always feel you're laughing at me?"

"I just think you're cute."

It was horrifying how I blushed, and there was nothing I c[...] do to stop it.

That afternoon Jonathan, Billie, and I went to a celebrity softball game. As it turned out, they didn't have enough players, so Billie and I got to play too. We did pretty well. By some miracle, Billie not only caught a fly ball hit by Alec Baldwin, she hit a home run too. She also spiced up the game by yelling her head off at the opposing team. "You suck!" she yelled every chance she got. I was happy just to stand at third base in the sunshine and be near Jonathan playing shortstop. Once he fielded a ball and threw it to me and we got someone out. As far as I was concerned, the secret smile he gave me after that was the high point of my year. Our team won by three runs.

I sat in the dugout puzzling about the coming evening. I hadn't told Billie about "the kiss" and I wasn't sure if she was still planning on making a move on Jonathan. I figured I should tell her what had happened. But I was afraid to. And I didn't know what it meant. And I didn't want to have to talk about it, or examine it, or reveal it. Not yet. But she should know.

I got up off the bench and went to her by the water fountain. "So what are your plans for tonight?"

"I was going to put my hooks into Jonathan tonight, but Mr. Baldwin asked me to dinner and I couldn't say no."

"But what about the plan?"

"I know. This is ridiculous. But I'm just having too much fun. You keep those skinny bitches off him for me, okay?" She nodded toward a cluster of young model types hanging out in the bleachers. I wanted to warn her that Alec's divorce from Kim Basinger had not been pretty. But she gave me a kiss on the cheek and was off and running. I waved good-bye to her as she drove off in his red Porsche.

* * *

...ng Jonathan and I had dinner with Lily, and then took
...e Sip 'n Soda in Southampton for ice cream. It was a real
...ountain, not much changed from when it opened in the
...s. We were sitting on stools at the counter sipping root beer
...ats when a friend of hers came in with her mom and they asked
...ily for a sleepover. When Lily begged Jonathan for permission,
he pretended to have to struggle with the concept and relent. Lily
jumped up and down with glee. Jonathan and I looked at each
other with quiet smiles. Lee had already gone back to the city.
That left us alone together for the evening.

We drove back to the house. It was too late to catch a movie or
go to one of the local plays. We'd already eaten. What was there to
do but turn on the TV? We settled into the couch, sitting quite
close to each other but not touching. I was flipping the channels.
I paused on PBS. There was Frank Sinatra in a tuxedo surrounded
by a set that was trying really hard to look "modern." I clicked on
the info button. It was a special he'd made in 1967 with Ella
Fitzgerald as a guest. The camera came in very close on his face as
he sang "Old Man River" from *Showboat*. His voice was so smooth.
And he sang it beautifully, going down into a deep register I didn't
associate with him. At one point he looked like he was going to
cry—or was that just part of his performance? A tear snuck out of
my right eye. I wiped it away quickly. It wasn't that I was unhappy—I was savoring that nostalgic feeling I loved so much.
Happy mixed with sad. Life mixed with death. It shouldn't have
been so possible to visit the past like this. Books and film and photographs had transformed death into something ephemeral, giving us the illusion that passing away was only temporary.

After the song was over, he introduced Ella Fitzgerald and they
made some jokes about being old. But, of course, they couldn't
know that more than thirty years later someone would be watching them *again*, after they'd *really* gotten old—after, little did they
know, they were dead. They did a medley of hit songs from the sixties. I recognized the one sung by The 5th Dimension about flying

up and away in a beautiful balloon. To us it was an oldie, them it was swinging sixties. And now we, the audience, cou~ only be entertained by Frank and Ella . . . we could also feer perior to them for the simple fact that we were still alive.

Little did we want to think about the fact that we were gonna be dead too.

Jonathan put his arm around me. "Is this making you sad?" he asked.

"A good kind of sad."

"Why?"

"Watching entertainers we idolize age, and then get old . . . and die. It's comforting. I think we all need to think about death more."

"Because we're in denial about it."

"Yeah. We need to keep rerealizing it. For our sanity."

We watched until the last song, and Frank thanked the audience, and the show ended. Good-bye, Frank. The screen went dark for a moment. Then this uptight guy with a gray beard and glasses came on asking "viewers like you" to send in money to support "shows like this." Jonathan aimed the remote and turned it off.

"Heckling people for money is even worse than advertising," I said, "don't you think?"

Without saying anything, Jonathan put his left arm around my shoulder, the other around my waist, practically lunged on top of me, and pressed his lips against mine. He pushed me so that suddenly I was on my back, and not only his lips but his entire body was pressed flat up against mine. It was clear that I was not going to find out his opinion on public television fund-raising practices. He was kissing me with this sense of urgency—it was almost alarming to know he wanted me like that.

At first, it was like I was watching from outside the situation. He was so in control, and I let him take charge. None of this was my responsibility; I was just a passive victim who should've spoken up but didn't.

Then I forgot about being outside the situation. We were kissing and grinding up against each other, and I was really wishing

as no clothing creating a barrier between us because all I
...d was to be right up against him. I wrapped my legs around
, and he cradled my bottom under his hands, and then lifted
e right up off the couch! I was about to warn him not to hurt his
back, but he had me and was carrying me to his bedroom. I
watched the carpet go by as he managed to negotiate around the
coffee table and down the hall. Then he lowered me onto the bed
without letting go, lying on top of me, our bodies, lips, and
tongues finding each other again.

Oh, god. This was really happening.

Would he want a blow job?

I was just going to have to do the best I could. At least I'd read
those sex tips recently. Would he expect me to deep-throat him?
Well, too bad for him.

But my anxiety about giving a good-enough blow job gave way
to my anxiety over the fact that he was making a trail of kisses that
went from my forehead to my nose to my mouth to my chin to my
chest to my belly to my . . . um . . . okay . . . it was obvious he knew
exactly what he was doing. Before I knew it, he'd unzipped my
pants. I lifted my bottom to let him pull my jeans off—even
though I knew we shouldn't be doing this, and I should put a stop
to this *right this second*, before this went *any farther*, because we
weren't going all the way here, of course not, w*ere we*? Apart from
the fact that I was going to have a hell of a time explaining this to
Billie in the morning—we'd just had our first kiss the night before—no way we were going all the way!

Thank god I was wearing my black underwear that didn't have
any holes. (Well, okay, I'd made sure of that just in case.) And it
was a good thing, because he was right there, kissing me on my
inner thighs, then all over my crotch, through my panties, the
light, soft pressure making me itchy and wet, and then he pulled
the elastic around my leg aside and lightly kissed underneath, his
breath making me want him to rip my underwear off and fling
them across the room and get on with it. I started to pull them
down, when he stopped me with his hand.

"There's no rush," he said. "Relax."

"But . . ."

"I'm enjoying myself."

"Are you sure?"

He came back up to face me, cupped my cheeks in his hand, kissed me on the lips, and said, so sweetly, "You're so beautiful." Then he gave me a long, deep, tender kiss. I was sinking . . . or was I floating? It was unsettling, to say the least. I was so relieved when he finally pulled my underwear down. I grinded against him, wanted to steer his penis into me. But he had other plans. Back down he went—it was making me totally crazy. I pulled on the shoulder of his shirt. "You don't have to do that . . ."

"I want to do it . . ."

"I think you should come up here . . ."

"Why"—he made a semicircle of kisses—"do women have such trouble"—completed the circle—"receiving pleasure?"

He had a point. A point I'd heard recently somewhere. Who had said that? Someone I knew had said that. No, not someone I knew. Someone . . . on *Boomers*. I'd read it in one of the episodes in the book of scripts Simon gave me. When Dennis was seducing Lisa. He'd made his huge confession that he used to suffer from premature ejaculation, so he'd specialized in going down on women as a way to prolong the event, and so he got really, really good at it.

I wanted to ask him, "Did you base that character on yourself?" It would be interesting to find out.

Eventually.

I kept my mouth closed and my legs open.

It was like he was lapping me up. And then he let his tongue linger. Inside. This light pressure. I felt like I was going to come just like this. But I felt so exposed. And I finally couldn't stand it anymore, and I said, in a not very poetic or romantic way, "Um, maybe you should put a condom on."

"Okay," he said, getting up. "Don't go away."

"Don't touch that dial," I said. (Wasn't I funny.)

"I'll be right back," he said.

"After a word from our sponsors." (Hilarious.)

He came back a minute later with a condom packet. "And now," he said, ripping it open, "on with the show."

Okay, at least he willing to stoop to my level.

So to speak.

I woke up in his bed alone. It was dark in his room, but as soon as I pulled the drape back, I could see it was blazingly sunny outside.

I got dressed and went out to the living room. No one there. The kitchen? Empty. The only sound was the hum of the refrigerator. On the table was a note from Jonathan. *Went to pick up Lily. Will stop at the bakery for muffins. Be back soon.*

I was grateful to have some time to pull myself together. My body was buzzing, as if his touch had sparked a current and jolted me into hyperdrive. I didn't want to deal with relating to a person. With any luck, Billie would still be sleeping. I went upstairs wondering if she'd come back late and seen my room empty. Probably. Her door was open and I peeked inside. She wasn't there. Maybe she'd never even come home to see my empty room.

I decided to take a shower. That's when reality seeped back into my brain. As I lathered up, I couldn't help working myself into a high state of anxiety. What had I done? How would I tell Billie? This was much worse than telling her I was going to marry Charlie. At least she'd only had disdain for Charlie. But Jonathan Hill? She'd be so jealous. I had always, always, *always* made sure to be involved with guys she would not find attractive. But now I'd be claiming the prize. Victory would never be worth the guilt. And for what? Most likely some passing flirtation with a man who was probably using me as some kind of diversion before hooking up with yet another famous actress.

As I dried myself off, the front door opened and closed downstairs. I heard Jonathan telling Lily he would take her swimming later. Lily refusing. "Billie and Daphne promised to take me into town."

Right. We had promised. And where the hell was Billie? If she'd just stayed around like she was supposed to, this never would've happened.

Not that I liked that thought either.

I went downstairs and joined them in the kitchen. "Good morning."

I couldn't quite make eye contact with Jonathan, and was glad Lily was there as a buffer. We could pretend, for the moment, nothing had happened.

"We got muffins!" she said.

"We didn't know what you liked," he added, "so we got one of each kind."

"Really?" I opened the pink box. Indeed, there was a blueberry, cranberry, raisin bran, almond. "Wow. Yum. How will I decide?"

I looked at him and . . . we made eye contact. There was no denying it. Something *had* happened. I could feel his kisses all over my body.

"Are we going to town?" Lily asked

"Billie isn't here right now," I said, breaking an edge off the almond muffin. The scent made my mouth water. Or was it proximity to Jonathan?

"When will she be back?"

"Soon, I hope."

"But I don't have anything to do!"

"Come down to the beach with me," Jonathan said, taking a piece of the blueberry. "Let Daphne have her breakfast."

I took a piece of blueberry too. "We'll go to town later, with Billie, I promise. And then we'll do the seventies."

As soon as they were gone, I poured myself some coffee and then looked in the box again. It was impossible to choose, so I risked being a rude guest and cut a slice of each one. Then I sat down and indulged (they were all good—buttery and not too sweet) while reading an article in the local paper about Renee Zellweger's interior decorator.

After I was done, I went down to the shore and watched

Jonathan and Lily throw a beach ball around in the shallow water. I couldn't believe his tanned body had been entangled with mine just a few hours ago. They both waved hello, and I waved back, sensing they were happy to have an audience. I indulged in a fantasy of the three of us being a family. As if that could happen. But what if it could?

"Good morning, Darling! So what's new? I had an amazing night. Did you see those muffins? Please don't let me pig out—I'm starving!" It was Billie, and she was buzzed.

I looked up, shielding my eyes from the sun. "Just getting home?"

"Can you believe it? I know, I know, you're going to say I'm up early, but I'm actually up late, seeing as I never went to sleep." She sat down next to me in the sand holding a piece of the bran muffin. If she was going to indulge, she'd do it with fiber involved. "Look at them playing with the beach ball. That's so sweet. You know what? I had the greatest idea for a show."

"For *Supermodels?*"

"For a whole new show. Jonathan is going to die. It is such a good idea—I can't wait to tell him."

"Tell me." I sure wasn't going to tell her I'd had an idea too. Along with every single person who came into contact with him. No wonder he was prickly about that. I regretted telling him the *My Cool Mom* idea, if only because I didn't want him to think I was like all the rest.

"*Hookers.*"

"*Hookers?*"

"*Hookers.* Listen up. You're gonna love this. We'll follow the stories of four women, each one a different age and social class. There's the single Hispanic mother with drug problems, the NYU student who has huge student loan debts, a quirky, funny housewife who does it to get out of the house, and last, but not least, an aging model desperately clinging to her washed-up career."

"Huh."

"And they all have the same pimp, who will be a businessman, maybe like Bosley on *Charlie's Angels*, and we'll never see him—I haven't decided—and they'll share a penthouse in some swanky Upper East Side high-rise. Not to live in, just to turn their tricks. So we can see them together at the penthouse, and then we can follow them as they go off on their separate lives, and we'll get into each character's individual struggle, so that we really feel for her and what she's up against—and, of course"—she laughed—"there'll be a lot of degrading sex."

My stomach clenched. "Wow. That sounds"—*disgusting and obnoxious*—"fun."

"I can't believe it hasn't already been done."

"That's when you know you have a really good idea." I marveled at how well I kept the scorn out of my voice.

"I can't wait to pitch it to him."

"You're aware that everyone is always pitching to him and it gets tiresome for him, right?"

"But this idea is brilliant! And it's incredibly commercial. And he's already eating up my ideas for *Supermodels*. What's the name of that agent you met? This could be something big. Maybe you can help me brainstorm some story ideas. You're good at this."

She sure did sound convincing. But did I want to participate? Could I help dream up a show that would make all the women and teenagers and little girls who watched feel just a little bit worse about themselves?

"Billie, *Supermodels* is fun, and it's trashy, but it's also kitschy and makes fun of itself, so I don't think anyone really takes it that seriously. But *Hookers*? Don't you think that's stooping a bit too low?"

"Is there such a thing these days?"

"But it's insulting. How are women supposed to feel watching these characters?"

"Forget the women. It's for men. Teenage boys would make up the largest audience. Isn't that what they want? Something to jerk off to? That's where the money is in this world, Honey, figuring out ways to get men to come."

"I suppose." It's true that teenage boys were the most desirable demographic. The more fart jokes, dumb blondes, and boobs the better. It probably *was* a very commercial idea. Perfect for HBO. Would Jonathan go for it? After all, the producer side of him was all business. *Supermodels* demonstrated that well enough. And here we were, at his beach house in the Hamptons, enjoying his good sense of business.

"Give it a shot," I said. "See what he says." God knows he wouldn't call it "nice" or "retro."

Lily came running into the kitchen. "Yay! Billie's back! Are we going into town?"

"Billie is exhausted," Billie said, "and must take a shower and a nap."

Lily pouted. "But that will take forever."

I offered to watch some shows with her. I understood exactly how she felt.

Jonathan came in. "The Queen of the Hamptons night life has returned."

"We need to talk," Billie said.

"Not now, though," Lily reminded her. "You have to get your nap done and then we're going to town."

"Tonight," she said to him. "Over dinner. I have a great idea I want to tell you."

"I can't wait to hear it."

I couldn't tell if he meant it or not. In any case, he probably thought she meant for *Supermodels*.

"We're on," she said, then went upstairs.

He turned to me. "You want to take a walk?"

Lily grabbed my hand. "Daphne is watching TV with me now."

I shrugged. "I promised her." Seemed like we were never going to be alone together. The part of me that was scared was okay with that. The rest of me was living for the moment.

"Then I'm gonna go do some work," he said. "See you girls later."

* * *

"The 1970s," I said to Lily, "was *the* decade of the sitcom. Sitcoms were at their most brilliant. There was *All in the Family*, *Taxi*, *Barney Miller*. . . ."

"Never heard of them."

"Ensemble acting, incredible writing, provocative humor . . . but unlike the wacky sixties we were back into heartwarming characters who learned from their mistakes. Some call it the era of the 'warmedy.' Sort of like the fifties but updated with more realistic characters and unconventional families. Workplace comedies were big. Single-parent families. Ethnic leads. Back then, almost all the highest-rated shows were sitcoms, believe it or not."

"Then people were dumb back then."

"I've brought you one of my old favorites. You remember Mary Tyler Moore, the wife from *The Dick Van Dyke Show*? Well, she got her own show in the seventies, as a single woman in Minneapolis. First she was going to be divorced, but then they worried people would think she'd been divorced from Dick Van Dyke and people wouldn't like that, so they made it so she was recovering from a broken engagement."

I put the DVD in. It occurred to me that I was recovering from a broken engagement.

Lily asked, "Did you used to watch it when you were my age?"

"I wasn't alive quite yet. But I saw it in reruns."

We saw the pilot, where Mary moves into her new apartment and gets her new job, and Lily was hooked. I took the opportunity to mull why I was so turned off by Billie's *Hookers* idea. I'd never gotten all politically correct when it came to *Supermodels*. The opposite, in fact. How many times had I defended the show to Charlie? So why was I "Miss Social Conscience" now? Yes, this was even trashier than *Supermodels*. But was that the main reason I was stewing? No. The main reason had more to do with the fact that if he really went for this, it might bond them in a way that I would find extremely annoying. Feeding him ideas for *Supermodels* was one thing, creating a show with him was another. Especially when my idea was so much better. Well, I liked it, anyway, even if it was "nice." And television was supposed to be my domain, not hers. She was trespassing on my territory.

Then again, she was the one who was supposed to be seducing him. And I hadn't yet told her about that development. So I was trespassing on her territory, too.

I really needed to go lie down.

"Lily, I'm gonna take a little nap, okay?"

"But if Billie wakes up, I'm gonna wake you up, too."

"It's a deal."

I went upstairs, lay down, listened to the waves crashing against the shore, and drifted off almost immediately. It seemed like minutes later that I woke to the sound of Billie knocking on my door.

"Shouldn't we get going? Lily is having convulsions down there."

I looked at the clock. An hour had passed. "Just let me wash my face."

I forced myself out of bed. I didn't remember having any dreams.

We drove into town—or, I should say, were driven in by Sam the caretaker guy—and did Main Street. Lily had five or six stores on her agenda. First up was the Canine Ranch Pet Spa. Lily was totally entranced by all the opulent dog accoutrements, such as a four-poster dog bed that was fancier than anything I'd ever slept in. (She had no dog, just the fantasy of one.) While she examined the merchandise, Billie regaled me with her nocturnal adventures.

"First Alec and I went to this party at Ron Perelman's. Julianne Moore was there, and Claudia Cohen and the Hiltons and Darren Star—it was amazing. Tori Spelling was smashed out of her mind and felt me up—"

"Tori Spelling felt you up?"

"She put her hand under my top . . . right on my breast."

"What did you say?"

"I said, 'may I *help* you?' She leaned over and tried to kiss me."

"Oh, my god! Donna tried to kiss you!" I couldn't help but still think of her as her character on *90210*.

"You think *I'm* wild?" Billie said. "That woman makes me look like Margaret Thatcher. Then they had a jam session—Ron on guitar, Richard Gere on drums, and Billy Joel at the piano."

"How cool."

"I danced, I pigged out on salmon, and then I went home with Karl von Richthofen, one of the richest men *in the world*."

"What happened to Alec Baldwin?"

"Who cares? Karl owns, like, half of Switzerland or something."

"Whoa." Had she found a replacement for Max already? Please let it be so.

"And I let him screw my brains out."

"Wow."

"When he woke up he didn't remember who I was, where I'd come from, or what I was doing there."

"Oh."

"Or what a great time I gave him. Asshole."

"Sorry."

"But enough of this. Tonight I'm focusing on Mr. Hill."

She began singing "Climb Every Mountain." Badly.

Lily was back, pulling on my T-shirt. "I'm ready to go." She dragged us next door to a teenybopper accessory shop that made me feel old because I could remember being able to browse with fascination at all these pink and purple girlie accessories and now it all looked like cheap crap. Even the doggie accessories were higher quality. But Lily was seeing total glamour in all the cheap jewelry, handbags, hats, and hair clips. . . .

I pulled Billie down onto a huge purple velour pillow. "There's something I have to tell you." Lily was on the other side of the store, turning a rack of pierced earrings.

"You're going back to Charlie?"

"No. It seems . . ."

"That . . . ?"

"Maybe he's interested in me."

"Who?"

"Jonathan."

"In you?" You'd think I was telling her I'd just been nominated to run for Mayor of Southampton. "What are you talking about?"

I took a deep breath. Exhaled. "We slept together. Last night."

Billie's eyebrows shot up. But before I could elaborate or get any verbal feedback, Lily had returned.

"I need your opinion," she said.

We got up from the pillow and dutifully redirected our attention. At least this would give Billie a chance to digest this information. Lily led us to two boxes. Each box had a pair of flip-flops, four tubes of glitter, glue, and an "activity mat." The idea was to decorate the flip-flops with the glitter. It was all about the packaging, of course, but at least it was something for her to do instead of watch TV. (Wow, I was thinking like some kind of conventional mom . . . had to watch out for that.)

"Do you think I should get the precious-metal one?" she asked. "Or the stars and stripes?"

"Precious metal," Billie said. "Always go for gold and silver when you can."

"Definitely," I agreed.

We paid for it and went down the street to a supertrendy clothing store. Lily was totally entranced with everything "hippie chic." While she tried on some bead necklaces, I pulled Billie aside again.

"Do you hate me?"

"You must really think I'm a creep."

"No. I just . . . he was supposed to be for you."

"To be honest, I think the guy is sorta boring. You may have noticed I haven't been killing myself to hang out with him."

"I know, but that doesn't mean you don't want him. I mean, he's rich, good-looking, *and* nice . . ."

She took both my hands in hers. "Daphne. You know what your problem is? You don't think I can handle the idea of you doing better than me. Am I right?"

"Sort of."

"But you know what? Give me some credit here. I want you to be happy, okay? I give you permission. I'm not a kid. I can handle it. Compete with me all you want. Go ahead. Do better!"

I felt a tremendous sense of relief. "You mean you won't be upset or get depressed or want to kill me or yourself?"

"Honey, if you get with Jonathan Hill, I'll have access to so many people it's not funny."

It was as if I'd been wearing a bulletproof vest for years and could finally take it off.

"You'll see," she said. "I'm gonna sell him on this *Hookers* idea, and then it's me and Hollywood, baby. I'm going all the way."

Now wait a second.

Maybe she was giving me the go-ahead on Jonathan. And yes, I wanted her to be happy, too. So now I was the one being immature and childish. But it would be *so not fair* if she ended up producing a show with Jonathan Hill!

"I'm gonna try on some clothes," I said. Yes. The only immediate solution was to divert my attention from the crisis at hand. Temporarily forget about everything. Juicy jeans, Scoop T-shirts, Gold Hawk silk camisoles. I tried on a pair of jeans and they fit me perfectly. They were $200. I'd never spent that much on jeans. But they fit so perfectly. . . .

"You're getting those," Billie said.

"They're too expensive."

"But you have to," Lily said. "They're perfect."

I sighed. "Not on my salary."

"It's worth it," Billie said. "As an investment in your future. I'm not kidding."

"I just can't."

We left the store and strolled down the street. I was still thinking about those jeans. How I couldn't allow myself to have them. Then we turned into an ice cream shop. Lily and I got cones. While we sat on the bench outside and watched the beautiful people walk by, I licked my chocolate chip cookie dough. I had to lick fast because it was soft and melting to begin with. Jonathan and his (ahem) licking skills came to mind. The memory made me tingle. My cell phone rang like an alarm going off. I saw by the caller ID it was Charlie. I was tempted not to answer, but knew I'd suffer with curiosity if I didn't hear what he had to say. "Hello?"

"Hi."

"How are you?"

I got off the bench and stood in front of a bookstore next door. I didn't want Billie and Lily to listen in.

"Sad," he said. He sounded sad. Had he called to try to reconcile? Billie was drawing an imaginary slit across her throat. I glared at her.

I took a lick of ice cream and held the phone to my ear. "I'm sorry."

"How is it out there?"

"It's okay. The house is nice. There's a view of the ocean from my bedroom." *Not that I'd slept there the night before.* "And the beach is nice." *Even if I did almost drown.* "It feels good to get direct sunlight on my skin." *Along with my host's kisses.* "But . . . it's hard to really enjoy myself under the circumstances."

"Yeah. So I wanted to let you know, my parents canceled Pearl River, so that's taken care of. They had to swallow the deposit, though."

The cone felt cold and sticky in my hand. "I'll pay them back."

"Don't be ridiculous. So I found a place to stay. An apartment in New Rochelle. I'm not sure what's going to happen with my grandma's house. That would be depressing to live there now— you know, by myself."

"Right." Drops of ice cream trickled down my fingers. There was no way to wipe them off. I had to let them keep trickling.

"And I hired a mover and got my stuff out of the apartment. I got pretty much all of it."

"That was fast." Ice cream dribbled onto my ring. I brought the sapphire to my lips and licked the stone with my tongue.

"I hope you don't mind—I took the TV from the bedroom."

"You did?" The trickles were now snaking down my wrist. There was a napkin around the cone, but it was already soggy, and it was stuck under my hand, in any case, so it was useless to me. I took another lick, more to get rid of some ice cream than to enjoy it.

"I know we bought it together," he said, "but you have the other one."

"It's so old." I'd owned the living room TV for like ten years. The power button was funky. Sometimes it got stuck, so you had to pry it out with a knife or use the remote.

"But it's yours."

"I know, but . . ." How could I complain when his parents were eating the deposit on the hotel? "Fine. Whatever." I forced myself to exhale. Forget about it. Let it go. "I can't believe this is happening." A drip ran down my arm halfway to my elbow.

"Yeah, I know. Well . . . take care."

"You too."

I closed my phone and put it in my pocket. Then I peeled the napkin off my cone to wipe my arm and hand. But the sticky mess was more than the napkin could absorb. And the ice cream now seemed disgustingly soft and sweet. Lily was still working on her cone, and Billie never went near the stuff. So I went back into the shop and threw it in the garbage. It landed with a plop. Then I grabbed a wad of napkins from the dispenser, wet them at the water fountain, and wiped myself clean.

Thirty One

*L*ily and I walked them to the front door. "You sure you two don't want to come with?" Jonathan asked. Billie was wearing a white baby doll dress that set off her tan.

"Daphne and I are doing the eighties."

He looked at me for confirmation.

"The eighties," I said, "was a very important decade."

"Well, in that case . . . I don't want to interfere with my daughter's education."

After they left, we ordered a pizza and settled in on the couch. "Okay," I said, "there were some interesting developments that happened in the eighties. Cable became available, which meant there started to be a lot more channels. And the VCR. I bet you can't imagine a time when you couldn't record the shows. If you missed it, you missed it."

"I totally can't imagine."

"And they didn't replay stuff all the time like they do on cable, either. Also, the remote control: Almost all TVs started to come with remote controls. Did you know people used to have to actually get up and change the channel when they wanted to watch something different?"

"Wow." She got this big smile, which was all the more cute because she was missing a front tooth. "I don't think I believe you!"

"It's true! So now there were a lot more channels to choose from, and people could change channels a lot more easily. So the big three networks—what were they?"

"ABC, CBS, and FOX."

"Not FOX. NBC."

"I knew that."

"They had to compete much harder for attention. Some say I actually got better as a result. It's known as the decade of 'quality TV' because of the hourlong dramas that were really popular then, like *Hill Street Blues* and *L.A. Law*."

"So nobody watched sitcoms anymore?"

"They did. There were lots of 'insultcoms.' *Cheers, Who's the Boss?, Three's Company*. Not so warm and fuzzy anymore." I didn't mention about how sexual innuendo and raunchiness were rampant. "I thought we might watch one of my favorites, *Kate and Allie*, about two divorced moms with kids who move in together. Lots of female bonding. Or I have the first season of *Who's the Boss?*" I'd brought that as backup, even though I didn't particularly like that show.

"*Who's the Boss.*"

"Are you sure? It's in reruns all the time."

"I like Alyssa Milano. I think she's so pretty."

"Okay." I put the disc in. Admittedly, there was something sexy about the employee–boss flirtation. But my eyes glazed over by the third episode. What were Jonathan and Billie talking about? Was he loving the idea of *Hookers*? Were they drawing up the contracts already? Was she drunk and blabbing to him all about me and Charlie? I'd made her promise, before she left, not to mention anything, but that didn't mean she'd remember she promised after her third blueberry margarita.

Lily was still watching when I went up to bed. "I'm really tired," I said. "I'm going to sleep."

"Good night," she said, not taking her eyes off the TV.

"You sure I can't tuck you in?"

"I'm just want to finish the season."

I had to wonder if I was corrupting her.

I took two Tylenols in case my brain wouldn't turn off, but it didn't do the trick. I was too anxious. Jonathan and Billie were out pretty late. Dinner couldn't have taken this long. Had they gone off to a party together? Were they brainstorming episode ideas? Demonstrating their oral sex skills on each other? It seemed that hen it came to imagining Billie and Jonathan alone together, sexual innuendo and raunchiness were rampant.

I was wide awake at midnight, when I heard them get out of Jonathan's car. I couldn't hear what they were saying, but the talk was animated, and Billie was laughing, and it was clear they were having a good time. I should've been glad they enjoyed being together, right? But it made me stiffen with jealousy. Would I have preferred them to share the animosity that had existed between her and Charlie? Maybe.

Billie knocked on my door and came in. "Are you awake?"

"Yeah."

She sat on the edge of my bed. "Guess what? He loved my idea."

"Really?"

"Totally. I think he's going to do it. I really do."

"Wow." I suddenly felt distressed. It wouldn't be fair for him to produce her show. It really just would not be fair. "Where were you all that time?"

"There was a humongo line at this restaurant. It took forever to get a table, and the service was horrendous. But guess what they had?"

"Really good crab cakes?"

"The best. He wants you, by the way."

"What?"

"He's waiting for you downstairs. Outside. On the patio."

"Oh."

She gave me a wink. "Do everything I would do."

I changed out of my pajamas and into a tank top and my jeans. At the last second, I grabbed my sweater out of my duffel bag. I practically galloped down the stairs and then slowed down as I went outside. He was on one of the lounge chairs.

"Hey," he said, standing.

"Hi." It was cool out. I put on my sweater.

"Feel like going down to the beach?"

"Okay." We walked down to the shore and sat down on the sand. The inky blackness and the waves crashing made it all seem very dramatic. I leaned back to get a good view of the stars and kept myself from saying something inane like "Wow, there are so many stars in the sky."

"How ya doin?" he asked.

"Good." It was windy. My hair was flying all over the place. I wished I'd brought something to tie it back.

"Were you sleeping?"

"Too much on my mind."

"Such as?"

I sighed. Well, I wasn't about to tell him I'd been lying in bed wondering if he'd been going down on my sister or vice versa. No need to go there! But I sure was overdue telling him about Charlie. Maybe it was time to confess.

"You regret," he said, "what we did?"

"No. No. It's just . . . I don't know, maybe we shouldn't have. . . ."

"Was it that bad?"

Was he kidding? "Of course it wasn't bad." I was blushing and glad he couldn't see in the dark. "It was wonderful. Don't you know that? I just mean I wasn't expecting us to go that far so soon."

"Was it soon? I thought it took forever."

I smiled and looked down into my lap. He was so sweet. Had it just been the day before yesterday that I'd felt the waves pushing me out to sea? Had it just been last night that his kisses had sent me to the moon? Was it just now that I began thinking like a romantic idiot?

"So what's going on?" he asked.

"Nothing's going on."

"*Something's* going on. You seem preoccupied."

"What did you think of Billie's idea?" I felt foolish for asking, but I was curious. Intensely. And it helped me avoid bringing up Charlie.

"You mean *Hookers*?"

"Yeah."

"It was good."

"You liked it?"

"Very commercial."

"I thought so too." I pushed a pile of sand with the side of my hand. "Are you going to do it?"

"So that's what's on your mind? *Hookers?*"

"No. There's something I have to tell you, and it's kind of embarrassing." The wind was whipping my hair in a frenzy. I had to hold it down with both hands. "You remember that ex-boyfriend I mentioned?"

"The teacher."

I looked toward him, still pressing my hands against my head. "He's been my ex for, like, a few days."

"Oh."

Using my pinky, without looking, I twisted the stone of my ring toward the palm of my hand. "We just broke up."

"Really. So . . . was this something serious?"

I cleared my throat. "We were engaged."

I heard the waves crash while he was silent.

"I wanted to tell you about him, but you have to understand—I couldn't let myself realize that it wasn't right with him, and I couldn't let myself believe that you really were interested in me."

"Because you were so busy trying to fix me up with your sister?" It was a statement as much as a question.

"Well, it was a plan. Not a very good one. I just thought you two might . . ." I paused. "Did you really like her idea?"

"Her idea?"

"*Hookers.*"

"Is that what this is all about?"

"What?"

"You wanted a chance to pitch your ideas?"

"No!"

"That's why you both came here this weekend."

Did he really think I was trying to use him? Was that possible? "You invited me here. I didn't even know about Billie's idea."

He shook his head, not believing me. "You make a good team."

"Wait a second. She just told me you love her idea, so why are you getting so weird about this?" I couldn't tell him I had nothing invested in him doing it. I couldn't tell him the truth was I really *didn't* want him to do it.

"You're telling me you're engaged, and I'm the weird one?"

"*Was* engaged."

"You're *sure* about that."

"Yes. He's moved out. It's over."

"You live together?"

"Lived. Past tense. He took all his stuff. Even the good TV. Okay, we bought it together, but he doesn't even watch anymore, except the Yankees. I mean, we should at least have joint custody, don't you think?" I thought I was being funny. Sort of. I thought he'd see that. He didn't.

"You know what?" Jonathan stood up. "I'm not interested in hearing about your problems with your boyfriend."

I stood up too. "I was kidding."

"Maybe you need to take some time to figure out where you're at."

I curled my toes in the sand. "Or maybe you're the one who needs the time."

"What are you talking about?"

The wind was gusting. My hair was flying in every direction. "Billie. You were out a long time with her tonight." My voice came out shrill. I wanted to shut my mouth, but it kept moving. "I heard you laughing when you got back. You had a good time together, didn't you." Deny it. Tell me you dreaded every minute of it. Couldn't wait to get back to see me . . .

"So?"

"It just seems like you two really hit it off." I gathered my hair together, pulled it into a ponytail, let it go again. "And now you want to produce her show. Maybe you're just more into her now than me."

"Is that what you think?"

"I don't know what to think." My body started walking toward the house. My body seemed to think he would tell me to stop, and then when I wouldn't stop, he'd follow after me and pull me into his arms and kiss away all this ridiculousness. But here I was, almost back at the house, and there was no one telling me anything.

At the porch, I made myself turn around. Maybe he was still standing there, looking at me, hoping I'd come back. But he was standing with his back to me, looking at the ocean. "Don't you know?" I said. "I'm in love with you." But from this distance he couldn't possibly hear. And my voice was carried away by the wind.

In the morning, it was hard to say good-bye to Lily. She was up before anyone watching *Kim Possible*. How much longer would she be innocent enough to watch the Disney channel? It was sort of sweet. I called a cab, and then went in to say good-bye to her.

"I'm taking an early train back to Manhattan."

"What about Billie?"

"Billie is still asleep. I'm not sure what she's doing."

"Will you be back?" she asked.

"I don't think so. But I'll see you in the city."

"We still need to do the nineties."

"Yes." The nineties. The decade her father made it big. The decade I got glued to my set. What show would I choose? There were so many good ones. *My So-Called Life. Daria. Roseanne. Seinfeld.* I'd have to think that over.

"You promise?"

"I promise. Say good-bye to your dad for me, okay?"

I left a note for him on the kitchen table. After obsessing over what to say, I'd settled for simply thanking him for everything. I figured the next time I'd hear from him would be an email telling me he didn't want to do the tribute anymore.

My goal was to escape without seeing Jonathan or Billie. And I succeeded.

Thirty Two

The TV in the bedroom was indeed gone. And the TV in the living room was still disconnected. I decided to leave it that way. Maybe with Charlie gone, I didn't need to hide in the airwaves anymore. Not to blame him. My dependency had certainly begun way before we met. But he was right. It had been a way to put a distance between us. No, not just us: Distance between me and my feelings. Now I was going to meet my feelings head-on.

I sat on the couch.

And felt lonely, sad, and depressed.

There.

I'd acknowledged my feelings.

Could I turn the TV on?

No! This was almost scary, how itchy I felt to turn it on. I could get through one day without the thing, couldn't I?

I unpacked my bag, went from room to room. It was so much emptier with his stuff gone. And so quiet.

I sat on the couch again. Glared at the dark screen. Could Jonathan Hill really think I was some kind of manipulative floozy who would try to use him to spawn a television-producing career? I mean, okay, yes, Billie was all those things. But *moi*? It wasn't exactly typical of me to jump into bed so quickly with a man. Not that Jonathan could know that. So maybe he really did think I was a manipulative floozy. Me. A manipulative floozy. What a joke. And here I was. By myself. Dying to turn the TV on and my thoughts off. I focused in on my own image reflected on the screen. *I have a life! And I can live it without you!*

I got up, went to the refrigerator, and opened the door. It was very nearly empty inside. *Hi, Mom. Crazy week, huh? Was I a fool to let Charlie go? Did I blow it with Jonathan Hill? I guess I'm not doing too well right now, especially seeing as I still seem to be imagining you're inside my refrigerator. I'll be mature and have a vegetable.*

I opened the vegetable drawer. Charlie had left me a head of broccoli. I took it out. Put on some hot water. Got one of those metal steamer things out. Chopped up the broccoli, stuck it in, put on the lid, and let it cook.

Oh, yes. I was going to be healthy. And strong. And virtuous.

When it was ready, I put some butter on it and sat at the table eating. It wasn't that bad.

But it wasn't that good, either.

I was at my desk pretending to read a book about the burlesque roots of the comedy/variety show and its gradual demise. There was a picture of Carol Burnett doing the famous Scarlett O'Hara skit, when she was wearing the dress made from curtains and the curtain rod was on her shoulder. Whoever thought of that had a truly inspired moment. I could use one of those.

An inspired moment. Not a curtain rod on my shoulder.

The phone rang. I saw on my caller ID it was Billie. "Hello?"

"You really should not have run off."

"He hates me."

"He's over it. I explained everything. He understands now that you didn't know about *Hookers*, and you're not trying to use him, and Charlie was never right for you, blah blah blah. Big sister fixed everything."

"You think so? Well, thanks." This sounded like a sitcom happy ending, and was just as believable. She probably wasn't even aware of how I'd accused him of wanting her instead of me. God, what an outpouring of insecurity. I must've sounded like a total idiot. And I still couldn't stand the idea that he might produce *Hookers.*

"You see how lucky you are to have me?" Billie asked.

"Does the theme music play now?"

"You better believe it. Come on, Babe. Fight for this guy. He's gonna get snatched up any second by someone so much less worthy."

"Billie, get real. I blew it. I'm sure he's realized he can do a lot better than me." Maybe even with her. I still didn't feel completely sure he wasn't into her.

"Look, he said he's going to call you. So don't lose your phone. In the meanwhile, I've been quite busy."

"Oh?" Had he optioned her idea? Told her to sit down and write that pilot? Maybe they were writing it together. I could just see them all cozy in his office taking turns at the computer.

"After you disappeared so ungraciously from Jonathan's house, I hooked back up with Karl von Richthofen."

"Really?"

"He must've remembered something about our night together, because he took the trouble to track me down and scoop me up. I'm still at his place."

"In the Hamptons?"

"Can't you hear the damn seagulls in the background? I'm on his boat. I hate boats. I don't even like waterbeds. Which reminds me. Can I move in with you?"

"Are you serious?"

"Max gave me two weeks' notice and cut off my credit card. Evidently I finally maxed out. Ha-ha."

Great. Hilarious. What timing. Charlie moves out. Billie moves in. "Sure. I guess."

"Don't worry," she said, "it's only temporary."

We said our good-byes and hung up. My sitcom ending suddenly seemed more like the premiere of a brand-new drama.

Two days passed. Jonathan did not call. It would seem big sister did not fix everything. But at least I knew she wasn't with him. And at least I had something to take my mind off my depressing life: the season finale of *Supermodels*.

There was so much hype about it everywhere. *US Weekly, En-*

tertainment Weekly, Star, all the showbiz "news" channels on TV—they were all speculating on what would happen to Mirage. No one seemed to know. It amazed me that the secret hadn't been leaked. Not even the obsessed blogger fans knew.

Taffy came over to see the last episode of the season with me. We sat on the couch with a bowl of popcorn between us. It was a relief to be watching with someone who didn't make me feel guilty about it. We should've been doing this all along.

"I met Simon's mother," Taffy said, as she took a handful. "She had me over for dinner. She's very nice."

"This is getting serious." I took my own handful. Maybe I'd be able to use my wedding-slash-bridesmaid dress after all.

"She's a big fan of *Supermodels*, by the way."

"Cool."

"She was very impressed that you knew Jonathan Hill."

I put a whole lot of popcorn into my mouth and didn't say anything to that.

"Are you going to call him?"

"No."

"I thought Billie smoothed things over."

"You never know if Billie is telling you the truth, or what she wants to *think* is the truth. And she said he would call me."

"So. He's probably been busy because of all the hype with the show or something."

"Forget it. I'm not calling him."

"Why?"

"Because I'm too afraid!" I nodded toward the TV. "It's starting."

"You have to call him."

I turned the sound up.

"You have to."

I turned up the sound some more. "It's starting!"

We settled into the show. Like the week before, they wasted a whole bunch of time up front with clips from the whole season. Then the first set of ads. Then they picked up from where it left off, just as the priest was about to pronounce them man and wife. Once again, Mirage screamed at the top of her lungs, "Wait!" Ashley and Niles both turned to face her. There was absolute silence. Mirage screamed, "Stop! You can't do this!"

Ashley stage-whispered back, "Please don't do this!"

"It's a mistake!"

"I love him!" Ashley yelled back.

All the guests looked on with relish and horror. Mirage stepped forward. "You don't know what love is! You're ambitious, just like I am, even if you're too stupid to admit it. He just wants you to pop out his children."

"I *want* to pop out his children."

Mirage gasped. "What about the stretch marks? You'll never do another swimsuit shoot in your life!"

"Get her out of here!" Niles fumed. "Take her away!"

Two men in tuxedos grabbed Mirage by the arm. "Don't do it," she shrieked as they carried her off. "You're making the biggest mistake of your life!"

A Target ad came on. I went to make more popcorn. Taffy joined me in the kitchen to get more soda. "Jessica Cox is such a bad actress."

"But the writing is so bad too," I said.

"Now you're dissing Jonathan Hill's writing?"

"I don't think he knows anymore if he's writing satire or just plain crap."

Or maybe I wanted a reason to dislike him.

After the popcorn was ready, we returned to the sofa and suffered through some more ads. Finally it was back. Mirage burst into her apartment and went straight to her medicine cabinet. Hands shaking, she emptied some pills into her palm and swallowed them down. Then she took a swig of vodka. Then she threw the bottle of vodka at the wall. Then she got in the elevator and went to the rooftop. First she cried hysterically while looking up at the sky and twirling and twirling and twirling. Her behavior was so ridiculous and melodramatic, but I began to cry. It was embarrassing. I mean, how could I, a theoretically intelligent person, be so emotionally involved with this dreck? Sure, Mirage reminded me of Billie. And yes, I was sort of like Ashley. But still. This was so over-the-top. Then Mirage stopped twirling and began to stagger to the edge. The music was going crazy. Taffy and I sat on the edge of the couch.

"She's gonna jump!" I yelled.

"Don't do it!"

"You'll never make it in features!"

Mirage stepped over the edge . . . and plummeted twenty floors down.

"Jesus," Taffy said. "Did they really have to show her bouncing off that awning?"

"She's dead." Even though I'd half expected it, I didn't really think he'd get rid of her forever. "He killed her off."

"Time for Jessica Cox to find a new agent."

They went to a commercial. Gap. Smiling dancers of every cultural persuasion were dancing around in khaki shorts. Good. I needed to collect myself. "She didn't leave a note," I joked to cover up the fact that her death had actually gotten to me. "That's so rude."

"You'd think people would at least have manners when they're committing suicide."

"They're too self-absorbed."

"Just thinking about themselves."

I ran to get the new popcorn. It was fun watching with Taffy—she got it in a way Charlie never would.

"So," she said as soon as I returned to the couch, "are you going to call him?"

"No."

The ads ended. Ashley and Niles were speaking to the doctor at the hospital. She was still wearing her wedding dress, but had removed the train and veil. "Doctor. Tell me the truth. Is she . . . ?"

"I'm afraid Mirage didn't make it."

"My god. The poor thing!"

"I'm very sorry," the doctor said, and then left. Ashley searched Niles's face for answers.

"You have to believe this is for the best," Niles said. "If she'd survived, her face and body would've been mangled beyond the scope of plastic surgery. Her employment opportunities would've been severely limited."

"So in a way . . . it's good that she died."

I groaned. "Has the show always been this bad?"

"Could you please not interfere with my happy ending?"

"Sorry."

"Do you still want to go on our honeymoon?" Niles asked.

"There's nothing I want more. But I do have one question. Is it possible to give birth without getting stretch marks?"

"Of course it is, Darling. Don't let that woman get to you. Despite the fact that she was a world-famous supermodel, deep down, she was very insecure."

"Deep down?" I said. "How about right on the surface?"

Ashley and Niles walked out of the hospital. The credits came on. Season over. Sigh. I couldn't resist looking for Jonathan's name to appear, as if it validated me somehow. "Can you believe," I said, as "Jonathan Hill" flashed on the screen for a moment and was gone, "I actually had sex with that man?"

"Maybe that's the problem."

"What do you mean?" I took one piece of popcorn. It was slightly burnt. I liked the charcoal taste.

"The sex. It was good. And now you're scared. Right? It's more intimidating than boring sex with Charlie. So you ran away."

I took another piece of popcorn. Bit off a piece of it. It was true that I'd freaked out. Gotten off that island before we could have a calm discussion in the light of day. "You know, you might have something there. How did you become so perceptive?"

"I saw every episode of *Frazier*. Major crush on Kelsey Grammer."

"TV therapists. Aren't they always the best?"

"You'd think they had writers to script their responses."

I chuckled. And then it hit me. This was a great idea for a seminar: TV shrinks. There was Lorraine Bracco on *The Sopranos*, Hank Azaria on *Huff*, Bob Newhart as Dr. Hartley in his seventies sitcom. There had to be more. I couldn't wait to research it.

"So you'll call him?"

I took a deep breath and let it go. She was right. The idea of getting close to Jonathan Hill was terrifying. But what was I going to do? Settle on watching his shows for the rest of my life? "I'll figure something out."

"Good. Would you like more soda?"

I nodded. "Thanks for being such a good friend."

"What would you do without me?"

She poured us each a glass. We clinked. Yeah. Everyone definitely needs an Ethel.

Thirty Three

Ben Kaplan was in a tizzy meeting and greeting everyone for the Bochco tribute. I had to give it to him: There was a sellout crowd, and he'd managed to get lots of actors from Bochco's past shows to come. To start the evening off, Ben gave a talk about Bochco's career, emphasizing the importance of *Hill Street Blues* and the *cinema verité* improvisational style that made it famous. Then Daniel Travanti, who played Frank Furillo for six seasons, went to the microphone and thanked Bochco for his creative genius—and for giving him a job that led to his comeback, two Emmy awards, and sex symbol status at forty-one. Everyone laughed. Then Bochco went on stage. After the applause died down, he thanked Ben and the museum before introducing his favorite episode, "Trial by Fury." In this one, Captain Furillo went up against lawyer Joyce Davenport, his lover and future wife, in a trial about a nun who'd been attacked. The lights went down, and we all watched the show.

After that was over, there was wine and cheese. The evening was a success. Except for one thing. I'd invited Jonathan. By email. He hadn't responded, but I was hoping against hope he would show up. I went to get a glass of wine. My own tribute to him was most likely dead in the water.

Wait a second. It was him. In the corner. Talking with Jennifer Tilly. She'd had some sort of recurring role on *Hill Street Blues*, if I remembered correctly.

My entire body stiffened. She was so sexy with that scratchy voice and exotic eyes. And he wasn't exactly going out of his way to seek me out. Maybe he'd brought Jennifer Tilly with him. Maybe they were lovers.

I smeared some Brie on a cracker, told myself to calm down. No reason to think he was sleeping with every actress he had a conversation with. I was the one who'd been hiding the fact that I was engaged. I was the one who'd hightailed it out of the Hamptons. I set down my wineglass and strode over to him and Jennifer.

"Hi," I said. "I'm so sorry to interrupt. . . ."

"Hi." He introduced me to Jennifer and told her I was a curator there.

"How interesting," she said, and seemed about to ask me a question, so I headed her off.

"I need to speak with him for a minute, do you mind very much?"

She seemed surprised, but graciously turned to Jonathan and shook his hand. "So nice talking with you."

"You too."

Good. They hadn't come together. "I'm sorry," I said, "I don't mean to be rude. I just really need to talk to you."

He nodded.

"Thanks for coming."

"Thanks for inviting me."

"Billie said she tried to smooth things out, and I was hoping you would call."

"I've been really busy."

I nodded quickly. "I'm sure you have been. And I really wanted to say I'm sorry, you know, about everything, and how I left. I guess it was all too overwhelming for me."

"Uh-huh." He was not making this easy. His face was totally neutral, and I had no idea what he was thinking.

"So," I went on, "I wanted to say that it was unfortunate how Billie and I both pestered you with ideas over the weekend. But it was not a plan. I really did think of *My Cool Mom* when we were riding in your car. I swear to god. And it just spilled out. I didn't mean to be, like, pitching to you or anything. I was just thinking out loud because I was excited about the idea. That's all."

"Okay," he said.

"I just wanted to be clear about that."

"I suppose I'm overly sensitive on that."

"Which is completely understandable. And I hope your mother forgives you for not using her idea someday, because she really shouldn't hold that against you."

He rewarded me with a tiny but tight smile. "Thanks."

"And if you want to produce *Hookers*, I just want you to know that I have nothing invested there. Either way. I mean, I'd actually prefer you *didn't* do it, because I don't happen to think it's the most wonderful concept in the world, but if you *want* to do it, that's fine too, because it would be great for Billie. I know I got jealous at the idea of you two and everything, but I see now that I was way overreacting."

"Okay, can I say something here?"

"Please."

"First of all, there's another show like that already in development. Second of all, that's really not what I want to be doing right now. Third of all, what am I gonna tell her—that I think it stinks? She's your sister. And as far as I can tell, she's all ready to pack her bags and move to Hollywood."

"Oh." I felt like tap-dancing around the room. Good thing I didn't know how to tap-dance. "That's wonderful. I mean, that's too bad. But . . ."

"Anyway, I should get going. Unless there's something else you had to say?"

Was he referring to Charlie? I really wanted to explain about Charlie. But here? Now? When he had his eye on the door? Maybe he really didn't care about me in any personal way, and he was going to go ask Jennifer Tilly to get a drink.

Maybe he'd just been using me for sex in the Hamptons.

Though somehow I doubted that. Men who used women for sex didn't—oh, god . . . I felt myself tingling again. "I was wondering . . ."

He raised his eyebrows.

I cleared my throat. I was about to ask him if we could still do his retrospective. But that's not what came out. "I promised Lily we'd do the nineties, and I don't want to disappoint her. Could we set something up?" Okay, yes, I was using Lily so I could see Jonathan again. But I *had* promised, and I *did* want to see her, and he wasn't making this easy.

"Okay," he said. "She'd like that."

"Great."

He told me to call and we would set up a time for him to bring her to the museum. And then he excused himself. I watched as he snaked his way through the crowd to the door. Good. He did not leave with Jennifer Tilly.

Thirty Four

I stood in line to buy my muffin and coffee. They were coming that day. I still didn't know what I was going to show her. The nineties were hard to sum up. There were the more traditional family-type sitcoms like *Home Improvement* and *Roseanne*. But then there was perhaps the best sitcom ever: *Seinfeld*. The show about "nothing," with its perpetual adolescent leads and postmodern sensibility. Compounding the challenge was the likelihood that Lily had seen all the important sitcoms in reruns ad infinitum.

I was finally at the front of the line. "Blueberry muffin, please, and a large coffee with half and half."

"Sugar?" the man behind the counter asked.

"No thanks."

When I'd called Jonathan to set this up, I still couldn't tell what he was thinking or where I stood. But the fact that he was willing to accompany her gave me hope. After all, he could've had Lee bring her, or the nanny.

The nanny.

Suddenly I knew exactly what show we were going to watch.

"The most important thing to be said about the nineties sitcom," I said, as Jonathan and Lily stared at the dark console screen in front of us, "is that at this point, the viewing audiences were so sophisticated, it became harder to transport them into a state of make-believe. Everyone was used to seeing shows over and over again, so everyone became an expert on the form. And the form had become predictable. No one believed in the quick happy ending anymore. So we didn't watch the shows to learn about ourselves anymore. We watched the shows to critique them."

"And most of them are stupid," Lily said.

"The most innovative show is probably *Seinfeld*. The writers had a philosophy. No hugging, no learning." I couldn't help but look at Jonathan when I said that. Would we hug? Would we learn? He looked back at me with a pleasant expression, and I still had no idea what he was thinking. I turned to Lily. "Do you know what they meant by that?"

"No quick, fake happy ending," she said.

"Exactly."

"Are we watching a *Seinfeld*?" she asked. "Because I only like Elaine."

"I had something else in mind. One of my very favorite shows. *The Nanny*. I used to watch it when I was a teenager."

"Not in reruns?" Lily asked.

"It was all new. And it starred an actress named Fran Drescher, who played a character named Fran Fine, who's hired to work for this millionaire theater producer named Maxwell Sheffield."

"I know, I know. It's on all the time. That's one of my very favorite shows too!"

Of course she knew it. We were on common ground now. History had caught up to us. "Have you ever seen the episode where they're on the plane?"

"I don't think so."

"And he finally tells her—"

"Don't tell her," Jonathan said.

"Yeah, you'll ruin it," Lily said.

"Okay. I'll cue it up."

Interesting trivia: Fran Drescher coproduced *The Nanny* with her high school sweetheart husband, Peter Marc Jacobson. By the sixth and last year, the character Fran Fine was happy, pregnant with twins, and had married the man of her dreams. Meanwhile, the actress Fran Drescher was miserable, had cancer, and was divorcing her high-school sweetheart husband.

I'd chosen the episode where Sheffield finally told Fran he

loved her. They were on an airplane, and Sheffield thought it was going to crash. He's so freaked out, he confesses his love.

I could still remember how profound it was the first time I saw it—as if it had been written with me in mind. It raised all sorts of questions. Did my parents have time to say anything before they knew they were going to die? Did they tell each other they loved each other? Did my mother have time to get mad at my father before impact?

My rational self knew there'd been no time for them to think or feel anything at all. These thoughts seemed to be a way to torture myself, a way to feel pain imagining their pain at feeling my pain.

The three of us watched the episode quietly. At the next console over, a man was laughing hysterically at Homer Simpson. I wondered what Jonathan thought of Fran Drescher's nasal voice and body-hugging wardrobe. (The show never explained how a nanny could afford all those clothes.) Her sexually flirtatious attitude was more blatant than I remembered. Funny how when you're young a lot of that stuff just doesn't register.

"That's the end?" Lily asked when the episode was over.

It was a total cliff-hanger.

"It was the last episode of the season. I remember having to wait *all summer* to see if they'd finally get together. But you don't have to wait. You can watch the next show right now."

"Goodie!"

After Lily settled into it, I asked Jonathan if we could talk for a minute. We went over to the windows and looked out at the offices across the street.

"So," he said. "Do they get together?"

"Nah. The plane didn't crash, and Sheffield took back what he said, and they started the flirtation all over as if he'd never said it. Isn't that evil of those mean television producers?"

"But effective," he said.

I shook my head.

"So," he said, "you've created a monster. Now that you've introduced Lily to the history of TV, she tells me she wants to direct."

"At least she doesn't want to act."

"True."

We both stared at a woman in the building opposite sitting at her desk, working at a computer. It felt like we were spying on a private moment, yet she wasn't doing anything interesting.

I took a deep breath and let it out. "I'm sorry I didn't tell you about my engagement thing."

"That's okay," he said.

"It's over. Really. He's a good guy. But there wasn't any . . ." I paused. I wanted to say the word "passion." But I couldn't, quite.

"What?"

"Electricity."

"Oh."

"I just didn't know how to tell you. Especially because I wasn't sure what was happening. Or if anything was happening. With us. Do you forgive me?"

He took a moment, and then finally said, "Yes . . ."

"Really?"

He turned toward me and took both my hands. "On one condition."

"Yes?" My heart was beating really fast.

"I've been thinking about *My Cool Mom*."

"Really?"

"Yeah. I love the idea. I was going to ask if I could pitch it to the network."

"You aren't serious."

"But I think the main character should be a teenager, if that's okay with you."

Okay with me? "I could go with that."

"I'd like you to come up with some more episode ideas."

"But you don't do sitcoms. And I thought you thought it was too retro."

"I've been looking for something Lily would like to watch. And . . ." He made a big deal out of clearing his throat. "I have something to confess."

"Yes?"

"*Mr. Ed* used to be one of my favorite shows."

"You? The talking horse?"

"Uh-huh." He did a horrible imitation of Ed telling Wilbur he wanted some sugar and then neighed.

I had to cover my ears. "Stop it!"

"Only if you agree to work with me."

Lily called out, "Did I hear a horse talking?"

"No such thing as a talking horse," Jonathan called back.

"I guess I'm just going crazy," she said.

We waited to see if she'd say anything else, but there was silence. Jonathan looked at me for my response.

"I'm not sure," I finally said.

"Why?"

I knew why. But I was scared to say it.

"Billie?" he asked.

"No. Well, I mean, yes. Billie is always a challenge. But that's not what I'm worrying about."

"Good. Because I know how to handle Billie. Could it be," he asked, "because we're . . . emotionally involved?"

"*Are* we emotionally involved?"

"I think we might be," he said. "Is that a problem?"

"Well, it's hard for couples to work together. It's already caused some tension between us."

"I'm over that."

"Look at Fran Drescher and Peter Marc Jacobson. Sonny and Cher. Hillary and Bill. Lucy and Ricky." I decided not to mention Jonathan's ex-wife and ex-girlfriend. I didn't want to make too strong a case against it. And, well, they were actresses. At least I wasn't an actress.

"What about George Burns and Gracie Allen?" he said.

"I read in his biography that he cheated on her once."

He put his arms around me and pulled me closer. "You don't think they had a good marriage?"

"I was surprised he confessed to it, actually. They did seem to be very much in love."

"And I," he said, kissing me once on the forehead, once on the nose, and once more on the mouth, "seem to be very much in love, too."

Oh, god. Did he just say that? "You are?"

"Uh-huh."

"I seem to be in love, too."

"Really."

"Did you know," I began to babble, "people used to believe Sid Caesar and Imogene Coca were married just because they were so good together on *Your Show of Shows*? Isn't that cute how people wanted to believe that?"

He put his arms around me and kissed me hard on the lips. To quiet me? Calm me? Whatever. I closed my eyes and turned off the sound. I was only aware of his body against mine and the sparks between us. We were most definitely broadcasting live.

Epilogue

*B*illie was all packed and ready to go. She picked up the phone and made the call, saying the number out loud as she punched in the numbers. "777-7777."

We were both grinning.

"Hi," she said. "Do you have a driver available? The airport. JFK."

She'd been staying with me since Max kicked her out. But it wasn't as bad as it could've been, because we knew it was temporary. No, she wasn't going to get to make *Hookers*. But Jonathan had promised her a guest spot on *Supermodels* when shooting started up again. And he'd arranged for her to meet with agents and casting directors out in L.A. Billie could not have been happier, and I was relieved of all residue guilt.

We went down to the sidewalk to wait for the driver to arrive. "I'm going to miss you," she said.

A wave of sadness hit me. She was going so far away. "I'll miss you, too."

"Even though I've been monopolizing your television set?"

"I told you. I'm trying not to watch so much anyway."

"Right . . ." She didn't believe me for a second. "And you aren't addicted to Jonathan's sixty-five inch screen, either, right?"

"Not in the least," I said with a fake smile, batting my eyelashes.

The limo pulled up. We kissed cheeks and hugged each other. "Maybe you'll come out and visit me," she said. "Even though the man you love is here and you hate L.A."

"I'll visit," I said. "And you can take me to all the fun places."

"You know I will."

I waited for the limo to drive away and then went back upstairs. The apartment was silent. Even though I wasn't hungry, I opened the refrigerator. *So, Mom, what do you think?* I took a baby carrot. *Are your girls going to be okay?* I let the refrigerator door close and crunched away. I didn't need an answer. Inside my heart, I already knew.

Acknowledgments

I'd like to thank David Bushman and Richard Holbrook at the Museum of Television & Radio in New York City for being so generous with their time. I hope the novel reflects our shared love of the history of television—if not a *completely* accurate picture of the inner workings of the museum. Thanks to Julie Carpenter for your early praise. Amanda Selwyn for your last-minute insights. Michael Lehmann for answering my questions and also the waffle. Elizabeth Kandall for that conversation in Georgina's. Steve, Madeleine, and Dave for letting me write in the kitchen instead of cook in it. Stephanie Kip Rostan, Kara Cesare, and Elaine Koster for your continued support. Minnette, as usual, you inspire me. And big thanks to Leah Pike on this one. Major thanks. I mean, really. Thank you.

About the Author

Photo by Madeleine Kronovet

Stephanie Lehmann is the author of *The Art of Undressing, Thoughts While Having Sex*, and *Are You in the Mood?* A playwright and contributor to Salon.com, she lives in Manhattan with her husband and two children. You can visit Stephanie at www.StephanieLehmann.com.